mary

NOW I LAY ME DOWN TO SLEEP

Patricia H. Rushford

ELM HILL BOOKS
A Division of Thomas Nelson Publishers
Since 1798

www.thomasnelson.com

Now I Lay Me Down to Sleep ISBN: 1-4041-8570-4

For additions, deletions, corrections or clarifications in future editions of this text, please contact
Paul Shepherd, Editor in Chief for Elm Hill Books. Email pshepherd@elmhillbooks.com

Products from Elm Hill Books may be purchased in bulk for educational, business, fundraising,
or sales promotional use. For information, please email SpecialMarkets@ThomasNelson.com.

This is a work of fiction. The characters, incidents, and dialogues are products of the author's
imagination and are not to be construed as real. Any resemblance to actual events or persons,
living or dead, is entirely coincidental.

Cover design by Patti Evans
Cover design by Mark Ross / MJ Ross Design

Previously published by Bethany House Publishers under ISBN: 1-55661-730-5

Printed in the United States of America

Dedicated to my ageless friends
and fellow writers.

Lauraine, Ruby, Birdie, Colleen, Sandy, Rev. Marcia,
Elsie, Gail, Marion, Gloria, and Woodeene

Acknowledgements

Sandy Dengler, Margo Power, Harry Russell, Michael Curtis, Judy Frandsen, and the Vancouver Police for their sage advice and expertise.

One

The phone rang for the fifteenth time that morning. Helen Bradley was beginning to wish Alexander Graham Bell had pursued another vocation.

Honeymoon Cruising in the Caribbean. She typed the title for her latest article on her laptop computer, determined to let the answering machine pick up the call. If her husband could ignore the phone, so could she.

Helen gave in on the third ring and reached for the offending mechanism. After all, it might be an editor, or family, or Uncle Sam with another assignment. "Hello."

"Mrs. Bradley?" The woman sounded as though she'd been running. "I need your help. My husband has been murdered."

Helen sat up in her chair. "Who is this?"

"I-lene."

"Irene?" Helen repeated, taking into account the Asian accent.

"Yes. Please, you must help me."

A dozen thoughts flittered through Helen's mind. The woman sounded sane enough, but . . . "Why are you calling me?"

"I understand you are a good investigator and I might be able to hire you."

Though Helen had once been a police officer and did take the occasional case, she didn't consider herself a private investigator—nor was she licensed as one. And she certainly didn't advertise. "Who gave you my name and number?"

"I cannot speak now. Meet me tonight at midnight at the north end of Waterfront Park."

"Midnight . . . I don't think—"

"At the Japanese-American Historical Plaza—do you know where that is?"

"Yes, of course, but—"

Helen's protest was met by a click, then a steady dial tone.

For several long minutes she stared out the window at the clear Oregon sky. Logic told her to ignore the call. Her softer side wouldn't let her. Helen knew all too well how it felt to lose a husband. Even though she'd recently remarried, her own heart still bore the wounds of her first husband's death.

Eleven years ago the State Department had sent Ian McGrady to Lebanon on a top secret mission. Helen had never learned the details, only that he'd been killed in a terrorist bombing.

Thoughts of Ian's death triggered an onslaught of feelings she'd been trying to suppress since the previous night when J.B.—her husband of six weeks—had gotten a phone call from the Pentagon pressing him into service. J.B. had taken a leave of absence from his post with the FBI and a ticket to Washington, D.C. was waiting for him at the Portland Airport.

On one hand, Helen didn't want him to go. On the other, she wished she were going with him.

Her concentration shattered, Helen turned off her laptop and padded into the bedroom to watch her husband pack.

J.B.'s sky-blue gaze met hers as she entered. It was a look she hadn't seen before—one filled with doubt, remorse, sadness. Though they'd only been married a short time, they'd been friends for over thirty years. She'd said good-bye to him a hundred times—but this time seemed different.

"Couldn't you have said no?" Helen sank onto the down comforter on J.B.'s queen-sized bed. Well, actually it was her bed too. She just hadn't gotten the his, mine, and ours thing down yet.

Her home sat on a ledge overlooking the Oregon coast near Lincoln City. It would be their permanent home when J.B. retired from his post with the FBI—if he retired. J.B. lived in a town-house on Portland's waterfront, which was where they'd been staying for the past three days.

"You know better, luv." He stuffed his travel case alongside his briefs in the black leather carry-on. He would be going into one of the world's hot spots—that much Helen knew. Bosnia, the Middle East, Russia—or perhaps Northern Ireland, their homeland. Though the cold war was supposedly over, the fighting never ended.

"Unfortunately, yes." Helen picked up a navy blue throw pil-low from the floor and threw it against the pillow shams behind her. "But a man's got to do what a man's got to do. Right?"

The pained expression on J.B.'s face made her wish she'd kept the last part of her sarcastic statement to herself. She didn't even know why she'd reacted so strongly to his announcement. It cer-tainly wasn't the first time the government had requested his help overseas, and it probably wouldn't be the last. Before they'd mar-ried, she'd taken his departures with a cavalier attitude.

Marriage had changed a lot of things.

"Aye, don't be giving me a difficult time of it now. You'd be going too if they'd asked." J.B. walked to the closet and retrieved a suit jacket and slacks, his large trim body nearly filling the doorway.

Helen didn't bother to deny his retort. They were two of a kind, but that didn't mean she had to like his absence. "How long will you be gone?"

J.B. transferred his suit to the carry-on's special hanger. "Two weeks, maybe three. At least that's what I've been told. I'll try to let you know if it will be more." His loving gaze caught hers and began to thaw her anger.

She didn't want it to and looked away. "And you still won't tell me what you'll be doing?" Helen swung her legs off the bed and paced to the window, warming herself in the wide swatch of morning sun.

"Helen, you of all people should understand. I can't tell you anything at this point." His broad shoulders rose and fell. "At any rate, I don't have all the details yet myself."

She folded her arms across her chest and watched a couple board a yacht in the boat basin below, wishing she and J.B. were still sailing in the turquoise waters off Jamaica. "I do understand. I just don't like it."

"Nor do I, luv." He wrapped his arms around her and drew her back against him. "I hate keeping things from you."

I hate keeping things from you as well, Helen started to say but didn't. She wanted to tell him about the phone call she'd just received, but he'd only worry. And there was really nothing to be concerned about. She'd meet the mysterious caller—this Irene who insisted her husband had been murdered—hear what she had to say, then come home. Simple.

Or was it?

Helen had awakened that morning in an odd mood and might have blamed it on PMS if she hadn't had a hysterectomy a few years back. She knew better than to pass off her instincts as nothing. Something terrible was about to happen. She'd had a similar feeling before Ian's death. Helen thought for a moment about begging J.B. to stay, but only for a moment.

"Shouldn't you be going?" she asked. "Your flight leaves in an hour."

"The limo will be here soon, but I can't go knowing you're angry with me."

Helen turned in his arms and placed her hands on each side of his handsome face, then wove them into his silver hair. "I'm not angry with you, darling. Not really. I'm angry with the government for taking you away from me so soon." Helen tipped her head back and closed her eyes as his lips met hers, his soft whisper reassuring, yet making no promises. They both knew the risks.

The doorbell rang. "That would be my ride." J.B. gathered his bags and admitted the limo driver, then handed over his suitcases. "I'll be right out," he said. When J.B. turned back to Helen his eyes declared his love for her more than words ever could. He gathered her in his arms for a final good-bye. "I'll call you when I get to Washington. I'll be getting my final orders there."

"I may drive to the beach in the morning." Helen reached up to straighten his blue-gray tie. "I can write better there."

He nodded, hesitated for a moment, then left.

Helen closed the door and leaned against it. Saying good-bye had never been that hard before—not even with Ian.

She pushed away from the door and the memory and headed into the bedroom to pack her own bag. With J.B. gone the townhouse felt cold and empty. She'd do better at the beach, where being alone was familiar. There, she'd stay busy, meet her deadlines on the articles she'd promised to several travel magazines, and slip back into the life she'd grown to love.

Her mind whirred with things to do. She'd take along most of her clothes and let her family know she was leaving town, then have a quiet leisurely dinner alone at a riverfront restaurant.

After her three-mile walk, she would have plenty of time to prepare for her late-night appointment with Irene. If all went well, she'd be at the coast tomorrow in time for lunch. Perhaps she'd go to Tidal Raves, her favorite restaurant in Depoe Bay. She'd walk along the beach at Fogarty Creek State Park, soak up some sun, and watch for whales.

Heavenly as it sounded, her usual enthusiasm evaded her.

Helen bit her lip, wishing the anxious feeling in the pit of her stomach would go away. She closed her eyes and uttered a prayer for J.B.'s safety—and her own.

Two

You shouldn't be doing this. Helen ignored the persistent inner voice, reached into the back of her sweater drawer, and pulled out her .38 special. From another drawer she retrieved the ammunition. Since quitting her job with the Portland Police Bureau ten years earlier to become a travel writer, she rarely needed the weapon. Not that she couldn't handle it. Regular practice at a shooting range had proven that her Smith & Wesson and her vision were both functioning as well as ever.

The phone rang. Helen glanced at it, knowing she wouldn't be able to let the answering machine pick it up. She dropped the last of five shells into the cylinder, snapped it shut, then reached for the phone on the fourth ring. Helen half expected to hear the voice of the mystery woman she'd agreed to meet and was surprised when her husband responded.

"There you are, luv." J.B.'s mellow Irish brogue, still present after all these years, temporarily dispelled the anxiety still churning inside her. "Did I wake you? I know it's late, but I wanted to hear your sweet voice one more time before I left the States."

"I was awake. Where are you?" Helen set the gun on the bedside stand. Though his call pleased her, she hoped it wouldn't make her late for her meeting.

"In D.C. My flight's been delayed."

Helen closed her eyes and sat on the edge of the bed, smiling as she envisioned him. "I miss you too. I wish you were here."

"I'd like nothing better, but it's not possible."

"I know. I wonder if the world will ever stop playing these silly spy games. I may as well have married double-o-seven. Same initials, same sort of job."

J.B. chuckled. "And do you find me as handsome and swashbuckling as well, luv?"

More so, Helen thought but didn't say it. "Don't you be getting any ideas. You're no longer a bachelor."

"There's no need to worry about that, now is there? You've captured me heart and soul." J.B. paused and cleared his throat.

"I'm not concerned. Not about that." It's your life I'm worried about. Once again she considered telling J.B. about the phone call from Irene. Had he been home with her instead of on some assignment for the Pentagon, she would have. Perhaps they'd have gone to see the distraught widow together. But J.B. didn't need another worry just now. Nor did she want him telling her she ought not to go.

Helen stared at the red glowing numbers on her radio alarm—11:42. Time to leave. "When is your flight?"

"I have an hour—providing they don't delay it again. I think I'll find a restaurant and have some coffee."

Helen picked up the gun and felt a mingling of excitement and trepidation about wearing it again. "J.B., I . . . be careful."

"I always am, luv."

After saying their I-love-you's, Helen hung up.

"You'd best be careful yourself," she warned the image in the full-length mirror on the closet door. She finger-combed her short salt-and-pepper hair, wishing this once she'd succumbed to the "get rid of the gray" ads. Though she rather liked her silver highlights, dark hair would have made her less conspicuous. Helen had donned a black turtleneck and matching jeans for her midnight rendezvous, but the silver streaks in her hair stood out like fluorescent stripes on a bicycle fender. Had she been home, she might have worn a black knit cap or a scarf, but she had nothing like that at J.B.'s townhouse. Well, too late to do anything about it now.

She slipped the gun into the holster. Odd. The shoulder holster had once felt as comfortable as an old shoe. Now it seemed heavy and awkward. She considered ditching it and using her pack that hung around her waist, then discarded the idea. If she needed the weapon, she wanted to be able to get to it quickly.

After one last look, Helen grabbed a black, lightweight cotton jacket from the hall closet and headed out the door.

Reaching the sidewalk she turned left and jogged past a number of riverfront shops. To her right the sidewalk bordered the Willamette River. She glanced down at the boats bobbing peacefully on the water, secured to their moorings for the night. A couple of late-night inline skaters buzzed past.

Making a left at the Alexis Hotel, Helen followed the sidewalk a block west to Front Street, then north again, angling back toward the river and into the park. About a mile long and a block or so wide, the park ran along Portland's seawall.

Moving quickly through the lights and shadows, she began to question in earnest the wisdom of Irene's time and choice for their meeting. Though the city had made a lot of improvements over the years and police officers patrolled the area regularly, the park was not the safest place for a midnight stroll.

She paused under one of the old-fashioned lamplights near the Salmon Street Fountain to tie a shoelace that had come undone. The comforting sounds of water splashing against the concrete wall were obliterated by a noisy Jet-Ski. The driver careened across the water, shattering the quiet and distorting the city's colorful reflections. She shook her head. Racing around out there at night was not a very smart thing to be doing.

Ironically the same could be said for herself.

Another jogger rushed by, hailing her with a breathless hello as he passed. She helloed him back and pressed on toward the Japanese memorial at the north end of the park. With each step away from the condominium her unease mounted. Her reason for meeting the woman at all escaped her at the moment. But to meet her at this time of night hardly qualified as a wise decision. But then neither had the time she'd gone bungee jumping for an article she never sold.

You could turn back, Helen reminded herself. She wouldn't, of course. Even in her younger days as a police officer she couldn't resist the caller's plea for help. The desperation and sense of urgency in Irene's voice would have compelled her then, perhaps even more than it did now. Although she didn't know the details, Helen had felt Irene's fear even in the few moments they'd connected over the phone and knew she'd do whatever she could to help.

Helen slowed to a walk and zipped her jacket to block out the chilly wind coming off the river. The park was well lit. Nothing to fear, really, she reminded her fluttery stomach again. Still, her heart thudded against the wall of her chest with a great deal more vigor than necessary.

Stopping in the shadow of a tree, Helen scrutinized the area in and around the Japanese-American Historical Plaza where she'd promised to meet Irene. Off to her left, one of the city's homeless lay stretched out on the grass. Three empty bottles lay on the ground beside him.

She glanced at the water. No boats marred the surface now. City lights danced on the ripples. The noisy Jet-Ski and its owner must have decided to call it a night.

The click of shoes on the sidewalk jerked Helen out of her reverie. She glanced around, seeing only the odd-shaped shadows cast by stones commemorating Japanese Americans. Helen ducked behind the largest of the stones. She unzipped her jacket and gripped the handle of her gun.

"Mrs. Bradley?"

Helen straightened and released her hold on the weapon when a woman moved into the light.

Helen walked toward her. "Irene?"

The woman nodded and tipped her head back to meet Helen's gaze. She raised a delicate hand to brush loose strands of straight black hair from her face. Irene had the exquisite features of an international model. Helen guessed her to be in her late thirties. The overall picture suggested both wealth and status—dark pant suit, white blouse, matching two-tone pumps, and exotic perfume—Calix, Helen guessed.

Irene looked familiar, but Helen couldn't place her. "Do I know you?"

"We met years ago at a dinner party honoring my husband, Dr. Andrew Kincaid."

"Kincaid? The gerontologist?" Helen stared at the woman's flawless porcelain skin. Irene hid her age well. She had to be at least sixty.

Irene's dark eyes misted. "Yes, as I mentioned on the phone, my husband is dead."

"I'm so sorry. I'm sure he will be greatly missed." Dr. Kincaid had received national acclaim for his work with the elderly.

"Many people owe their lives to him."

"When did he die? I try to keep up with the news, and I'm sure his death would have made the headlines—especially if he was murdered."

"Four weeks ago. It was not well publicized. I—" Irene glanced behind her, then turned back, apparently satisfied no one was listening. "They say he had a heart attack, but I have recently discovered the truth. My husband was murdered."

"Why come to me? You should be talking to the police."

"They do nothing. Even after my home was burglarized and my husband's files searched, they do not believe me. They are sympathetic but tell me they do not have sufficient evidence to warrant a murder investigation."

Helen scrutinized the woman's face, not sure what she hoped to see. Honesty, maybe. Or mental stability. "What do you want from me?"

"I would like to hire you to find my husband's murderer."

"I'm not sure I can do that. I'm not with the police anymore, but my son, Jason McGrady, works in the homicide division. I could talk to him."

"No, it will do no good. Paul, Andrew's son, has turned them against me. I thought perhaps you would investigate more thoroughly and not be swayed by his lies. I know you have done this type of work before." Irene drew the strap from her shoulder and reached into her handbag.

"I'm not sure I can help you. If the police—"

"I have evidence. I believe Paul . . . " She hesitated, peering nervously into the darkness.

Helen whipped around at the sound of footsteps. A figure approached. At first glance, she dismissed the man in shorts, T-shirt, and tennis shoes as another late-night jogger. When he neared the light under which she and Irene stood, she saw the nylon mask distorting his features—and the gun.

"Don't try anything stupid." He waved the semiautomatic pistol between the two of them. To Irene he said, "Give me your purse, lady. Now!"

Irene hugged the handbag to her side. "No."

"Do as he says," Helen urged, unhooking the leather pack from her waist and letting it drop to the ground. If he stooped to pick it up, she'd gain the advantage with a kick to his knees and a fist to his throat.

"No!" Irene shook her head, still clutching the bag. "I cannot."

The assailant yanked the bag out of Irene's hand and backed away, not bothering to pick up Helen's pack. "Stay put and you won't get hurt." The handbag swung wildly from his arm as he ran back in the direction he'd come.

"Don't let him get away!" Irene called, pursuing the thief. "He has the disk!"

"Irene, stop!" Helen drew her gun and sprinted after them.

The thief vaulted over the railing onto a boat ramp. A moment later, he popped back up and opened fire.

"Get down!" Helen pushed Irene aside, managing to fire off three quick shots.

The gunman returned fire. Helen dove for the sidewalk as a bullet tore into her right arm. Pain exploded through her shoulder when she collided with the concrete. The gun fell from her hand and skittered out of reach. Blood pounded in her ears, nearly drowning out the motor of what sounded like a Jet-Ski.

Helen rose to her knees. The lights merged into a fuzzy gray— then black.

Three

The high-pitched squeal of police cars and a rescue unit from the nearby fire station drew Helen back into consciousness.

"What have we got?" a woman asked.

"Two victims, both gunshot wounds," a man answered. "This one got it in the chest—lost a lot of blood."

"Irene—?" Helen scrunched her eyes shut to minimize the glare from the flashing lights and tried to sit. The pain in her arm and shoulder drove her back to the ground.

"Take it easy, ma'am." A police officer who looked no older than her sixteen-year-old granddaughter knelt beside Helen. "The EMTs are looking after your friend. They'll get to you in a minute. Can you tell me your name?"

Helen did.

"What about your friend?"

"Irene Kincaid. Is she...?" Helen gritted her teeth as another jolt of pain scattered her thoughts.

"She's alive. Just rest now, ma'am."

"The gunman," she panted. "Did someone go after him?"

Helen didn't know whether he answered or not as a wave of nausea rumbled through her and sent her world spinning. Consciousness stayed just out of reach as paramedics cut the turtleneck and jacket away from her wound, hooked up an IV, and transported her to the hospital.

When Helen awoke more fully, the sirens had been replaced by the din of an emergency room. At least a dozen green-clad figures bustled around her, poking and prodding.

A sturdy gray-haired woman in scrubs stood to her left, pump-ing up a blood pressure cuff. Another nurse hung a bag of fluid.

A young man in wire-rimmed glasses scrutinized Helen's shoulder. "Better get an x-ray. And clean up this wound so we can see what we're dealing with. Looks like she might have a dislo-cated shoulder under all that blood."

"Sure thing." The curtains swished apart as one of the nurses stepped out.

His blue-green gaze moved to Helen's face. "I'm Dr. Long." He shined a light in her eyes and checked her ears, then asked her name. She gave it.

"How are you doing?"

"Not bad as long as I don't move—or breathe."

He nodded. "We'll get you something for pain and throw in a muscle relaxant. Are you allergic to anything?"

At the shake of her head, Dr. Long called out an order, and a few seconds later a nurse stood over her with a syringe and deft-ly deposited the contents into Helen's hip.

Helen drifted in and out of consciousness as various techni-cians, doctors, and nurses drew her blood, x-rayed her, and injected her shoulder with a local anesthetic. Once she'd suppos-edly relaxed, Dr. Long popped her shoulder back into place and sewed her up.

"Mrs. Bradley," the gray-haired nurse told her. "There's a police officer outside who wants to talk to you—if you're up to it."

"Up to it?" Helen managed a smile.

"I could put him off."

"No. I'll talk to him."

Helen's son approached the gurney looking none too pleased. Jason McGrady's still-handsome face bore the scars of serving his country in the war on drugs. He'd recently quit the Drug

Enforcement Agency to take what he thought would be a less demanding job with the Portland Police Bureau as a detective in the homicide division. Jason came forward and kissed her cheek. "What happened?"

Helen took a deep breath, wishing she hadn't. She waited a moment for the pain to subside, then told him about Irene's phone call.

Jason shook his head. "I can't believe you went out alone like that. Why didn't you call me? I'd have come with you."

Helen attempted a smile but didn't quite make it. She patted his hand, then let her arm drop back on the sheets. "I don't suppose you caught the gunman?"

"Not yet. We do have an eyewitness—a vagrant. I'm hoping you can give us a more accurate account. With all that booze pickling his brain, his testimony isn't worth spit. According to him the guy jumped over the seawall and took off on a Jet-Ski."

"That's possible. I thought I heard one. I . . . " It was getting harder and harder to keep her eyes open—and to think. "I saw someone on a Jet-Ski a few minutes earlier—seemed odd he'd be out that time of night." She recounted as best she could the incident with the purse snatcher. "I wouldn't have gone after him, but Irene—how is she?"

"Don't know. She's in surgery. The doc said she had a punctured lung, among other things." Jason rested his elbows on the raised bedrail and rubbed his chin. "Want to tell me why you were meeting Mrs. Kincaid in the park at midnight?"

Helen's eyes drifted closed. Her mouth felt dry. "Irene insisted her husband had been murdered . . . wanted me to . . . investigate. I'm . . . sorry, I can't . . ."

"I'll have to ask you to leave now," someone said. Helen didn't bother to open her eyes when the gurney moved.

The rest of the night, she wavered on the edge of awareness. Nurses and aids bustled in with pain medication, ice packs, and miscellaneous equipment at regular intervals to assure themselves and her that she was still among the living. At times Helen found herself thinking that at least the dead got some sleep.

The light pouring into the room made the memories of the purse snatcher and the shooting seem like a bad dream. Helen winced as she turned her head to look at her shoulder. Pain and the white gauze dressing bore witness to its reality.

Little by little her other senses awakened. Despite the occasional sips of water, her mouth felt as if it had been left in a food dehydrator all night.

Her vision cleared and focused on a blank television screen. Not blank exactly. In it, she could see her reflection. The unflattering image startled her and she looked away.

Helen chewed on her lower lip. Oh, Lord, how could I have been so stupid? She wondered what J.B. would say when he found out she'd been shot. He'd probably lecture her for not confessing what she'd planned to do, but only after he'd kissed her and given her flowers and put her fears to rest. He'd take good care of her—nurse her back to health.

Helen bristled—partly because J.B. wouldn't be there and partly because she hated the thought of needing care at all. She'd become fiercely independent after Ian's death. Now a buried fear assaulted her. Would this injury put an end to that independence?

She glanced back up at the reflection and murmured, "Helen Bradley, how could you even think such a thing?"

A movement to her right startled her. The curtain parted to admit Jason. "How are you doing this morning?"

Without waiting for an answer he approached the bed, bent over the rail, and kissed Helen's cheek. "I have to admit I've been pretty worried." He looked exhausted.

"No need to concern yourself about me. The wound isn't that serious. I'll be up and around in no time." Helen followed her announcement with a silent prayer.

"I haven't been able to get a hold of Kate or J.B."

"I'd rather you didn't try." Helen's daughter and Jason's twin, Kate Calhoun, her husband, Kevin, and their two children, Lisa and Kurt, were on their way to Montana for vacation. Since they were driving and sightseeing along the way, they wouldn't arrive at their final destination—a dude ranch—for another three days.

"Are you kidding? Kate would have a fit if we didn't let her know."

"It's not necessary. I don't want to interrupt their vacation. They've been looking forward to it all summer."

Jason shrugged. "I suppose you're right. But what about J.B.? He'll want to know. I called his office. They wouldn't tell me anything."

Helen pursed her lips. "He's on assignment. Top secret."

Jason raked long slender fingers through his nearly black hair. "Did he say when he'd be back?"

"Three weeks, maybe."

"Hopefully he'll call me when he can't get you at home." Jason lifted up a burgundy overnight case. "By the way, Susan sends her love and said you might need this. She'll be in later."

"That was sweet of her."

Jason nodded. His dark blue eyes had taken on that haunted look they often did when he talked about his ex-wife. Helen started to ask how his quest to win her back was going but didn't. It wasn't something she wanted to deal with at the moment.

"Could I get you anything?"

"Water."

"You got it." He hurried into the hall and had only been gone a few minutes when the door to her private room opened. The man who entered wore a white lab coat over a pale blue shirt and khaki trousers.

"Mrs. Bradley?" The morning sun illuminated his blond hair, giving him a halo effect. Only this man was no angel. From the set of his square jaw and look of pure displeasure in his pastel blue eyes, Helen figured he was either constipated or terribly annoyed. "I'm Dr. Kincaid."

"Andrew?" Helen shook her head to dispel the notion she was seeing a ghost. "But you can't be . . . oh, of course, you must be Irene's son, Paul." Looking closely she could see his father's features—the high forehead and sandy hair. But blue eyes? That seemed strange considering Irene's Asian ancestry. A former marriage or adoption? "How is Irene?"

"Alive, no thanks to you." The creases in his forehead grew more severe.

"Excuse me?"

"How dare you lure her out at that time of night?"

"Now wait a minute." Helen grabbed the bed rail and tried to sit up. Pain forced her to retreat. Her stomach rebelled. She took several shallow breaths, willing the nausea to pass. It didn't.

Dr. Kincaid grabbed a small plastic tray from the nightstand and placed it under Helen's chin, holding her forward while she vomited.

After she'd emptied her stomach of what little it had in it, she fell back against the sheets. Moments later, she gratefully accepted the warm wet washcloth the doctor handed her.

"I'm sorry if I've upset you—perhaps I should have waited until tomorrow." His anger had been replaced with a look of concern. "Are you feeling better?"

Helen was afraid to answer—afraid to move.

"Here's your water...." Jason set the pitcher on the bedside table. He looked at Helen, then shifted his gaze to Dr. Kincaid.

"What's going on? Are you her doctor?"

"No, I'm . . . look this isn't a good time. I'll come by later."

"No, wait!" Helen's plea came out as little more than a whisper. She couldn't let him go without clearing up his obvious misconception. "I didn't lure your mother anywhere, Dr. Kincaid. She called me and asked me to meet her."

He stared at her for a moment, his frown returning. "Why would she do that?"

"Irene believes your father was murdered."

He shook his head. "And you believed her?"

"I had no reason not to."

"Mrs. Bradley, my mother—stepmother"—he added the phrase as if disowning her—"lives in a fantasy world. My father had a massive coronary. It happened in the presence of several colleagues—medical doctors. I arrived within seconds of the attack, but we were unable to save him."

"But she seemed so certain."

Paul sighed. "Look, Mrs. Bradley, I'm sorry she dragged you into this. The truth is, Irene is an Alzheimer's patient."

"But she's so young," Helen gasped. "I mean—I know it can affect younger people, but . . . "

Dr. Kincaid smiled for the first time. "Yes, she does look young. Irene has been using some of our anti-aging products. They've worked wonders on her." He sobered again. "She may look young, but she's actually sixty-nine. She's had symptoms of Alzheimer's for five years. We thought she'd stabilized, but apparently she's getting worse."

Helen closed her eyes for a moment, picturing the woman she'd met the night before. She tried to superimpose the image Irene's stepson had painted over the impression still fresh in her mind. The two didn't fit.

Four

Dr. Kincaid exited, looking rather like a peacock with his tail feathers at half-mast.

"What was that all about?" Jason asked.

"I'll tell you later." Helen's interest in the Kincaids vanished as her aching body reminded her all too abruptly where she was and why.

The rest of the day went by much as the previous night, with the same regularity of interrupted naps, medications, ice packs, and periodic checks by nurses. Then there were the walks. Four times nurses who could have passed as army sergeants ordered Helen out of bed to walk to the toilet, then up and down the halls.

By midafternoon the desire to be put out of her misery had dissipated. After a tedious bath, she'd ditched the open-backed hospital gown and, with the aid's assistance, donned the new cotton nightgown and teal velour robe Susan had packed for her. The clothes, a little makeup, and a brush through her hair made her feel and look almost normal. Helen eyed the reflection in the television screen. Much better.

As much as she hated the idea of letting J.B. know what had happened to her, she had to try. If he'd been the one injured, she would want to know immediately. There had to be some way to get in touch with him. Helen eyed the telephone sitting on a bedside stand just out of reach. Jason had already called J.B.'s office. Even if they knew, they probably wouldn't tell her anything. Maybe she'd try later. Helen tipped her head back and closed her eyes, then put her fears about her husband on God's much broader shoulders.

The door opened and Susan McGrady entered with a bouquet of flowers. "Jason said to give you his love. He'll be back when he gets off work."

"Thank you." Helen buried her nose in one of the half-dozen red and white carnations and inhaled the blend of sweetness and spice. "So, how are you and Jason getting along?" After Jason had been missing and presumed dead for five years, Susan had filed for divorce and become engaged to another man. Jason's surprise homecoming had forced her to reexamine her plans.

Susan set the vase on the bedside stand and lifted her thick auburn hair off the back of her neck. "All right, I guess. The kids have been pressuring me to remarry him. He's been surprisingly patient." She glanced down, then slowly lifted her gaze to meet Helen's. "I wish I knew what to do. I still love Jason, but I'm afraid to go back."

"He's changed—for the better," Helen said softly.

"I know. But he's still in law enforcement. I honestly don't know if I can handle that kind of life again. Never knowing. Hoping the next phone call isn't the one telling me he's dead. It was so awful before . . . yet I want to do what's best for the kids." She offered Helen a wistful smile. "But then you know all about that, don't you?"

Helen grasped Susan's hand. "I wish I could help, but it's a decision you have to make on your own."

"True. I wish you'd tell that to Jennie and Nick. Nick especially. He's always wanting to know why Daddy can't move back to our house."

Helen glanced at the door. "Which reminds me, where are they?"

"The receptionist said Nick was too young to visit, so Jennie's watching him. They're probably upstairs at the nursery window by now."

"Did someone you know have a baby?"

Susan grinned and shook her head, taking a seat on one of the tan vinyl-covered chairs against the wall. "No. Nick's been obsessing on babies lately. He's gotten it into his head that as soon as Jason comes home we're going to give him a little brother."

"I see." Helen resisted adding her own thoughts on the subject, since they were probably much closer to Nick's than Susan's.

Susan's blush faded. "Helen, I . . . um, Jennie's anxious to talk to you. She's playing detective again. I'm worried she might try to find the person who shot at you."

"And you want me to dissuade her."

"If you can."

Helen smiled. The sixteen-year-old had not been an easy daughter to raise. Not because she was rebellious or disobedient. Jennie was just pure McGrady—from the indigo eyes, slender build, and dark hair to her stubborn nature and penchant for solving crimes. She'd already made a name for herself locally— and worrying Susan to distraction. "I'll do my best."

"Well, I'd better go rescue her. She's anxious to see you."

Susan had been gone no more than five minutes when Jennie arrived. She approached the bed warily.

"Does it hurt much?" Jennie asked.

Her eyes held an all-too-common gleam, and Helen suspected her granddaughter had already begun to investigate the shooting.

Jennie gave her grandmother a kiss. "Are you sure you're going to be okay? You don't have an infection or fever or anything, do you?"

"I'm going to be just fine. In fact, I should be out of here by tomorrow." Helen paused as the implications of what Jennie had said hit her. "Why would you ask if I had an infection?"

Jennie shrugged. "I guess because Mrs. Kincaid has one—a bad one. The paper said she might not make it."

"Really?" The information unnerved her. "Would you save the

article for me?" Helen asked, deciding to put her ambitious detective to work on a safe project. "And while you're at it, maybe you could clip anything you find pertaining to the purse snatching and the Kincaids."

"Sure. Do you think we could work on the case together?" Jennie asked.

Helen chuckled. "Do I look like I'm in any condition to go after a mugger?"

"I could help."

"I think it might be better if we leave this one to the police."

Surprisingly, Jennie didn't argue. "Mom said I shouldn't stay long." Her gaze darted toward the closed door, then back at Helen. "You are going to be okay, aren't you, Gram?"

Helen grasped Jennie's hand and gave it a firm squeeze. "I'll be fine."

By the time Jennie left, Helen could hardly keep her eyes open. Loneliness and a feeling of dread inched their way into her fading thoughts as she drifted off. J.B. still hadn't called.

The nurse roused her an hour later for a dinner of creamed soup, applesauce, and custard. Evening came and went as did her visitors—Jennie and Susan. Jennie reported that Irene was doing better and that her fever was down. Susan brought her a new devotional book on St. Theresa of Avilla.

Jason dragged in at nine, looking even more weary and glassy-eyed than he had that morning. He dropped down in the chair and stretched out his legs.

"Would you like my bed?" Helen shifted the covers to the side. "Looks like you could use it more than I."

He wiped a hand down his eyes and over his unshaven face. "Do I look that bad? Don't answer. We had another homicide today. That makes a dozen since I've been here."

"I know, I watched the news during dinner. You're not having second thoughts about the job, are you?"

"I'm not planning on going back to work for the DEA, if that's what you mean. I like the job. It's just that I'm not getting to spend much time with Susan and the kids. At the rate I'm going she'll never take me back."

"Oh, I have a feeling she will. She needs time to adjust to your coming back—to your being alive. You have to admit you've given her plenty of reasons not to trust you."

Jason glanced at his watch. "Yeah, and these hours I'm putting in aren't helping much. I told her I'd come by around nine—it's after that now. I hate to rush off."

"It's okay. I'm not in the mood for a long visit anyway. Did you find out anything about J.B.?"

He shook his head. "Put calls in to some key people. I should hear something soon." He pushed himself to his feet. "I'll let you know."

"Thanks. Have a nice visit with Susan."

His haggard look almost disappeared when he smiled. "Oh, I will."

"Jason," she called him back. "We need to talk about Irene."

"I know. You want me to follow up on her accusations. I did some checking today on the case. I've asked for a full report. Should have it by tomorrow."

———

The following morning, Dr. Long signed her discharge papers on the condition that she not stay alone. Helen finally agreed to staying with Susan and the children for a few days.

"Now, you see that she behaves herself," he said to Jason in a tone that made Helen feel like an errant child.

"Don't worry. We'll take good care of her." Jason winked at her.

Dr. Long turned to Helen and gave her a lopsided grin. "And

no late-night trysts with armed purse snatchers. That shoulder needs time to heal. You've got a fair amount of muscle and soft tissue damage."

"I meant to ask you earlier—I know I won't be doing any push-ups or cartwheels, but what about writing? I have several assignments with deadlines looming and . . . "

"You're a writer!" He eyed the sling that supported her wounded right shoulder. "Wait, don't tell me. You write mysteries—just like Jessica Fletcher."

"No. Nothing so exciting, I'm afraid."

"I wondered, with the gunshot wound and all."

Jason cleared his throat. "Don't give her any ideas." Then in a tone that made him sound almost proud he added, "Actually, my mother is a travel writer. She gets paid to visit these great vacation spots and write about them."

"Sounds like fun."

"It is, most of the time." Helen eased back into the conversation. "But what I need to know is, when will I be able to write? At the moment it hurts to move anything."

"I'll get you started on an exercise program in a couple days. You may even want to consider checking yourself into a rehab center for a month or so. In the meantime, you can try writing for short periods—just make sure your arm is supported and don't overdo it. In another six weeks that arm and shoulder should be good as new."

Helen winced at the six weeks. She wasn't used to being restricted, and the thought depressed her. Of course, six weeks wasn't really that long. It would be a good time to catch up on some reading and enjoy her grandchildren. And maybe she'd quietly look into Andrew Kincaid's death.

As she settled into the wheelchair for the ride to the car, Helen set her anxieties aside and vowed to make the best of things.

"Gram is here! She's here. She's here." Nick bounced across the wide porch and down the stairs. Bernie, his St. Bernard pup, followed.

Helen's heart flip-flopped as she watched him race toward the car. "Oh, Jason, Nick looks more like you every day."

"Mmm. I know. He's a great kid. I just wish I'd been able to come back sooner." Jason set the emergency brake and unfastened his seat belt.

"Well, you're here now. That's what matters."

Jennie's welcome was a bit more controlled than her younger brother's, but her eyes glowed with enthusiasm as she opened the passenger door.

Nick darted in front of Jennie with his arms stretched out to receive a hug. Jennie grabbed him before he could plow into Helen. "Be careful, big guy. Gram's got a major owie on her arm."

"I know. Daddy said we have to be real careful 'cause when people are old they get flag—fagile." He sighed. "You know—they break easy."

"I didn't mean that like it sounded," Jason said, offering her a hand out of the car.

"Humph." Helen swung around in the seat. "I am neither old nor fragile. Come on, sweetheart." She motioned to Nick with her left hand. "Give your gram a big hug."

Bernie stuck his nose between them, begging for a little of the attention she'd been lavishing on Nick. Helen complied.

Once settled in the spare bedroom of the large Victorian home, Helen's first official task was to take a nap, which she did. She was awakened sometime later by the phone ringing.

Seconds later Jennie tapped on the door and stuck her head

into the bedroom. "Just checking to see if you're awake." She held up a cordless phone. "It's for you. Irene Kincaid. Do you want to talk to her?"

"Sure." Helen grabbed the phone and cradled it between her chin and left shoulder. "Hello?"

"Helen." Irene's frantic voice lowered to a whisper. "Helen, please, you must help me. They are trying to poison me."

Five

Helen pressed the phone against her ear and tried to sit up. "Irene?" When she didn't answer, Helen asked, "Are you still there?"

"Yes . . . yes." She paused. "Please, help me."

"Where are you?"

Irene didn't answer. The rasping breaths ceased, followed by a click and a dial tone.

"What's wrong?" Jennie placed a sturdy arm behind Helen for support.

"Irene may be in trouble. She just told me someone was trying to poison her." Helen sucked in a deep breath to ward off the dizziness. "Get me the number for the hospital. I need to call—"

"I'll get it, but you'd better let me do the calling. You look like you're ready to faint."

Helen eased back against the pillow. "I'm . . . I'm all right," she panted. "Just make the call."

"Be back in a couple of minutes."

The encounter with pain and an overdose of adrenalin sent Helen's heart skittering. Her skin felt cool and clammy. She concentrated on slowing down her breathing and relaxing her tense muscles.

Five minutes later Jennie came in carrying a fresh ice pack and a glass of water. "I talked to Irene's nurse and everything is okay—well, not totally. The nurse said she's been delusional. She's even been accusing the nurses of poisoning her when they try to give her medication."

"She sounded so desperate."

"Who are you talking about?" Susan came in and handed Helen two pain pills. "I thought you might want these. You're overdue."

"Thanks."

Jennie told her mother about Irene while Helen reached for her water. She thought about refusing the pills. She needed a clear head. But then how could she think at all when her shoulder protested so loudly? Propping herself up, Helen took the pills, then sank back into the pillows and placed the ice pack over her shoulder. How long would she have to put up with the pain and inconvenience? The brief flurry of activity had left her exhausted and frustrated. She hated being laid up. Helen McGrady, she caught herself before the pity party could begin in earnest, how could you even think of feeling sorry for yourself? At least you're out of the hospital and improving, while Irene . . . Only God knew what was happening to Irene.

Jennie pulled an armchair closer to the bed and dropped into it.

Susan picked up the empty water glass and headed for the door. "I'm so sorry about your friend."

"I wish I could see her for myself, but . . . "

Jennie's gaze met hers. "Why don't I go? Mom won't mind. I could easily be back before dark."

"I don't know, Jennie. I'd rather not have you involved in case there is a problem."

Jennie rolled her eyes.

"Why don't I call Jason?" Susan continued. "He's coming for dinner, so we could ask him to stop on his way."

"That makes sense," Helen agreed. "He'll be able to get more information than either of you. Ask him to talk to the nurses—find out as much as he can. Something doesn't mesh. If Irene is that delusional, how did she manage to find me at your number?"

After her nap, Helen managed a short walk, exercised her arm, and was beginning to feel somewhat human again. The wonderful smells coming from the kitchen drew her there.

"Can I get you anything?" Susan lifted the lid from the electric frypan and turned the chicken.

"A cup of tea would be nice, but I can get that myself."

"Don't be silly. I've already got water on the stove." Susan poured two cups of hot water and set a canister of various teas on the table.

"Where is everyone?" Helen glanced around. "It's so quiet."

"Jennie took Nick to the library. Said something about looking up information on Dr. Kincaid." Glancing at the clock, Susan added, "They should be here any minute."

"I hope you don't mind my asking Jennie to do some research for me."

"Not at all. Wonderful idea, actually—keeps her busy and out of trouble." Susan dunked her orange spice teabag and set it on the saucer. "Helen, I . . . I've been meaning to ask you something."

"Yes . . ."

"I know you'd like Jason and me to remarry, but . . . " Susan stared at the rosy brew in her cup, then closed her eyes. "This is so hard for me. I feel like a traitor for even having questions. But the truth is, I don't know if I want to go back. I'm not like you, Helen. You're always so understanding and calm. I mean, here J.B. is gone on some assignment somewhere and you're not the least bit worried."

"Susan . . . "

"No, don't say it. I'm sure it would be best for the children, and maybe I'm being selfish, but I hate the thought of losing him again. Every time I look at him and see the scar on his cheek, I'm reminded of the danger he faces."

"I do understand—more than you know. It tears me up inside not knowing where J.B. is—not having him here with me."

"I'm sorry—I didn't mean to imply you didn't care." Susan drew both hands through her thick natural curls, then settled them on the table. "You just seem to be so much better suited to that kind of life."

"The secret, for me at least, is not dwelling on what could go wrong, but to focus on what is."

Susan nodded. "Easier said than done. I guess the question I'm asking is whether love is really enough."

Funny, Helen had been asking herself that same question. She squeezed Susan's hand. "I don't know, darling. I really don't know. What I do know is that you don't have to decide right now. Pray about it. Ask God to help you make the choice. That may seem simplistic, but sometimes we just need to back off and let life happen. You're trying entirely too hard."

"Okay, so you're saying I should just relax and not worry about making a decision right now?"

"That about sums it up."

"How will I know when I'm ready?"

"You will."

About halfway through tea, Bernie's deep woof announced Jennie and Nick's arrival. Jason showed up a few minutes later. Between Nick's excitement over his new books and getting dinner on the table, they were well into their chicken and mashed potatoes and gravy dinner before the subject of Irene Kincaid came up.

"Did you stop at the hospital, Dad?" Jennie forked an asparagus spear and nibbled at the tender head.

"No, I'm sorry." Jason's dark brows nearly touched when he frowned. "I'll have to go after dinner. Just couldn't work it in this afternoon. I did call though, and the nurses assured me that Irene was doing a little better."

Helen nodded. "I'm relieved to hear that at least."

"I also did some more checking into the case, but I'll fill you in on that later." He gave her a for-your-ears-only look.

"That Kincaid family is something else," Jennie said. "Dr. Kincaid developed all this anti-aging stuff. And they are extremely wealthy. We're talking billions."

"I knew about his work in gerontology." Helen set down the drumstick she'd been nibbling and wiped her hand on her napkin. "His son mentioned that Irene had been using some anti-aging products."

"What's ger-a-tology?" Nick asked.

"Well, ology is the study of something," Jennie explained. "And gerontology is the study of—"

"Gerbils?" Nick tipped his head to the side.

"Close, Nick," Jennie chuckled. "It's the study of aging."

"What's aging?"

Jennie sighed. "When people get older."

"I'm getting older. I'll be six next May fifteenth. On my last birthday I axed for my daddy to come back and he did. Next time I'm axing for a new baby brother."

Jason's hopeful gaze swept to Susan, who ignored it and tried to change the subject.

"Nick, are you ready for another piece of chicken? Or how about some dessert—I made your favorite—chocolate cake."

Jennie cleared her throat. "Anyway, I brought you lots of articles about the Kincaids and the stuff they were working on."

Helen thanked her and promised to look it over later.

After dinner, Jason left for the hospital. Helen joined Susan and the children in the family room. While they watched television, she browsed through some of the articles and notes Jennie had gathered.

The articles verified that the well-known doctor had indeed died of a heart attack. Helen felt remiss at not having heard about Andrew's death, but it had happened while she'd been in Paris with J.B., where he'd proposed. Remembering back to those glorious few days, the news could have been broadcast from every satellite dish in the galaxy and she'd have missed it.

Another interesting piece of news was that Edgewood had been Dr. Kincaid's dream child—a utopia of sorts for the older generation. It consisted of an elite multilevel facility, offering senior citizens every imaginable alternative. Clients could buy or rent state-of-the-art condominiums set high on a hill overlooking the Columbia River Gorge. The facility featured golf, fishing, hiking trails, a restaurant, swimming pools, and fitness centers. Expensive, but the package included an insurance policy that provided lifetime care for those who needed it.

Edgewood also offered assisted living apartments along with a complete care facility, rehabilitation center, and nursing home.

All of this, Helen realized, fell to Andrew Kincaid's heirs. Irene, Paul, and a daughter, Mai Lin Chang, had inherited Kincaid Enterprises, which consisted of Edgewood Estates and Kincaid Laboratories—a multimillion-dollar organization. Reading through various articles, Helen gleaned bits and pieces of information that helped her get to know the Kincaid family a little better. Dr. Mai Lin Chang, for instance, was married to David Chang, also a doctor. They had an eighteen-year-old son. And Paul Kincaid—though never married—was engaged to Adriane Donahue, another gerontologist. All of the doctors seemed highly esteemed among researchers, or so the articles said.

When her body could no longer tolerate being up, Helen

excused herself and went to her bedroom for a brief rest. She'd just climbed into bed when the phone rang. A few seconds later Jennie brought in the phone. "Dad wants to talk to you."

"Jason, I was about to give up on you. Is everything all right?"

"I'm afraid I haven't made it to the hospital yet. Got a call on the way. It looks like we may have found the purse snatcher."

"Oh, that is good news. So you've made an arrest?"

"No." Jason cleared his throat. "He's down at the morgue. A fisherman found his body washed up over at Kelly Point, where the Willamette flows into the Columbia. Mrs. Kincaid's purse was still hooked around his neck. Looks like he made his getaway on a Jet-Ski. We found one beached about a quarter of a mile upstream. Guy's name is Charlie Dupay. He's got a couple of pri-ors—petty theft and possession. Crack user—which might explain the violent behavior."

"What about the contents of the purse? Irene had mentioned something about a disk."

"Nothing like that in it. Just the usual, wallet—a couple hun-dred in cash—credit cards, makeup, that sort of thing."

"How did he die?" Helen glanced at Jennie, whose expression oozed curiosity.

"Aside from the drowning, he had a nasty dent in his skull. The medical examiner thinks he may have lost control of the Jet-Ski. No way of knowing for sure. I'll let you know if we find anything else."

After thanking him and saying good-bye, Helen handed the phone back to Jennie.

"It was about the gunman, right?" she asked.

"Yes. Looks like they found him." Helen reiterated part of the conversation, then added, "I guess that's the end of it."

"But what about Mrs. Kincaid's husband? She thinks he was murdered. And where's the disk she was going to give you?"

Helen shook her head. "There may not have been a murder or a disk."

"Do you think Mrs. Kincaid lied?" Jennie dropped sideways into the arm chair and dangled her long legs over the arm.

"No. Not lied. I think she believed everything she said. It's just that her story may not be based on reality."

"So it's over?"

"Looks that way." Helen winced as she adjusted her pillow.

"Can I get you anything?" Jennie swung her legs around to the front of the chair and sprang forward.

"The usual—pain pills and an ice pack."

Jennie hurried away and Helen's heart ballooned with pride. She almost wished she could involve Jennie in her investigation. Investigation? Now why had that word surfaced? Hadn't she just told Jennie it was all over? They had found the mugger and retrieved Irene's purse intact. No disk, but Paul Kincaid had said his mother was suffering from Alzheimer's. Still, Helen couldn't quite put the incident to rest.

She took her medication and slept for two hours. When she awoke it was dark. Susan had come in to check on her.

"Sorry, I didn't mean to wake you."

"You didn't. Did Jason come back?"

"Yes. He's anxious to talk with you but didn't want to wake you. I'll get him."

"How is Irene?" Helen asked the moment Jason entered the room.

"It's a long story." In two strides he reached the mauve arm-chair and sank into it. "I guess I should start with how she knew where to call you."

"Sounds like a good plan." Helen scooted back to a sitting position and set an extra pillow behind her back.

"Irene has had times, usually in the morning or late at night, when she is quite lucid." Jason stretched out his long legs and hooked his hands behind his head. "The nurse I spoke with said she'd given Irene the number. Irene wanted to thank you personally."

"But instead she tells me she's being poisoned?"

Jason leaned forward and rested his elbows on his denim-clad knees. "Yes, although everything can be explained. Irene made all sorts of accusations against the hospital staff. That mostly happened while she was running a high fever. They thought the fever might have caused the delirium—at least part of the time. Of course, since she has Alzheimer's . . . "

"Yes, so I heard. I understand that the only way to tell if someone definitely has Alzheimer's is with an autopsy. The diagnosis is a guess based on a person's symptoms."

Jason leaned back again, loosening his tie. "Her son specializes in geriatrics. He should know."

Helen nodded, meeting her son's concerned gaze. "Did you think to ask about visitors—like who and how many?"

"As a matter of fact, I did." He shrugged. "She had a lot of them—mostly family. Dr. Chang, Irene's daughter, stayed there the first couple of nights."

"I get the feeling there's something you're not telling me."

Jason hesitated, then asked, "How's the shoulder? Do you need something for pain—an ice bag?"

"No, I'm fine. Jennie brought me some just after you left. Quit trying to change the subject."

"I'm sorry. It's just that I know when I tell you what happened you'll want to investigate on your own."

"Jason, look at me. I can hardly get up to go to the bathroom. Now tell me. Did you see her? How is she?"

"She was gone. The family signed her out and took her to Edgewood Manor."

"The nursing home? But she was in critical care."

"It didn't make sense to the nurses either. They said her condition had deteriorated. Late this afternoon she went into cardiac arrest. They were able to resuscitate her, but she's still in danger. About an hour later Paul Kincaid showed up with an ambulance and checked her out."

"Why on earth would he do that?"

"He's threatening to file a lawsuit against the hospital for negligence. Kincaid thinks Irene was contaminated in surgery, and he's taking her to his facility, where he claims she'll receive better care. He thinks Kincaid Laboratories will be able to find an antibiotic to fight her infection more efficiently than anything they have at the hospital."

Helen stared at her hands and loosened her grip on the bedspread. "You're right about my wanting to investigate. I can understand Paul's frustration, but to have her transferred out when she's critically ill—that's negligence."

"To be honest, I might have done the same thing if I had the resources he does. And I'd be furious with the hospital for letting an infection get out of hand."

"I suppose we'll have to see what comes of it. There isn't much we can do tonight. Maybe I'll call out there tomorrow and see how she is."

Jason nodded. "There is one more thing I should probably tell you, although it's entirely possible the nurses are saying it to protect themselves."

"What's that?"

"One of the nurses I talked to on the unit seemed especially worried about Irene being discharged—not so much about the quality of care at Edgewood, but the lack of it."

"What do you mean? From what I've read, Edgewood has one

of the best geriatric and rehabilitation facilities around."

"It does. But the nurse said with Dr. Kincaid being such a strong advocate for assisted suicide, she's afraid he may have taken Irene to Edgewood to die."

Edgewood Manor, how may I direct your call?" The crisp pleasant voice was almost as bright as the early morning sun. Except for a dull ache in her right shoulder, Helen felt almost like her old self. She'd already made coffee, read from her new devotional book, and single-handedly typed two pages of an article on whale watching along the Oregon coast.

"Good morning." Helen smiled despite her concern for Irene. "You have a patient there—Irene Kincaid. I'd like to find out how she's doing."

"Mrs. Kincaid? Of course. She's in the north wing. I'll connect you with the nurses' station."

Helen sipped at her coffee while she waited. After a few moments a woman identifying herself as Stephanie answered. Helen asked again about Irene.

"You said you were a friend?" This time the response was cool and abrupt.

"Yes...."

"I'm sorry, but Dr. Kincaid has asked that we not release information to anyone other than family."

"I'm Helen Bradley, the woman who was with her Sunday night when she was injured. I've been concerned about her." Helen watched her daughter-in-law shuffle into the kitchen. Susan's bright floral print robe reminded her of a field of tulips and made the morning even brighter.

"I wish I could help you, Mrs. Bradley, but . . . "

"All I want is a brief update on her condition. Is she the same, doing better... ?"

Stephanie sighed. "Well, I guess it wouldn't hurt to tell you that much. She's stable. It's too soon to tell, but I'd say she's looking better."

"Is she still delusional?"

"Excuse me?"

"Irene called me yesterday from the hospital. She insisted someone was trying to poison her. The nurses there said she'd been confused. They thought it may have been caused by the high fever."

"Oh, I . . . I . . . um . . . no, I've seen no signs of confusion. Mrs. Bradley, I don't mean to be rude, but I have patients waiting."

"Certainly. Thanks so much for your time. Oh, one more thing. When are visiting hours?"

"Our doors are always open to friends and family. We just ask that you check in at the desk first."

Helen thanked her again and hung up.

"How is she?" Susan set a steaming mug of coffee on the table and went back to the counter to retrieve the stack of toast she'd been preparing.

"Apparently better." Helen frowned.

"You don't sound convinced." Susan brought over the coffeepot and topped off Helen's cup.

"I'm puzzled. Stephanie—the nurse I just spoke with—sounded surprised when I asked about Irene being delusional. Of course, she may not have had time to read the chart. Still, you'd think . . . "

Susan warmed her hands on a hand thrown-mug before taking a tentative sip. "Sounds like you were having a hard time extracting information from her. Maybe she knows and didn't want to say."

"Maybe." Helen let her gaze drift from Susan's peaceful countenance to the light streaming into the kitchen from the dining room windows. "Why don't we sit out on the porch? It's a gorgeous morning."

Susan raised her eyebrows in surprise. "Sure. You're looking pretty chipper. I take it your shoulder's better."

"Much. I've decided to stop the codeine—except maybe at bedtime—and switch to the less potent pain medication the doctor recommended." Helen picked up her cup and carried it outside. Susan followed with the toast, butter, and jam after pausing to retrieve a wooden tray from the pantry.

When they'd settled on the white wicker chairs, Susan spread strawberry jam on the hazelnut toast and handed one to Helen. "I know it isn't any of my business, but don't you think it's a bit too soon for you to visit Irene?"

Helen chuckled. "Am I that transparent?"

"Not really. It's just that Jason asked me to keep an eye on you."

"So Jason told you about Irene being moved to Edgewood?"

"Hmm. And he's quite concerned. So am I, for that matter. Even though the bill passed to make it legal, assisted suicide hasn't been accepted as law. Jason's worried he may have to contend with another suicide doctor."

Susan slipped into a rhetoric about the latest case of the famous suicide doctor back east. Being pro-life, most of the family had given a great deal of money and time to keeping the assisted suicide bill from passing in Oregon.

Helen held strong views herself, yet struggled with the issue—especially since her friend Mary had opted to end her life before cancer completely destroyed it. Mary had given up. She'd refused all treatment except pain medication. After two days with no food or water and a self-administered overdose of morphine, she'd passed on. Had God understood Mary's anguish and granted her grace?

"Helen? Are you all right?"

"Wha—? Oh, I'm sorry." Helen shook her head. "Just wool gathering. I was thinking about Mary—you remember my friend in Lincoln City."

"She committed suicide, didn't she?"

"In a manner of speaking, yes."

"You're not thinking it's okay, are you? I mean—I know she was your friend, but surely you can't be siding with the proponents of euthanasia?"

"No, of course not." Helen paused and took a drink of her now lukewarm coffee. "My head says Mary made the wrong choice. My heart isn't quite so sure."

"Personally, I feel suicide is a cop-out—the ultimate act of self-ishness."

"But people kill themselves every day. How is Mary's choice any worse than that of the alcoholic or drug addict or even a smoker who poisons himself a little at a time? They know their choices are going to kill them someday, but they do it anyway. It's not a black or white issue."

"That's true, I suppose." Susan tipped her head to one side, her hair turning to fire in the morning sun. "I thought you hated shades of gray."

Helen, weary of the turn the conversation had taken, smiled and ran her fingers through her graying hair. "Some gray you learn to live with."

"You could color it."

"I could, but it would still be gray underneath."

Susan chuckled. "You are definitely getting better."

"Let's hope."

"As much as I'd like to stay here and visit with you all day, I have to get to work." After Jason's disappearance, Susan had started up an accounting business out of her home, allowing her to bring in needed income and still stay home with her children. Helen rose and followed Susan back inside.

"You haven't mentioned J.B. since you got home," Susan said, refilling her cup. "Is there a problem between you two—I'm surprised he hasn't called."

"Problem?" Oh yes, there was definitely a problem, but nothing she could discuss with Susan. Although the family knew about his job with the FBI, they were unaware of his occasional missions for the State Department. Nor did they know about her own undercover work. "I'm sure everything is fine. He may have been trying to call the apartment. Unfortunately, I don't have the code, so I can't retrieve my messages by remote."

"He didn't give it to you?"

"Well, yes, and I wrote it down, but it's at the apartment."

"Do you want Jennie to run over and check the answering machine?"

Helen decided she'd rather go herself. The messages, if there were any, might be for her ears only. "Better yet, I'll have her take me by the apartment after I see Dr. Long this afternoon."

At one-fifteen that afternoon, Helen ducked into Jennie's red Mustang car and fastened the seat belt, adjusting the shoulder strap so it wouldn't press against her wound. "I sure appreciate your driving me around."

"No problem. I love hanging out with you." Jennie paused before she backed down the driveway. "Gram? Are you really giving up on the Kincaid case?"

Jennie's question took her by surprise. "Well, I . . . I suppose. The suspect is dead."

"But—oh, I don't know. I just keep thinking about what Mrs. Kincaid told you—about her husband being murdered. Don't you think we should look into it some more? I know you can't do anything right now, but I could."

"What did you have in mind?"

"I could go out to Edgewood and snoop around."

"Why do I get the feeling we're talking past tense here? What have you been up to?"

"Nothing terrible. I just went out to Edgewood this morning and talked to some people. Told them I might be interested in working out there until school starts. Don't look at me like that! I might be."

"Sure, then what happened?"

"The guard said I should go to the personnel office. Well, I parked right next to this guy. You'll never guess who—" Jennie tossed her grandmother a sly grin and answered her own question. "Turns out his name is Chris Chang. He recognized me from those stories in the paper and the television coverage after Nick's kidnaping. Remember when we had that press conference?"

"Clearly. I also remember how you almost got yourself killed going after the kidnapper."

"Yeah, well, anyway. Chris wanted to know what I was doing out at Edgewood."

"How convenient that you should run into Irene's grandson." Helen vacillated between pride and fear where Jennie was concerned. The girl had assisted the police in solving several crimes in recent months and two of the stories had made the national news. You have only yourself to blame, Helen reminded herself. Jennie wanted to follow her father and grandparents into law enforcement. Apparently, there'd be no stopping her.

Jennie shrugged. "It really was luck. I got there about the time people were coming in to work. He offered to show me around, and by the time we finished the tour, he'd asked me out."

"And you're going?"

"Of course. Don't you see? I'm in a great position to find out what's going on with your friend Irene. Maybe I can even—"

"Jennie," Helen interrupted. "I won't stop you from seeing this young man, but I don't want you fishing around out there."

"You think it might be dangerous?"

Helen wasn't sure how to answer. "Not really," she finally said, afraid an affirmative response would fuel Jennie's cause even more. "Just unnecessary."

Jennie pulled into the parking garage adjacent to the four-story medical building. If she was disappointed, she didn't show it.

Helen extricated herself from the car, careful not to bump her shoulder, and accepted Jennie's hand. "Just promise me something," Helen said as she leaned on her granddaughter for support. "If you do find anything amiss at Edgewood—and I'm not suggesting you will—I want you to tell me or your father straight away."

Jennie's grin nearly covered half her face. "I know the rules, Gram."

———

Dr. Long changed Helen's dressing, then demonstrated several range-of-motion exercises for her to try. She could easily accomplish most of them. The hard one was raising her arm. Helen stood an arm's length from the wall and reached out to touch it, then finger-walked up it. By the time she'd done the exercise two times, she felt as if she'd run a marathon. "It looks a lot easier than it is." She pulled a tissue from the box on the counter and wiped the perspiration from her forehead. "Will I ever have full movement in my shoulder again?"

The doctor tapped his pen against the chart. "I'd like to give you a definite answer, but it could go either way. Time will tell. I do know this, if you don't exercise, your shoulder will freeze up."

"Then I guess I have a lot of work ahead of me."

Helen supposed she should put the business about Irene out of her mind, but she saw an opportunity too good to pass up. "Dr., how long have you been practicing in this area?"

Dr. Long set her chart aside, crossed his arms, and leaned against the counter. "About ten years. Why?"

"Did you know Andrew Kincaid?"

"Sure did. Played golf with Andrew once a week. He was a good man—tragic end to a great career. Over the years I sent a lot of my older patients his way. In fact, I was going to suggest you go through their rehab program."

"What about his son, Paul?"

Dr. Long rubbed his chin. "Don't know him near as well, but from what I hear he's brilliant—one of the best geriatric specialists in the country. Why do you ask?"

Helen explained her meeting with Irene in detail. "Irene's accusations may be the result of dementia, but I'm having a hard time accepting that analysis."

"Murder, huh?" Dr. Long shook his head. "I'm afraid I have to side with Paul Kincaid on that one. In fact, I was at the hospital when they brought Andrew in. He'd had a heart attack all right. Now as far as his wife is concerned, Andrew never mentioned that she had Alzheimer's, but that isn't something he'd necessarily confide to a golfing buddy. Tell you what, though. I'll ask around. Some of my colleagues might have seen or heard something."

"I'd appreciate that."

Armed with a packet of instructions on how to care for her shoulder, Helen left the clinic. Fifteen minutes later, she and Jennie turned off Front Street toward the Riverside complex, then made a left into the garage beneath J.B.'s condo.

On the drive over, Helen's inquisitive granddaughter had been asking far too many questions about J.B. With her imagination in full bloom, Jennie had come up with a number of possible scenarios about her new grandfather's whereabouts. She was still at it when they took the elevator to the second level.

"Maybe J.B.'s working on a drug case like Dad used to." She beamed as the words tumbled out of her mouth.

"I don't think that's likely, dear."

"It could happen. The DEA and the FBI work together sometimes."

"Yes, but J.B. isn't working for the FBI just now. He's gone overseas." Helen unlocked the door, then stood for a moment in the entry. Traces of her husband—the scent of his cologne, the sight of his chair—washed over her. So strong was his presence that Helen felt the ground shift beneath her.

"Gram?" Jennie grabbed Helen's good elbow and led her to the sofa. "You don't look so good. Better sit down."

"I think that would be wise." Helen dropped to the couch and tipped her head back against the cushions. "Seems rather stuffy in here. Would you mind opening the windows?"

Jennie complied, then came back. "Are you going to be okay? Can I get you anything?"

"Something to drink. There should be some iced tea in the refrigerator. Maybe you could pour us each a glass."

A cool breeze coming through the open windows revived her. She looked around for signs that J.B. had been there but found none. Just wishful thinking on her part. He'd said himself he'd probably be gone three weeks. The blinking red light on the answering machine drew her forward. She pushed the rewind button, then playback.

Several clicks and beeps later, J.B.'s rich baritone voice filled the room. "Helen, darling, 'tis your wayward husband. I'm at

Heathrow in London on this dreary Monday morning wishing with all my heart I'd chosen another line of work. I'm missing you greatly, luv." He paused, and Helen held her breath. "This will be my last call until I'm stateside. Security, you know. I'm wishing I could tell you what it's all about. I only hope . . . " Another pause. "Ah, Helen, light of my life. I'd like nothing more than to be lying in your arms at this very moment. God willing, we'll be together soon."

"Was that J.B.?" Jennie wandered back into the living room as Helen, having made certain there were no more messages, rewound the tape.

"Yes. He called Monday." Only three days ago. It felt like a lifetime. Helen popped out the cassette and replaced it with a new one from the desk drawer. Wanting to listen to the message again in private, she placed the tape in a protective case and dropped it into her bag. The gnawing feeling in the pit of her stomach told her that J.B.'s message might have to last for a long time.

Did he say when he'd be back?"

"No," Helen answered absently, then straightened and smiled, giving Jennie a reassuring hug. "But I'm sure it will be soon. Come on. Help me pack, then we'd better head to your place. Your mother will be wondering what's happened to us."

After packing a suitcase and an overnight bag with clothing and other necessities for what she hoped would be a short stay at Susan's, Helen locked up the apartment. Walking back to the car, she purposely steered the conversation away from herself and J.B.

"Your mother tells me she and Jason are still trying to work things out. How are you feeling about that?"

Jennie shrugged. "What's to feel? I know they love each other. I just wish Mom would hurry up and remarry Dad so he can come home. I don't think it's fair to make him stay in that little apartment."

"She needs time, Jennie. He was gone a long time."

"Yeah. I guess I should just be happy she didn't go through with marrying Michael." Jennie hesitated as she changed lanes and drove onto the Steel Bridge. "I think it's worst for Nick. He's really excited that Dad's back, but he doesn't understand why he can't live with us."

Helen watched a motorboat race along the Willamette River beneath them. "Your mother and father were having problems long before he disappeared."

"I know." Jennie went on to talk about memories—both the good and the bad—of their life before Jason had disappeared. Helen listened and empathized. Fifteen minutes later they pulled up in front of the McGrady home. After taking Helen's bags in,

Jennie helped unpack, then left to go swimming with friends.

Weary from her day's activities, Helen picked up the novel she'd been reading before her life had taken its unfortunate turn. She stopped by the kitchen for a cool drink, then settled on the wicker chaise lounge on the porch. So many things to do. So little energy . . . and far too much time.

The next day Helen did little more than eat, sleep, and exercise. "Your body needs rest in order to heal," Dr. Long had told her. The rest must have done some good, because Friday morning brought about a welcome change.

She awoke at five a.m., too full of anticipation to sleep. Today she and Jennie would drive out to Edgewood to see Irene. Helen had called daily, and each time the report was the same. "Mrs. Kincaid is resting comfortably. I'll let her know you called."

Helen had asked numerous times to speak with Irene, but each time the answer was the same: "I'm sorry, she's not taking calls." Helen had an odd sense they weren't being entirely honest. Today would be different. One way or another she'd get into Irene's room and see for herself.

Rolling over onto her left side, Helen eased out of bed, wrapped an afghan around her shoulders, and moved to the chair. Once settled, she reached for the devotional book Susan had given her. She read for twenty minutes, then closed her eyes, giving thanks for her family and improving health, for J.B.'s safety—and for Irene's.

Through a bit of creative manipulating Helen managed to ease her sore arm and shoulder into some loose-fitting sweats. She winced when her shoulder resisted her efforts to raise it. Bending at the waist, she swung her arm in ever-widening circles. Soon the stiff muscles began to loosen up. The shoulder needed a lot of work— she still couldn't raise her arm higher than chest level. Amazing how a gunshot wound and dislocated shoulder could set a person back. Fortunately, Helen had been no stranger to exercise and had kept up a daily regimen since her police academy days. This past week, however, her body acted as though she'd never moved a muscle. She paused ten minutes into her routine to catch her breath, then forced herself to go on. "Time," she panted. "It just takes time."

At seven, Helen covered the gauze bandage with plastic wrap and took a shower. Dressing primarily for comfort, she'd slipped into an ankle-length white cotton dress and accessorized it with the silver chain belt and sandals she'd purchased in Acapulco after helping officials close down a drug ring there.

She'd been recruited to infiltrate the operation by posing as a tourist. When the Federales closed in, they'd arrested her along with all the others in the Ortiz cartel. It had taken J.B. and the DEA four days to locate her.

The earthen-wall pit and her rodent roommates bore little resemblance to the places she wrote about for Tour and Travel. About the only amenity it had was water and what she loosely termed as food. The combination had cleaned her out and stripped her of ten pounds. Definitely not a diet she'd recommend to friends.

"I don't want you taking any more assignments like that one, luv," J.B. had told her later over dinner. "Much too dangerous."

"Oh really? Maybe you should let me be the judge of that."

"Now don't be giving me that look." His cerulean blue gaze had lingered on hers as he took her hand and brought it to his lips. Helen's protestations had skittered away like startled butterflies as she recognized the first pangs of love for him.

Helen closed her eyes and held the memory—wishing she were holding him instead.

Picking up a brush, she yanked it through her wet hair. Now, more then ever, Helen understood the concerns he'd felt all those times she'd been in the field while he'd been stuck behind a desk.

After breakfast Helen took a walk through a nearby park with Nick and Jennie, then headed for bed and a much-needed nap. Jason arrived minutes before she and Jennie were scheduled to leave for Edgewood and insisted on taking her himself.

"I'm sorry, Jennie. I know you were looking forward to the outing with Gram, but I'd like to see the place for myself." His dark brooding offered no argument.

Jennie protested anyway. "Could I go along?"

"Not this time."

"You're expecting trouble, aren't you?" Her dark eyes brightened. Helen suppressed a smile.

"Not really." He turned to Helen. "Ready to go?"

"More than ready." Helen gathered her purse and followed him to the car. Jason may not be expecting trouble, but he wasn't eliminating the possibility.

After a pleasant lunch at the Multnomah Falls Lodge, they headed southwest on the winding road that took them into the hills high above the river and the main highway. "I've always been curious about this place." Helen braced herself as Jason negotiated a sharp curve. Her shoulder slammed against the door. She grimaced and sucked in a deep breath.

"Sorry, Mom. That one took me by surprise. You okay?"

"I will be when I stop seeing stars."

"Do you want me to pull over?"

As the pain dulled, Helen forced her muscles to relax. "It's okay." A high brick wall to their left pulled her attention back to their mission. "This must be Edgewood."

Jason raised a questioning eyebrow. "Looks like a prison. Are you sure you want to go in?"

"Of course. Security is one of their selling points." A black-and-gold metal sign, flush against the brick, read Edgewood Estates.

"I don't know. This doesn't give me a feeling of security—it gives me the creeps."

Helen shared Jason's uneasiness but didn't say so. She'd waited for days to see Irene Kincaid and had no intention of turning back now.

They took a left into a two-lane driveway and stopped at the guardhouse just in front of a closed iron gate. A young woman in an official-looking uniform leaned out of the window and smiled. "Welcome to Edgewood. I'm Andi Spence. What can I do for you folks today?"

"We're here to visit a patient in Edgewood Manor," Jason responded.

Andi pulled up a clipboard and pen. "Who might that be?"

"Irene Kincaid."

She frowned. "Oh, now, I'm not sure we can let you do that. Dr. Kincaid left orders that Irene couldn't have any visitors."

Helen leaned forward so she could see the guard's face. "I spoke with the nurse—Stephanie—on Wednesday. She said we could come in anytime."

"What was your name?"

"Helen Bradley, and this is my son, Jason McGrady."

"Helen . . . " Andi paused. "Hey, you're the lady who was with Ms. Kincaid the night she got shot. Saw your picture in the paper. You're an ex-cop, right?" Admiration lit up Andi's hazel eyes. "I heard how you went after the guy."

"I tried."

"Paper said they found his body down by the river. Bet you're glad it's over."

Helen agreed and added, "I'd very much like to see Irene."

Andi pursed her lips, then reached for a phone. "Tell you what. I'll check with Stephanie—see what she says. Sometimes we get orders from the brass, then they change their minds and the message doesn't trickle out this far."

Helen nodded. "I know how that feels."

While she waited, Helen leaned her head back against the seat and massaged a sore spot on her neck.

Andi stepped out of the guardhouse and peered into the car. Her official uniform came equipped with a holster and gun, Helen noticed. "Dr. Kincaid is out of town today, but Stephanie said it would be okay, seeing who you are and all."

After looking at their I.D.'s, Andi questioned Jason about his position with the Portland Police Bureau. Duly impressed, she jotted down the license number of Jason's black Camero, handed them a map, then punched a sequence of numbers that set the wrought-iron gate into motion.

"Have a nice visit," Andi called as Jason moved the car forward. They followed the paved road for about a quarter of a mile into the woods. According to the map, the forested area to their left covered ten acres and provided a network of foot trails. Three stair-step rows of new condominiums bordered the forest to the north—each with a view of the gorge.

Jason slowed the car as the road forked. "I take back what I said. This place is unbelievable. Living out here would certainly take the edge off growing old. So, which way do we go?"

"Right, I think." Helen pointed to a signpost that directed visitors to various locations. A turn to the left would take them into Edgewood West—the condominiums, golf course, club house, an entertainment pavilion, and community center.

Shortly after they made a right turn, the two-lane road split. They followed a one-way arrow past emerald lawns and into an older section of the estate that looked like an Ivy League campus. Each of the brick buildings had been marked with discreet signs similar to the one at the gate. The road curved in a horseshoe, with the median serving as a park. Several trees, benches, a pond, waterfall, and half a dozen swans and ducks completed the serene picture. Edgewood Manor lay on the other side of the park.

The magnitude of the place left Helen speechless.

"I had no idea it was this large." Jason slowed in compliance with the ten-miles-per-hour warning and a speed bump.

"Neither did I, but then, I guess it would be with all they offer." Helen checked the buildings against the map. They passed Edgewood Apartments, the assisted living quarters. At the east end of the campus lay Kincaid Laboratories, a square three-story brick structure. A large warehouse sat behind it.

The next driveway led them into a paved parking lot that apparently gave access to both Kincaid Laboratories and the nursing home.

Edgewood Manor had the look and feel of a well-maintained convalescent facility. The linoleum floors had been shined to a high gloss. Their footsteps echoed as they crossed the foyer to the information desk. After getting directions to the north wing, Jason and Helen started down the wide hallway.

It was quiet. Nap time for many, Helen suspected. They passed a large day room where several residents sat on sofas and love seats reading, talking, or watching a television talk show.

The sight of a frail white-haired woman in a wheelchair triggered a distant memory. Helen's own mother had spent the last month of her life in a nursing home not nearly so grand as this one on the other side of the Atlantic. At eighty-five, she had taken a fall and shattered a hip. Surgery revealed bone cancer. Poor Mum deteriorated quickly after that. A month later they'd buried her beside her husband in a little plot near Dublin.

When they reached the nurses' station, Helen shook aside the memory. The square cubicle with its tray of charts was empty.

"Hello?" Helen directed a hushed voice to a back room. "Anyone here?" No one answered.

"I'll see if I can find someone." Jason went around the corner, then stopped when he heard a loud mournful wail. "Ah—maybe we should just wait here."

"We may not need to." Helen reached over the ledge and flipped open a card file on the desk.

Jason glanced in both directions. "What are you doing?"

"Relax." Having found what she needed, Helen flipped the cards back. "She's in Room 130—right here on the corner."

Helen crossed the hall and stepped cautiously through the partially open door. The room was modest, but nice. A single bed faced a large plate glass window. Had Helen not been so intent on the woman in the bed, she might have admired the view.

"Oh, dear God," Helen breathed. "I—" She covered her mouth to keep from crying out.

The woman in the bed bore little resemblance to the Irene Kincaid she'd seen on Sunday night. Irene had been animated, vibrant, and beautiful. This woman was Asian, yes, but far too old. An IV tube ran through an electronic pump and into an emaciated arm. Another tube protruded from a dressing above her left side and sucked rust-colored drainage into a clear bottle. "There's some mistake. I read the card wrong. This couldn't be . . ." But it was. The plastic bracelet wrapped loosely around the woman's bony wrist verified it.

Jason squeezed Helen's shoulder. "What's wrong?"

Helen couldn't answer. A dozen thoughts swarmed through her mind. What was it Paul Kincaid had said? His mother had been using their anti-aging products. Irene was sixty-nine. She'd looked closer to forty. Now she looked more like eighty.

Helen glanced around the room and stepped over to a pair of blue wing-backed chairs, sinking into the nearest one.

Jason dropped to one knee beside her. "Would you mind telling me what's going on? I haven't seen you this upset since Dad died."

"It's—I'm just so shocked to see her like this. Irene looks like she's aged at least forty years. When Paul told me she'd been using an anti-aging agent, I assumed he meant some kind of skin care, but what kind of product would change a person so dramatically?"

Jason glanced over at Irene's still form. "Are you sure? You only saw her once, and it was at night."

"True. And she must have been wearing a wig—and makeup. That could certainly account for some of the difference, but . . . " A soft groan pulled Helen's attention back to the frail figure on the bed.

Helen rose and moved to the woman's side. Irene's dark almond eyes opened. A single tear, then another and another trailed down a wrinkle in her parchment skin, dripping into thinning white hair.

Helen's gaze moved back up the trail of tears and rested on Irene's face.

Irene raised her hand and let it fall to the bed. Recognition ignited her dark eyes.

Helen cradled the woman's skeletal hand in hers. "Irene, I'm so sorry...."

"You . . . " Irene rasped as she gripped Helen's fingers and strained to lift her head off the pillow. "You must . . . h-help . . . me."

"Of course I will." Helen leaned closer so she could hear.

Irene's head fell back. Her chest rose and fell in heaving

breaths. She murmured something Helen could barely hear. Helen backed away, but Irene's words pierced her heart like shards of glass.

"What did she say?" Jason's glance flitted from Irene to Helen.

"I'm . . . I'm not sure. All I could make out was 'kill me.'

Eight

What are you doing in here?" A woman Susan's age, maybe younger, leveled an accusing gaze at Helen and Jason as she approached Irene's bed. She had short ash-brown hair and matching eyes. The black lettering on a rectangular white pin introduced her as Stephanie Curtis, RN. Her adept fingers encircled Irene's wrist.

"I'm Helen Bradley. We spoke on the phone, and I believe you told the guard we could come. This is my son, Jason." When Stephanie didn't answer, Helen went on. "There was no one at the desk so—"

"Her pulse is racing." Stephanie made a notation in the chart she carried. Her rose-framed glasses slipped down to the bridge of her nose. Pushing them back, she said, "You've upset her."

"I don't think so. But something certainly has." Helen took a deep breath to slow down her own racing pulse. "Perhaps we'd better talk outside."

"Yes, I think that might be wise." Stephanie escorted them to a visitors' waiting room two doors down. "Go ahead and get yourselves some coffee. I need to finish with Irene and check on my staff. I'll be back in a few minutes."

Jason and Helen didn't speak as they poured coffee into Styrofoam cups. Helen stood at the window and watched a tugboat push a barge upstream on the Columbia River far below them.

"You're awfully quiet." Jason came up beside her.

"Just thinking." Helen turned from the window to look at her son. "How would you feel about my coming here—as a patient?"

Jason scowled. "You're not serious."

The question had surprised Helen as well. But now that she'd given voice to her thought, it made perfect sense. "Yes, I am."

"But why? You don't need—"

"I know. It isn't a matter of needs. A woman I barely know has given me a burden I'm not sure I can carry." Helen set her cup on the windowsill and adjusted her sling. Her shoulder was still feeling the effects of the hairpin turn.

"Then don't carry it." Jason left the window and settled on the sofa against the wall. "I know you want to help her, but I don't see that there's much we can do."

"Maybe not, but if I'm here as a patient, perhaps I can get a better idea of what's going on and determine whether or not the claims that her husband was murdered are valid. Find out whether someone really is trying to kill her." Irene's words sliced through her again. The sentence had been disjointed—barely audible—but it didn't take a genius to fill in the blanks.

Jason shot her a parental look. "I can't let you do that. If—"

Stephanie walked into the room before he could finish.

"Sorry to keep you waiting. I needed to let my aids know where to find me." The nurse poured coffee for herself and added sweetener. "Please have a seat, Mrs. Bradley."

Helen joined Jason on a pastel print sofa. Stephanie perched on the edge of the armless chair facing them. Her snug lavender pants matched the lavender, blue, and pink print of her top. The clothes, Helen guessed, were a size twelve. Stephanie was easily a fourteen.

"We prefer that visitors check with us before going into our residents' rooms. Having an unexpected visitor can be embarrassing for them."

And possibly for you. "I can certainly understand that, and I'm sorry." Helen glanced down at the bitter drink, then fixed her gaze on Stephanie. "How is Irene doing? Have you been able to find an antibiotic to treat the infection?"

"That information is confidential, Mrs. Bradley. Suppose you tell me what upset her."

"Irene asked for my help."

"Why would she do that?" Stephanie sipped the hot liquid and grimaced.

"I was hoping you could tell me."

"She's very ill and tends to be confused."

"She said something else," Helen told her, "but all I could make out was `kill me. 'Now I could be wrong, but if I insert the missing words, I come up with 'Someone is trying to kill me.'"

Stephanie fingered the stethoscope that hung around her neck. "You must be mistaken. No one here would want to kill Irene."

"Not even to silence her?"

"Silence her? I don't—oh, you mean that business about her husband's murder. We've been through all that with the police. There is simply no evidence to substantiate her accusations. I was on duty the day he died. We tried to resuscitate him, but—"

Jason leaned forward and set his still full cup on the glass surface of the coffee table. "I wonder if we aren't making too much of this. After all, the nurses at Good Sam agreed that she'd been delusional."

Helen stood and walked back to the window. The tug had disappeared from view. "Something tells me it isn't that simple."

"There is another possibility," Stephanie said.

Helen turned around. "Which is?"

"Irene may have been asking you to help her die."

The words jarred Helen—literally. Hot coffee sloshed over the rim of the cup and dribbled onto her fingers. Stephanie jumped up and retrieved napkins from the counter.

"Are you all right? It didn't burn you?" She took the cup and set it in the sink, then dabbed at Helen's hand.

Helen pulled her hand back. "I'm fine. Thank you." Helen refocused on Stephanie's interpretation of Irene's request. "Do you really believe Irene would ask that of me? She hardly knows me, and I'm certainly not in a position to—"

"Oh, but you are. Everyone is. You could help her if you chose to."

Helen folded her good arm across the one in the sling. She would have liked nothing better than to get in Jason's car and drive as far from Edgewood Manor as possible—all the way to her home in Bay Village. "You sound as if assisted suicide were a normal occurrence. It may be acceptable to some people, but—"

"Mrs. Bradley, I can assure you that Edgewood operates well within the limits of the law. Many of our clients, however, believe that there comes a time when the quality of life has deteriorated and dying is the preferable choice. Irene is one of them." Stephanie took her half-empty cup to the counter and refilled it.

"You seem rather sure of that."

"Oh, I am. Mrs. Kincaid came to the manor two afternoons a week as a volunteer. She'd do a lot of the extra things our staff members don't always have time for—make-overs, hairstyling, reading, social activities. Sometimes after she'd been working with one of our advanced Alzheimer patients, she'd get rather depressed and tell me how she never wanted to be a burden. 'I don't mind growing older,' she'd often say, 'as long as I can be healthy.' One time she even asked me if I'd put her out of her misery if the time ever came when she couldn't take care of herself."

"Like now."

"Yes, like now. I won't though, not because I don't think it's right—but because it could cost me my nursing license."

"I see." Helen rubbed her forehead. She didn't see at all. Had Irene asked Helen to kill her or to prevent her being killed? Under the circumstances, Stephanie's explanation seemed plausible.

"Would it be so terrible?" Stephanie asked. "I've been in geriatrics for a long time, and I can't tell you the number of times I wish I could have pulled a plug or overmedicated to put a client and the family out of their misery. Surely you can understand that."

"It must be an enormous ethical dilemma for you." Helen glanced at Jason, wondering if Stephanie would be quite so open if she knew he was a homicide investigator. Though Helen had no intention of helping Irene kill herself, she wasn't certain she wanted Stephanie to know that at the moment.

"We'd better be going, Jason." She lifted her wounded arm. "I'm getting rather tired." To Stephanie she said, "Do you suppose we could stop and see Irene one more time?"

"Possibly. Let me make a quick check." Stephanie left the room, and Helen and Jason followed as far as the hallway. Within a few seconds the nurse came back out of Irene's room. "You can go in. She's resting quietly now."

"We'll only be a minute." Helen braced herself and walked into the room. This time seeing Irene's snow-white hair and wrinkled face came as less of a shock. Helen stepped close to the bed and examined the frail woman lying there.

What kind of anti-aging products had Irene used to make her look so young? And even more perplexing, how could anything work such wonders, then cause such a drastic change when it was stopped? At least she'd assumed the usage had stopped. Another possibility hit her. What if the rapid aging had been caused by something else?

Suppose someone had given Irene something to accelerate the aging process? Insane, she told herself. Helen tried to steer her train of thought down another track, but it plunged ahead. If Kincaid Laboratories could produce products that reduced the effects of aging, couldn't they also develop something to age people more quickly? The ultimate in assisted suicide—no more lingering deaths.

Irene's eyes opened. They stared glazed and unseeing. She opened her mouth as if to say something, then coughed. Her rattling breaths came in spasms. Rust-colored phlegm spilled from the corner of her mouth.

"Oh no. Irene, hold on." Helen punched the call button.

"Stay with her, I'll get a nurse." Jason ran into the hallway. Seconds later he returned with a tall slender woman. A name badge introduced her as Barbara James, LVN.

"She probably just needs suctioning," Barbara said in a voice so calm Helen wanted to shake her.

The nurse's glance flitted from Helen to Jason. "I'll have to ask you to wait out in the hall. Or better yet, why don't you have a seat in the waiting room."

Helen stood in the hallway for a moment. She could hear Irene's gagging cough above the sickening slurp of the suction tube. Unable to tolerate the sounds, Helen took hold of Jason's arm and headed toward the room they'd been in earlier.

While she waited, Helen tried to read an article in Modern Maturity about a youthful eighty-year-old who led exercise classes and climbed mountains. Unable to concentrate, she finally set the magazine down. "I wonder what's going on."

Jason lowered a copy of Newsweek. "Want me to go check?"

"Yes . . . no—" Helen shook her head. "I don't know. She looked terrible, Jason, just terrible." Helen eased out of her chair and walked across the hall to a drinking fountain, then paced up and down the hall.

Five minutes later, Helen watched as both nurses left Irene's room. They spoke in hushed tones.

"I'll call him as soon as I talk to Mrs. Bradley." Stephanie made her way toward Helen. Barbara returned to the nurses' station.

As Stephanie approached, she opened her mouth and closed it again. The flicker of grief in her eyes when she finally met Helen's gaze said it all, but Helen needed to hear the words. "She didn't make it, did she?"

Stephanie's gaze dropped to the floor. "I—no, Mrs. Bradley. She didn't."

Nine

Jason wrapped an arm around Helen's shoulders.

The gesture had been meant to comfort, but it did little to stop the churning in her stomach.

"If you'll excuse me, I need to call Dr. Kincaid."

Stephanie was halfway down the hall when Helen caught up with her. "Stephanie, wait!"

"What is it?"

"Why didn't you call a code—isn't that the normal procedure?"

"It depends." Stephanie hesitated before answering. "Some of our clients are considered a no-code."

Helen remembered the conversation she'd had with Jason and the fears they'd voiced about Paul bringing Irene to Edgewood Manor to die. It looked as though those fears had been realized. "And Irene was one of them? I was under the impression that Dr. Kincaid had brought her here to save her life."

"Mrs. Bradley, I'm not sure I should be answering your questions. Maybe you should talk with Dr. Kincaid. Why don't I have him call you later?"

"I'd appreciate that." After giving Stephanie the phone number, they left.

Once outside, Helen breathed in a lungful of fresh crisp air. The horror of the last hour threatened to topple her. Setting one foot in front of the other, she managed to walk to the car. Her limbs melted into a liquid mass the moment she folded herself into the leather seat and secured the seat belt.

Jason tossed several questioning glances at her as they drove back to the guardhouse, but he said nothing. They stopped at the entrance, where Andi greeted them like old friends and waved them through.

Apparently word about Mrs. Kincaid's death hadn't made it to the guardhouse.

As they drove back to Portland, the idea of checking herself into Edgewood still darted in and around the periphery of her mind, but Helen ignored it. Part of her wanted to stay at Edgewood and investigate Kincaid Enterprises. Part of her never wanted to go through those gates again.

There'd be no point now anyway, would there? Irene was dead. Guilt gripped her heart with an icy claw. A line of if-onlys marched across her mind. If only I hadn't agreed to meet Irene Sunday night. If I'd come to Edgewood sooner, maybe . . .

"I'm beginning to think it was a mistake to bring you out there." Jason's cobalt eyes filled with concern.

"Mistake? No, I'm glad I got to see her."

"I know there isn't much I can say, but if you want to talk about it, I'm here."

"I appreciate that. I'm not sure there's anything to say at the moment. I have a lot to process."

Jason nodded and, like a dutiful son, left her to her thoughts.

Once home, Jason returned to work and Helen excused herself to take a nap. She'd intended to sleep, but Irene's face and pleas for help haunted her thoughts. Youthful and healthy one moment—frail and elderly the next.

"All right, that's it," Helen grumbled after thirty minutes. Tossing off the floral pastel afghan, she headed for the telephone. Jason wasn't in, so she left a message for him to call. Their brief encounter with Irene had left too many questions and loose ends.

While she waited for him to call, Helen wandered around the

house, chatted a moment with Susan about dinner, and ended up in the living room where Nick was watching Mr. Rogers. She stretched out on the recliner and seconds later drifted off to sleep.

Jason called around eight that evening. While filling him in on the status of her own health, she carried the phone to her room and closed the door with her foot.

"I wanted to talk to you about Irene's death. I think you should consider handling it as a suspicious death."

"We are. All gunshot wounds are—you know that."

"Yes, but I'm concerned that since you already have the shooter, the exam won't be as thorough as I'd like it to be."

"I'm not sure I follow you."

"You have the man who stole her handbag and wounded her. But I'm not sure you have the real killer. I keep thinking about what Stephanie said about assisted suicide. Someone at Edgewood may have killed her."

"I've already considered the possibility. I'll talk to the medical examiner and let you know what develops."

"Thanks, darling. I owe you one."

Helen felt herself relaxing some. Knowing the medical examiner would look beyond the obvious reassured her. Her smile remained as she hit the disconnect button and tapped the phone against her hand. It felt good having Jason home again and back in her life.

She wondered what it would be like to come out of retirement and go back to work as a police officer. But the longing passed. Helen had her writing career now—among other things—and loved it. She'd begun writing after Ian's death when her pastor had told her to start keeping a journal. "It'll help you heal," he'd said. It had.

Helen took a deep breath and rose from the chair. Not only had writing helped her heal, it had launched a whole new career.

Speaking of which, articles did not write themselves. She
returned the phone to the kitchen, read Nick a bedtime story,
then told Susan she'd be working for a couple of hours. After
plugging in her laptop, she settled into a chair at the dining room
table, waited for her word processing program to kick in, then
called up the "whales" file and began writing.

It was nearing midnight by the time Helen finished the article,
proofed it, and printed it out on Jennie's desktop computer. Jennie
had gone out earlier that afternoon and still hadn't come home.
The concern that had tugged at her intermittently throughout the
evening returned, demanding attention. Some grandmother she
was. Helen didn't even know where the girl had gone.

"Still at it?" Susan nudged open the door and came up behind her.

"Finished." Helen tucked her eight-page article into a Priority
Mail envelope.

"Great. I fixed us some tea. Thought you might want a cup
before bed."

"Sounds wonderful. Is Jennie back yet?"

"No, but she should be coming in any minute." Susan led the
way to the kitchen. "I told her to be home by eleven-thirty. She's
usually good about coming home on time—or at least calling.
Guess I need to have a talk with her."

Helen waited until Susan had poured the tea, then asked,
"Where did she go?"

"She was meeting a friend at the library and called about nine
to say they were going to a late movie. I suppose I'm being silly
to worry. Sometimes the movies don't let out until twelve."

"Who is the friend?" Helen took a sip of tea to calm her growing apprehension.

"Chris something." Susan frowned.

"Chang?" Helen remembered Jennie's comment about seeing

him again.

"I don't remember." Susan brushed a hand through her thick curls and shook her head. "You must think I'm terrible, letting her meet someone I don't even know. I usually get a life history on all her friends. This time the name just went in and out." Susan paused for a breath. "I'm rambling—I never ramble. It's just that things have been so crazy around here. With Jason coming back and I'm a week behind in my postings and—"

"And me coming to stay with you certainly isn't helping."

Susan shook her head. "Oh, I didn't mean that."

Helen reached for Susan's hand. "I know. Don't be so hard on yourself. I'm sure Jennie's fine."

"But you're worried. I can see it in your eyes."

"A bit, yes. Chris Chang is—was Irene's grandson."

"You don't think Jennie's in danger—maybe I should call Jason." When Susan rose to retrieve the phone, a car pulled into the driveway. Seconds later, Jennie sauntered in, oblivious to the fact that she'd taken a year off her grandmother's life and given her mother several new gray hairs.

"Hi. How come you're up so late?"

"Waiting for you." Susan raised an eyebrow and gave her daughter a formidable you-are-in-big-trouble look. "Do you have any idea what time it is?"

Jennie sighed and sank into the chair next to Helen. "I was hoping you hadn't noticed. I meant to call, but we got to talking and—"

"I was getting worried. Especially when I realized who you were out with." Susan eased back into her chair.

"You were worried about Chris? What for? He's a really nice guy—you would both like him." Jennie poured some tea into an empty cup. "He told me about his grandmother dying. In fact, that's almost all we talked about. He's pretty upset about it."

Susan's anger defused in a deep sigh. "I'm glad you could be there for him, Jennie. I really am. But next time please try to call me if you're going to be late."

Jennie apologized and promised to be more careful. The threesome sipped a little more tea, then headed off to bed.

When they reached Helen's door Jennie paused. "I'll be up in a minute, Mom. I need to ask Gram something."

Susan wished them pleasant dreams and headed upstairs.

Jennie followed Helen into the room. "Gram? Did you know they found an antibiotic for her?"

"For Irene? Are you sure?" Helen sank onto the bed.

"Yeah. Chris told me he'd been working with about four other people to isolate the bacteria in Irene's wound and find the right combination of drugs to fight it. Two days ago, they found something that would work—I think he called it exo- or echo-cyllin—something like that."

"They found an antibiotic and the doctors were giving it to her?"

"They should have been. Chris seemed surprised that she died. According to him, Irene should have started getting better twenty-four to forty-eight hours after getting the new drug. Only she didn't."

Although Helen didn't especially want to encourage Jennie's participation in the case, she couldn't ignore what could be a crucial source of information. "I'd like to talk to Chris."

"I knew you would. He wants to meet you too. Got it all set up for Sunday after church. He'll meet us at Salty's on Marine Drive."

Helen chuckled. "If you were a little older, I'd consider hiring you as my assistant."

"You don't have to hire me, Gram. I am your assistant."

"Jennie . . . "

"I know. Be careful. If I had a nickel for every time I've heard that lately, I could buy Microsoft." She laughed. "Just kidding, Gram. I know the rules."

Helen cautioned her again. Jennie might know the rules, but there were a lot of criminals out there who didn't play by them.

Ten

Getting ready for bed took far too long. Though Helen wouldn't admit it to her family, her shoulder felt as if it'd been slammed into a concrete wall.

She completed her bedtime ritual by taking the more potent pain medication. As soon as her head hit the pillow her body began to relax. Unfortunately her mind couldn't do the same. Sorrow over Irene's death surrounded her like a shroud. It seemed strange that she would mourn so deeply the loss of someone she barely knew.

Helen, an inner voice reminded, you're not only mourning her death—you're mourning your own losses as well.

Funny how losing the use of one's limb—even partially or temporarily—could cause such a stir. She'd often shared her bed with grief. As before, it wrestled with her all night, dredging up memories and opening old wounds. By morning she felt more exhausted than when she'd gone to bed.

At five-thirty, Helen gave up and trudged into the kitchen to make coffee. While the coffee dripped, she stood at the living room window and watched the sun rise over the lavender hills to the east. Closing her eyes, she imagined herself leaning back against J.B.'s tall muscular body. He'd have rested his chin on her head and wrapped comforting arms around her. She'd tell him about her restless night and her concerns about Irene's death. She opened her eyes and spoke into the dawn's rosy hues. "What do you think we should do about it?"

"About what?"

Helen started and whipped around. "Susan! You scared me half to death."

"I'm sorry. You were talking and I thought you knew I was here." Susan yawned and finger-combed her fiery curls. "Who were you talking to?"

"Myself, God, J.B. Anyone who had a notion to listen, I suspect."

"Hmm." Susan joined her at the window. They watched for a few minutes in silence, each entranced by God's handiwork. As the sun came up, the coffee maker gave its last sputter. The morning paper hit the front porch with a thud, signaling an end to their musings. While Susan poured the coffee, Helen retrieved the paper, wandered into the kitchen, and began scanning the front section.

"Looking for anything in particular?" Susan returned to the table with warm cranberry scones, butter, and jam.

"I thought there'd be an article on Irene's death, but I don't see anything."

"You'd think they'd run a follow-up story."

"Maybe her son doesn't want the publicity." Helen turned to the obituaries.

Susan picked up the section of paper Helen had set aside. "Are you done with this?"

"Hmm." According to the obituary, Irene died of complications from a gunshot wound sustained in a robbery. Nothing new there—or in the list of family members left behind. Helen frowned. "She's being cremated."

Susan glanced at the scone in her hand and grimaced.

"I'm sorry—not exactly a breakfast topic."

"That's okay. Is there a service?"

"Monday at ten—I'd like to go."

Susan nodded. "Jennie or I could take you."

By ten, Helen had the house to herself. Jennie had taken Nick and Bernie to the park, and Susan had gone shopping. Having already completed her exercise routine and walked a mile, Helen stretched out on the lounge chair with her laptop and began writing. The article was one she had researched during a recent trip to Jamaica and featured a lovely resort overlooking Ocho Rio Harbor. It was the honeymoon article she'd begun when she'd gotten the call from Irene.

The trip had been her and J.B.'s honeymoon cruise, and writing about it washed up dozens of memories, each more precious than the next. She collected them like seashells, then wrote about the experiences she thought her readers might want to share.

By noon, she'd finished the rough draft. During the writing, her tears had come and gone, leaving only a trace of salt on her flushed cheeks. Writing the article had given her an entirely different perspective about J.B.'s absence. Her husband's love reached beyond the barriers of time and place and dissolve her worries. As soon as J.B. completed whatever mission he was on, he'd be back. And they'd celebrate his homecoming as they'd done so many times before.

Helen saved the file and exited the program. Her arm hurt, but not nearly as much as it had the day before. She padded to the kitchen and fixed a salad. The newspaper, still lying open to the obituary column, snatched her mind from the Caribbean back to Irene.

Or more precisely, Irene's death. That death, morbid as it was, occupied her thoughts through lunch and during her exercises. She fell asleep replaying her meeting with Irene and awoke more convinced than ever that she needed to dig deeper.

"Oh, Lord," she murmured. "I hope I'm doing the right thing."

The answer, though not audible, seemed to come from somewhere outside herself. Her decision brought a sudden sense of elation and excitement. Jason would be upset, of course, but that couldn't be helped. Besides, she was beginning to feel like a burden to Susan. With all the disruptions the woman had in her life, she didn't need to be looking after her mother-in law—ex-mother-in-law.

When Jason showed up at five with plans to take her out to dinner, Helen was ecstatic. She showered and dressed, and by six they were heading for the Olive Garden near Clackamas Town Center.

"What do you mean, you're going to investigate?" Jason peered down at her from his six-inch height advantage as they walked toward the restaurant. "You're in no condition to do a ridiculous thing like that."

Helen quickened her steps to keep up with her son's long strides. She'd intended to bring up the subject in the car, but Jason had monopolized the conversation with his concerns over Jennie's dating Chris. He was not a happy man.

"My condition"—Helen raised her injured arm slightly for emphasis—"gives me a perfect excuse to check myself into Edgewood. As a patient I can see for myself what goes on there."

"Sounds as though you've made up your mind."

"I have. As much as I'd like to forget about this whole thing, I can't. Irene's death is just too convenient. I think her accusations warrant a more complete investigation."

"I'm not so sure about that. We aren't getting much cooperation from the brass on this. Just today we had a meeting, and they're wanting it wrapped up ASAP."

Jason opened the door and ushered her in, putting their conversation on hold.

Once they were seated Helen took up where they'd left off. "I'm right and you know it, Jason McGrady. Even if Dr. Kincaid did die of natural causes, why would Irene come to me for help—and what about the disk we've never found?"

"If there was a disk. You never saw it, right?"

"No. Irene was reaching for it when the purse snatcher came along—as though someone were listening to our conversation. The timing couldn't have been more accurate. Then of course there was the burglary."

"Ah yes, the break-in at her apartment. The report on that said Irene seemed confused. Apparently nothing was missing, although Irene claimed someone had riffled through her husband's desk. The son—Paul Kincaid—came in the next day and explained that Irene tended to be paranoid at times. I guess it's part of her dementia."

Helen felt her frustration mounting. "Maybe you can write this all off as coincidence, but I can't. And this business about her having Alzheimer's—"

"I suppose you have a theory as to what's going on." Jason's dark hair and eyes, along with his slightly rumpled suit, gave him a Columbo look that Helen would have found comical had she not been feeling on the defense.

"My guess is that they're operating some kind of scam to rip off the elderly. Could be they're helping some of their long-term patients into an early grave to collect insurance and cut costs. Edgewood is a big operation. The money has got to come from somewhere."

"That's possible, but I still say you should let us handle it."

"I disagree. There may be nothing going on at Edgewood at all, but if there is, I have a better chance of discovering it than the police. An open investigation would warn off Kincaid and his people. I, on the other hand, wouldn't pose much of a threat to them. Besides, from what you've told me, I doubt the bureau will put a high priority on this—and I'm sure they don't have the funds to initiate the kind of investigation I have in mind."

Jason blew out a long breath. "You're right about that."

"Good, then it's settled."

"Wait a minute. I didn't say I approved."

Helen stopped. "Darling, I don't need your approval. I plan to go with or without your blessing."

"I still don't like it. If nothing's going on you'd be wasting your time. If you're right it could be dangerous."

"I'm not fond of the idea myself, but I've given it a lot of thought." Helen hesitated, then said, "I owe it to Irene to investigate her death and her allegations about Andrew's murder." Helen glanced at the menu, then at her son. "Jason, I have another reason for going."

Jason's gaze met hers. "Which is?"

"Susan really doesn't need an extra burden in her life right now."

"Mom, you're not—"

"Let me finish." Helen closed her eyes to collect her thoughts. "You and Susan need this time to concentrate on each other. You have a lot to work out. At Edgewood I'll have a comfortable room and, from what I hear, a wonderful rehabilitation program."

"Okay." Jason held up his hands in a gesture of surrender. "When do you plan to go?"

"I'm not sure. Since it's the weekend, I may have to wait until Monday. But that's the day of the funeral...."

"Ah, we'd better table this discussion for now, Mom."

Helen followed his gaze to an attractive woman in a navy blue silk blouse and matching pants. She seemed to be looking their way.

"Who's that?"

"Our dinner guest."

"Anyone I know?"

"Could be." A smile tugged at the corners of her son's mouth, turning him ten years younger—far too young to be interested in the middle-aged woman coming toward them.

Helen frowned. "What's this all about?"

"You want to know about the autopsy, right?"

"Right."

"I saw the preliminary report this afternoon."

"And you brought me a copy?"

"Better than that." Jason flashed her a wide grin. "I brought you the medical examiner."

Eleven

I see you made it okay." Jason slid out of the booth to let her in, then sat beside her. She looked vaguely familiar, but Helen couldn't place her.

"Sure did. Thanks for the invitation." She glanced at Helen. "It's great to see you again. I couldn't believe it when Jason called."

Helen wasn't sure how to respond. Apparently they'd met, but Helen had no idea who she was.

With an odd look of amusement, Jason glanced from Helen to his guest.

Helen's gaze drifted over the woman's matronly form, high cheekbones, and a turned-up nose and into her sea-green eyes. "You look familiar. Have we been introduced before?"

Jason chuckled. "I can't believe you don't recognize her, Mom. Twenty-five years is a long time, but with you being friends and all—"

"Don't let him kid you, Helen. Jason didn't have a clue as to who I was until I told him. Unlike you, I have changed."

Twenty-five years? Friends? Helen did a quick calculation, taking her back to her police academy days. "No, it can't be. Sammi Cooper? It is you. I can't believe it." Helen had lost track of Sammi after she and her husband had moved to California. They'd vowed to keep in touch, but life had intervened.

"I would have called you sooner if I'd known the Mrs. Helen Bradley I've been reading about in the paper was you. Jason says you recently remarried."

"Very recent. What about you?"

"My name's changed a couple of times since I last saw you. It's Fergeson now."

Helen glanced at Jason, then back to Sammi. "You're the medical examiner?"

"In the flesh."

"I still can't believe it," Helen said. "You look great. Different, but great." Sammi's once red hair was now a warm golden blond. Her slender figure had thickened to the pleasant roundness of a Michelangelo Renaissance woman.

A young girl set glasses and a basket of soft garlic bread sticks on the table, then scurried away. After she'd gone, Helen took a moment to look at the menu, then focused back on her old friend. "Tell me about yourself."

"So much has happened," Sammi said. "It will take weeks to catch up. You realize that will mean a lot of lunches and coffee breaks."

"Sounds good to me."

Jason's cell phone rang. He pulled it out of the holder on his belt, flipped it open, and greeted the caller. He listened for a few seconds, muttered under his breath, excused himself, and left the table.

"So where were we?" Sammi unfolded her napkin and placed it across her lap. "Tell me about your daughter. Jason and I didn't have much time to talk about family."

"Kate's doing well. She and her family live here in Portland. They're on vacation right now, but I can't wait for you to see her."

Sammi's smile faded as her gaze drifted to Helen's sling. "How did you injure your—oh, yes, the shooting. I'd read about it, but like I said earlier, I didn't realize it was you. How are you doing?"

"Not bad considering. Ah, Sammi, are you doing the autopsy on Irene Kincaid?"

"Yes, why?"

Helen filled her in on the details. "I can accept her battling an infection and developing pneumonia. What I can't understand is the rapid aging. Sammi, that woman aged a good twenty years in five days. I know it sounds bizarre, but it's almost as if she'd been given something to speed up the aging process."

Sammi gave her an incredulous look. "It's an interesting premise and a great plot for a novel, but . . . you're serious about this, aren't you?"

Helen nodded, feeling rather foolish now that she'd voiced her thoughts. "It makes sense in a twisted sort of way. With her body in such a weakened state, she'd succumb to complications from the infection much sooner." She crossed her legs and sank back against the cushions. "I take it you disagree."

Sammi's green eyes narrowed into a frown. "I've done my preliminary report. So far I haven't found anything to contradict the diagnosis on her hospital records. Her lungs were full of fluid. Infection is putting it mildly. It's a wonder she lasted as long as she did. I won't have a full report for several days. Off-hand I'd say she developed septicemia—a staph infection—and pneumonia. I'll do a full blood work-up and toxicology screening. If there's anything suspicious, I'm sure we'll find it."

"That's all I ask."

Sammi took a couple of deep swallows from her ice water. She obviously felt uncomfortable talking about Irene, but Helen couldn't let it go just yet.

"How did the family react to your performing the autopsy?" Helen asked.

"The daughter was against it, but they know the guidelines—seeing as she'd been shot initially, we didn't have much choice. I didn't get the impression the family was trying to hide anything." Sammi leaned back against the seat cushions. "But enough shop talk. I'm anxious to hear about you and your family—your career. You're still with the police, I take it. What are you now, a lieutenant?"

"Actually, I retired a year after Ian died—about ten years ago." Helen wrapped a napkin around her glass to mop up the moisture forming around the outside.

"Ten years? Then why all the interest in the Kincaid case? Don't tell me—you're a private investigator."

Helen didn't particularly want to go into detail just yet. Fortunately Jason chose that moment to come back to the table.

"Something's come up on a case and I have to go." He gave Helen a sheepish look. "I don't know if I can make it back before you finish eating."

"Don't worry about it, darling," Helen said. "I can always call a cab."

"You'll do no such thing." Sammi turned to Jason. "I'll be happy to drive her home."

"Thanks." He eyed the breadsticks, grabbed a couple, then took off, nearly colliding with their waitress in his haste.

Sammi and Helen ordered, then slipped back into their conversation—with Helen deftly keeping the focus on Sammi.

Their lives held similarities. Sammi had married a police officer, Aaron Dunn, and a few years later he'd been killed by an irate motorist he'd pulled over.

"Aaron's death really messed me up," Sammi confessed. "I started drinking. And to make a long story short, after a year, I realized I couldn't go on being a cop or an alcoholic. I went into treatment and met John—my second husband."

"How did you come to be a medical examiner?" Helen broke one of the breadsticks in half before taking a bite.

"John was a doctor, and since medicine was his life, it became mine. I went to nursing school and ended up in med school. It's perfect for me, really. I'm a pathologist and an investigator all wrapped up in one."

"So is it as exciting as the *'Quincy'* show portrayed?" Helen asked with a smile.

Sammi shrugged. "Not really, but I like my work. Makes me feel good when I can come up with evidence that links someone to a crime. I guess the old saying is true—once a cop always a cop."

Their salad arrived, then pasta dinners. Between bites their talk drifted from careers to family. Sammi had waited until after thirty to have children. Sarah, her oldest, was in college, and her youngest, Jonathan, was a junior in high school.

Though Helen and Sammi were close in age, hearing her friend talk about having a child the same age as her granddaughters made her feel rather old. Her gray hair didn't help, nor did the fact that her arm had started aching and she'd begun to tire from the day's activities.

"Can I get some dessert for you?" The waitress collected their empty plates and waited expectantly.

"Oh, goodness, I don't know if I can eat another bite." Sammi patted her ample stomach.

"We're having a special tonight—key lime pie."

They decided to share. The pie and a cup of Earl Grey tea revived Helen and brightened her mood. After paying their bills and using the rest room, they made their way through the crowded parking lot. Sammi stopped beside a black Lincoln. Using a device on her key chain, she clicked open the locks and disarmed the alarm.

"Nice car," Helen murmured as she folded her long frame into the plush leather seat. "Smells new."

"It is." Sammi drew her seat belt forward and fastened it. "Picked it up this morning. I've been driving around an old clunker and finally decided to put my money into something besides clothes for my kids." Leaning forward, she pushed her key into the igni-tion, bringing the powerful engine to life. Sammi backed down the driveway and headed toward the freeway. "You're lucky yours are grown, you know. Everything is so expensive these days."

"Hmm. Actually I do know. I have grandchildren, remember?" Helen adjusted her shoulder strap so it rested lightly across her chest. "I contribute quite a bit to their care. Susan, Jason's wife—well ex-wife at the moment—thinks I spoil them, but I like to help as much as I can."

Sammi shook her head. "You're too young to have grandchil-dren." Her wide mouth spread in a teasing grin. "It must make you feel terribly old."

"Not really. They make me feel alive, needed, loved."

"If you say so." Sammi chewed on her lower lip, then glanced at Helen. "Tell me more about your involvement in the Kincaid case. I know you suspect Irene may have been murdered, but do you have any proof?"

"No, I'm hoping you can provide that. All I have right now is questions."

"What about suspects?"

"Nothing there either, I'm afraid, just an unsettling feeling about Paul Kincaid taking his stepmother out to Edgewood. And all that talk about anti-aging products."

"I'm glad we got a chance to talk. I'll know better what to look for. Paul Kincaid has a reputation for being honest as well as bril-liant. Even though she ended up dying, taking his mother to Edgewood made a lot of sense. If anyone could have come up with a cure for her, they could."

"I understand the doctors there found an antibiotic."

"Yes, according to her records, she'd gotten several doses, but it looks like a case of too little, too late."

Helen watched her old friend's face grow light and dark from the headlights of oncoming cars. "Sounds as though you know a lot about the Kincaids."

Sammi shrugged. "Actually, I do. Andrew Kincaid and my husband were friends. When John reached the point where I couldn't care for him at home, he insisted I admit him to Edgewood Manor. Edgewood has a wonderful hospice program."

"John is ill?"

"Was. He's dead."

Twelve

It took Helen a few moments to find her voice. "Your husband is dead?"

Sammi stopped at a red light. "Didn't I tell you?"

"No." Helen's stomach churned as she mulled over the implications. "I—when . . . ?"

"Two years next month. He had cancer." The light changed and Sammi made a left onto the ramp that would put them on I-205 northbound.

"I'm so sorry. I had no idea."

"I don't talk about it much. I suppose I should—my therapist tells me I hold in too much. John and I had ten wonderful years together. I'm still furious with him for leaving me, though. Silly, isn't it?" Sammi reached up to catch her tears. "Being angry after all this time."

"Not exactly. It's been eleven years since Ian's death, and sometimes I still catch myself asking why." Helen closed her eyes and blinked away her own grief. As she watched the long string of taillights wind their way along the freeway, she thought about a dozen questions she'd like to ask Sammi, but they all seemed too intrusive. "I imagine Irene's death and the connection to Edgewood must be difficult for you."

"Not really. Even though John died there, Edgewood evokes pleasant memories. They let me stay there with him. We'd spend hours talking and watching the river. I've never known a more empathetic and supportive staff." Sammi shifted her gaze from the road to Helen and back again. "I have to be honest with you.

I'd be very surprised to find anything amiss in Irene's autopsy."

"I suppose we'll find out soon enough."

"Yes." Sammi sighed. "So, tell me more about this FBI man of yours. He sounds intriguing."

"Oh, J.B. is that. As I mentioned before, we've known each other since we were kids. He and Ian were best friends. When Ian and I started dating there was a lot of friction between them. But that soon changed."

"Let me guess—he was in love with you as well."

Helen chuckled. "Yes, only I didn't know that until recently. His confession is what finally convinced me to marry him. Do you know he never married?"

"Waiting for you?" Sammi glanced at Helen and gave her a knowing smile.

"So he says." She sighed and told Sammi about wanting J.B. to seek an early retirement.

"Does that mean you'll be retiring as well? Somehow I can't picture that."

"No," she mused. "Sammi, I feel like such a fool. I don't really know what happened, but marrying J.B. seemed to bring back all the old fears I had about losing Ian. For the first few years of our marriage I tried to talk Ian into finding a safer job. One day I realized I'd never be able to change him. That's when I decided to become a police officer."

"If you can't beat them, join them?"

"Something like that. I guess I finally realized that Ian's work as a special agent was so much a part of him, he couldn't change. J.B.'s work is a part of who he is as well. I should have learned my lesson, but now I seem to be repeating the same pattern."

"If it's any consolation, I can empathize. I knew that fear all too well with Aaron. After he died, I vowed I'd never marry another cop—too dangerous, I told myself. So what happened? My husband, the doctor, dies of cancer."

"You just never know." Helen paused. "Listen to us go on. Here we've just met after thirty years, and we're talking about death. How did we get onto that?"

"We're both widows. It was bound to come up."

"I suppose." They were approaching the turnoff to Susan's house and Helen gave her directions. When Sammi pulled into the driveway a few minutes later, Helen rummaged through her bag for a business card and scribbled Susan's phone number on the back. They exchanged cards and promised to keep in touch.

"I'll call you if I find anything unusual on Irene's autopsy," Sammi said.

"Thanks. If you'd like to get together sooner, give me a call. I have very little on my agenda for the next couple of weeks."

Sammi nodded. "Are you going to Irene's funeral on Monday?"

"Yes. I'd planned on having Susan or Jennie take me, but if you're going . . . "

"Say no more. I'll pick you up at nine-thirty."

"Are you sure?"

"Absolutely. It'll give us a chance to talk again."

Helen agreed, then closed the passenger side door and waved as Sammi backed down the drive. She watched the car until the taillights disappeared around the corner. Seeing Sammi again had been wonderful, but having her old friend turn out to be a medical examiner was a mixed blessing.

As she entered the house, Helen had a spring to her step. It was the best she'd felt since the shooting.

An odd crinkling sound awakened her the next morning. Helen opened one eye and found herself staring at a blur of words. The night before, she'd taken to bed a copy of a Journal of the American Medical Association article written by Dr. Andrew Kincaid. The combination of ten-letter words and pain medication had successfully put her to sleep.

She focused on the small print and tried to remember what the article was about. Something to do with gerontological advances in the treatment of the aged and an upcoming cure for Alzheimer's.

Though Helen had taken several first aid courses and knew a little about medicine, the article was too technical to glean any useful information. Maybe Sammi would translate. Or perhaps Irene's grandson Chris could enlighten her.

Helen tossed the covers aside and picked up the scattered pages. She'd hoped to go over the rest of the information Jennie had gathered, but too much of the morning had already slipped by. The family would be leaving for church in an hour.

Helen did some stretching exercises, showered, and after much deliberation finally settled on a loose white cotton blouse and pants. She selected a silver-and-gold braided belt and a gold chain from her minuscule collection of jewelry.

"Gram?" Jennie knocked on the door. "Mom said to see if you needed any help."

"Come in, dear. You're just in time. How about helping me with the latch on this belt?"

"Sure." Jennie deftly hooked the belt together and adjusted the blouse. Her ponytail swayed to one side as she examined her handiwork. "You look super."

"Why, thank you." Helen picked up the drab canvas sling, slipped it over her head, and settled her right arm in its cradle. She eyed herself in the mirror and frowned. "Sort of ruins the effect, doesn't it?"

"Maybe a little." Jennie chuckled and gave her a hug. "Want me to do your hair?"

"Sure." Helen sat on the chair while her granddaughter brushed through her silver-and-black hair and drew a few strands forward for a partial bang. A quick shot of hair spray and she was done.

Helen sent Jennie ahead when she'd finished, applied some eye makeup and a touch of blush, then headed to the kitchen for breakfast. Since church started at ten, they were out the door by nine-forty.

Helen spent most of the service watching Nick draw and practice writing his letters—and thinking about Irene. What she did catch of the sermon seemed to be a direct message from God. She'd heard the words many times before, but this time they held a slightly different connotation. The pastor had based his sermon on Psalm 139:5-10.

You hem me in—behind and before; you have laid your hand upon me . . . . Where can I go from your Spirit? Where can I flee from your presence? If I go to the heavens, you are there; if I make my bed in the depths . . . even there your hand will guide me.

Hearing the spoken word gave Helen reassurance on two fronts. Wherever J.B.'s assignment had taken him and for whatever reason, God would be there with him. And the Spirit would guide and accompany her as well—even at Edgewood Manor. There'd be no guarantee of survival for either of them—at least not in the human sense. But they would not be alone.

After church, Jennie, eager to meet Chris, hustled Helen away from friends and family. The morning clouds had burned off, and it looked as though they were in for a scorcher. Having sat in the late morning sun for over an hour, Jennie's Mustang felt like an oven. They spent the first few minutes of their drive to Salty's cooling off and chatting about Jennie's frustration with her parents.

"They're both upset 'cause you're moving out to Edgewood."

"How do you feel about it?"

"Are you kidding? I'm surprised you didn't go out there right away." Jennie paused to make a left turn. "'Course I guess you couldn't do much with your shoulder being hurt." Without missing a beat, Jennie asked, "Did you get a chance to look through the articles I found for you on Kincaid Laboratories?"

"Some. I appreciate all the work you did."

"No problem. I like doing research. Besides, the librarian was a big help. When I told her what I wanted, she gave me a bunch of topics and medical terms to look up."

"Want to give me a quick rundown?"

Jennie's dark eyebrows knit together in a frown. "I can try. A lot of it was like reading Greek—especially the medical journals."

"So I noticed. One of the journal articles put me to sleep."

"Yeah, but there were some write-ups in The Oregonian and regular magazines. Kincaid Laboratories is known all over the world for the experiments they have been doing. One of the articles said they were close to finding a cure for Alzheimer's. Another one had to do with anti-oxidants." Jennie glanced over at Helen. "None of the articles I read was negative—you know, implying weird experiments or anything. Except . . . well, I did find one by an animal rights group that criticized their use of animals for experiments, but that was it. Most of them had to do with different drugs and face creams, vitamin therapy, and finding ways to slow down aging and keep older people healthy."

"I'm looking forward to reading the rest and hearing what Chris has to say. You mentioned that he works in the lab."

Jennie pushed down the blinker signal and turned onto Marine Drive. "He's learning the business, so he's into a lot of different things. Mostly he works in the product development lab." She paused for a moment. "Gram, Chris is a really nice guy and everything, but I get the feeling he's hiding something—like maybe he knows more than he's letting on."

"What makes you think that?" Rolling down her window, Helen gazed longingly at the colorful sails as boaters and wind-surfers skimmed over the water. When J.B. came home maybe they could take his boat out—their boat. She half dreamed and half listened as the cool wind caressed her face.

"It's a feeling I get when I talk to him." Jennie slowed and turned into the parking lot. The restaurant overlooked the Columbia River. Helen recognized Chris immediately. He moved away from the silver convertible he'd been leaning against and walked toward them. Chris Chang had the attractive Asian fea-tures of his grandmother—dark hair and almond eyes—and the height of his Caucasian grandfather.

"Hi, Jennie. How's it going?"

"Great."

His smiling gaze swept from Jennie to Helen as he helped her out of the car. "You must be Mrs. Bradley. I'm glad to finally meet you. My grandmother told me about you."

"Really?"

"Yes, before she . . . " The words seem to catch in his throat. "She had told me of her intention to call you."

"Then you knew . . . "

"About her murder theory? Yes." He glanced around as though he suspected someone might be watching. "Let's talk inside. I reserved a window table."

"Chris," Helen began after they'd been seated, "if you suspect your grandparents may have been murdered, why haven't you talked to the police?"

"I didn't say I believed Grandma. I only said that I knew of her suspicions. As I told Jennie, I'm not certain what to believe. I go back and forth—primarily because she had begun to accuse

Uncle Paul and my mother of killing him. I know they would
never do such a thing. My parents and Uncle Paul say
Grandmother was confused because of the Alzheimer's."

"Do you agree?"

His hesitation came in a deep sigh. "Mrs. Bradley, this is very
difficult for me. Why don't we order, then I will explain why I
wanted to meet you."

Helen watched Chris as he ducked his head to peruse the
menu, then turned her attention to the luncheon specials.
"Everything looks wonderful," she said absently, "but since they
specialize in seafood, I think I'll have a salad and the grilled
salmon."

Chris opted for steak and Jennie for a crab Louis. After they'd
ordered, Helen sipped at her water while she waited for Chris to
continue.

"It is all very confusing for me," he said finally. "While I feel my
family is innocent of any wrongdoing, Grandma Irene may have
been right about the disk and the burglary. You see, Grandfather
always recorded his latest experiments on the computer and kept
his disk with him so he could work at the lab and in his office at
the house. Someone may have stolen his files on the new drug he
had formulated to slow down or reverse senile dementia."

"That's not much of a motive." Helen pulled a warm slice of
sourdough from the basket Jennie passed her, then reached for
the butter. "Why would anyone want to stop that kind of
progress?"

"Perhaps not to stop it, only to delay or perhaps to claim it for
themselves. It was never made public, and the disk on which
Grandfather kept his notes is missing. Which means we have no
way of going on with his project. Grandma told me just before
she met with you that she'd found the disk. She claimed it not

only contained the information on his latest experiments, but also proof that someone murdered him."

"Only she was conveniently robbed and shot before she could show it to anyone." Helen leaned back when the waitress brought their drinks.

"Yes." Chris leaned forward, resting his arms on the table. "If Grandfather was right and actually did have a cure for Alzheimer's, that disk could be worth millions."

"And you think that's a possibility."

"More than that. My grandmother has proof that it worked."

"He experimented on her?"

"Normally he wouldn't—we never use humans unless the treatment is approved by the government. Grandmother insisted he test the product on her."

"Chris and I have a theory." Jennie set down her drink. "It's possible that when Dr. Kincaid had his heart attack, someone who worked in the lab took the disk, planning to sell it to another drug company. Irene could have found out who it was and somehow gotten the disk back. Then whoever it was shot her— before she could show it to you."

"It doesn't seem likely she'd be able to do that," Helen said, "but she may have found another copy. It seems to me that with such important records, your grandfather would have had a backup."

They suspended conversation while the waitress delivered their orders. When she'd gone, Helen continued. "Chris, did you ever actually see the disk?"

"No. Grandma had it hidden in a safe place. She planned to give it to you when she hired you to investigate." Chris sawed off a piece of his charred steak and paused to chew it. "My grandmother wanted to hire you. I would like to hire you as well."

"I'd like to help, Chris, but . . . ."

"I have money."

"It isn't that. I don't know where Irene got the idea I am a private investigator—I'm not."

Chris frowned. "Grandma seemed to think you were. She showed me a couple of articles in the newspaper about how you helped the police solve a murder. I thought . . . "

"It's kind of a hobby, isn't it, Gram?" Jennie waved an empty fork in Chris's direction. "She used to be a homicide detective."

"True. But it's not exactly a hobby either. Having been a police officer, I try to stay abreast of crimes committed in the area. It usually goes no further than looking at the evidence and trying to determine who's guilty. From time to time, however, I've actually cracked a case."

"Do you think you could work on this one, Mrs. Bradley? Like I said before, I don't know for sure if anyone was murdered. Grandfather may have hidden his disk, and we have yet to find it. And Grandma might have been confused. But I owe it to them to find out for sure."

"Of course she will," Jennie intervened. "And I'll help her."

"You'll do no such thing, young lady." Helen tossed her a stern look. "Chris, I want very much to discover whether or not your grandmother's claims were true. I've already decided to get involved—at least I plan to check myself into Edgewood Manor. However, I don't expect any payment."

Chris's eyes flashed to high beam. "So you'll do it?"

"I can't promise results. There's still the possibility Irene may have been the victim of a senseless random act. But yes, I'll do what I can. I'll come to the funeral tomorrow and hopefully meet some of the family and people who worked with your grandfather."

"That's perfect." Jennie speared a chunk of lettuce. "We can go to the reception afterward as Chris's guests.'"

"We?"

Chris looked from one to the other. "Well . . . I asked Jennie to come. I hope you don't mind."

Helen shook her head. "No, I guess not."

They finished eating and paid the bill. On the way out to the car, Helen asked one of her many questions. "Chris, you said Irene told you about the disk and her suspicions that someone had murdered your grandfather. How many others knew about her allegations?"

"Almost everyone who works at Edgewood. She started asking the nurses at the manor all kinds of questions, and one day she came into the lab to talk to Uncle Paul. Turned into a huge fight. He kept trying to calm her down. She came storming out of his office yelling, 'Someone here murdered my husband, and I'm going to find out who.' Uncle Paul sat everyone down and explained that she had Alzheimer's disease and that's why she was acting so strange."

"And what about her intentions to hire me? Any idea who may have known about our meeting?"

Chris shrugged. "Could have been anyone. She told me a couple of times that someone was following her and tapping her phone lines. I never noticed anyone."

After promising to pick up Jennie for the funeral, Chris vaulted into his convertible and sped away.

During the drive home Helen chatted with Jennie, trying not to think about what lay ahead. The prospect of going to Edgewood Manor haunted her. If Irene was killed because she knew too much—if Andrew really had been murdered—what would she be facing?

Thirteen

"Irene must have had a lot of friends," Helen remarked as Sammi parked her car near St. Mark's Episcopal Church after driving through a full parking lot.

"I doubt that. She wasn't what you'd call friendly. Most of these people are probably business associates—or just curious acquaintances. That's why you and I are here, isn't it?"

"In part, I suppose." Helen grasped the door handle and pushed it open. "But on the other hand, her death truly saddens me. I felt drawn to her. I think if she'd lived we could have been friends."

Sammi tossed her a skeptical look. "Don't be too sure."

They left the car and began walking the block and a half back to the church. "That seems an odd thing to say. How well did you know her?"

Sammi frowned. "It's funny. If people were honest about it, they would have to admit that what we call friendship is often nothing more than a devious way of getting something we want. Like with the Kincaids. After John died, I stayed on friendly terms with them—not because I particularly liked being with them, but because Andrew and Paul had connections. They helped me land the medical examiner's job." Sammi shook her head. "I'm sorry. I didn't answer your question, did I?"

"No, but you've succeeded in making me feel guilty." Helen frowned. "I hope you don't think I'm using you by asking about Irene. Here we finally meet after all these years and I'm groveling for favors."

"Oh, I didn't mean to imply that. I don't feel at all used. I was just confessing my relationship with the Kincaids. I thought Irene and I were close, but I really know so little about her. Doing the autopsy made me realize I had no real bond with her. Otherwise I would have turned it over to someone else. She was basically just another body." Sammi gave Helen a contrite look. "That sounded terrible, didn't it?"

"I suppose you harden yourself to it after a while."

"In my line of work we have to develop some sort of emotional shield or we'll never last. It's not that I'm callous or indifferent. Some of these cases really get to me—especially when child abuse is involved. But usually when I examine older adults, well, death is part of the life cycle and you learn to accept it."

"I suppose." Knowing what an autopsy required, Helen shuddered. "I can't imagine myself examining anyone's dead body, let alone someone I knew."

Sammi chewed her lower lip. "I do what I have to do. You of all people should know that."

"That's true enough. So what can you tell me about Irene?"

"As I was saying earlier, having performed the autopsy, I know all the physical details, but I didn't know that much about her personal life. Irene was beautiful and lonely, I think. Isolated. Everyone around her lived for science, always experimenting with a new drug or a new cure. She was a homemaker—devoted to her husband and his work, and the family. She doted on Chris, her grandson." Sammi paused as they ascended the church steps. "That's him now. With the cute dark-haired girl. Must be a new girlfriend. I don't remember seeing her before."

Helen glanced at the couple heading into the sanctuary, admiring the tan young woman wearing a white sundress. "She is darling, isn't she?" Helen's lips twitched in an effort to repress a smile. "I'll introduce you after the service."

"You've met her?"

"Mmm. Sixteen years ago in a birthing room at Good Samaritan—we've been best friends ever since. That's my granddaughter, Jennie McGrady."

"I should have known. Jason's daughter. She takes after you—but then so do your twins."

Helen warmed to the compliment. "Sounds like the service is starting. We'd better go in." One of several ushers greeted them and handed them each a bulletin as they entered the sanctuary. On the front was a picture of Christ as the Good Shepherd. Inside were brief program notes and a couple of paragraphs entitled "Remembrance." After being seated in a back pew Helen scanned the epitaph. It contained little more information than Sammi's initial assessment and the obituary.

Helen closed her eyes as the organist played one of her favorite hymns, "Have Thine Own Way." Irene's family would be sitting up front where Chris had escorted Jennie. She'd hoped to observe them herself, but with so many people attending the service, Helen doubted she'd have a chance to see them, much less talk with them until after the service. Perhaps having Jennie involved wasn't such a bad idea. The teenager had exceptional instincts.

After the hymn the priest stepped up to a pulpit. He opened with a prayer, then reminded them why they'd come. He called Irene's death "a random act of violence." Violent? Yes. Random? Helen had her doubts.

After the memorial service Helen and Sammi spoke briefly with Jennie and Chris.

"It's good to see you again, Chris," Sammi said. "Sorry it is under such unhappy circumstances."

Chris nodded. "I'm glad you could make it." He cleared his throat and reached out to grasp Jennie's hand.

Helen sensed a difference in him from the day before. More sullen—less confident. She attributed his change to the funeral.

"You really went to the police academy with Gram?" Obviously not used to wearing dresses and heels, Jennie slipped off one of her white pumps and rubbed the bare foot against her leg, looking a bit like a stork.

"Sure did," Sammi responded. "Your grandmother tells me you plan to go into law enforcement as well."

"Law school first, then I might become a detective. I haven't really decided yet." Jennie eyed Sammi with curiosity and respect. "Are you a police officer?"

"Not anymore. I'm a doctor now."

"Oh." Jennie sounded disappointed.

"We should go." Chris pulled Jennie toward him and she hurriedly slipped her shoe back on. "Ah . . . about this afternoon, Mrs. Bradley," he went on, "I told my parents you'd be coming. They're anxious to meet you." His gaze dropped to the ground, then back to Sammi. "Are you coming too, Dr. Fergeson? If you aren't, Jennie and I could give Mrs. Bradley a ride."

"Thank you for asking, but I'll be there."

"It was nice meeting you, Dr. Fergeson." Jennie turned around to wave.

Walking to the car, Helen puzzled over Chris's response to Sammi. She'd picked up subtle animosity in his tone. Had he not wanted Sammi to come? More than likely he'd simply wanted an opportunity to talk with her alone. Helen dismissed the incident, promising herself she'd ask him about it later.

As they merged with the processional to Edgewood, where family and friends would be gathering, Helen considered how best to approach Chris's parents and others connected with Irene and Andrew Kincaid. Though she had a lot of questions, Helen felt the best way to get answers was to listen and observe. She didn't want to put the family off by sounding too much like an investigator.

"You're awfully quiet," Sammi said. "What are you thinking about?"

"Irene's death and how I'm going to find out what really happened."

Sammi sighed audibly. "Although I can't be a hundred percent certain, the evidence I've found suggests that Irene's death was preventable. The gunshot penetrated her lung and lodged against a rib. The surgeon at Emmanuel did a great repair job, and if everything had gone well, she should have survived."

"But it didn't go well."

"No. Somehow bacteria was introduced to the wound—possibly a nurse who didn't wash before changing the dressing. My original cause of death still stands. She succumed to pneumonia and to the septicemia brought on by wound contamination."

"And you didn't find anything else?"

"Nothing that would have caused her death. Paul was right about her having Alzheimer's disease. I found evidence of that in her brain. She was on several medications—Septral for hypertension, estrogen, and a rather wide assortment of vitamins and herbs. Irene was a guinea pig of sorts—using a number of antioxidants and face creams, but nothing that I'd have considered harmful, and certainly nothing that contributed to her death."

"What about the change in her appearance? How could she have aged so drastically in such a short time?"

"After we talked Saturday night I headed back to the lab to more carefully examine her skin. I found several spots on her face and hands that still had the residue of a waxy substance—nontoxic," Sammi added with emphasis.

"You're sure?"

"Absolutely. I called Paul and he told me it was a special skin cream. Mai Lin—that's Irene's daughter—and her team developed it a couple years ago. It's called Renovare. They're very excited about it. If the experiments continue to produce the positive results they've seen so far, they expect it to be released to the public within a couple of months."

"So Irene was using this Renovare?"

"That's what gave her skin its youthful appearance. For years scientists have been working to develop products that reduce the signs of aging. Renovare works somewhat like a mask. You put it on in the morning as a foundation and wash it off at night. The effects are unbelievable. Wrinkles literally disappear."

"You're sure it's safe?"

"As far as I can tell. I drove out to Edgewood yesterday to talk to Mai about it, and while she wouldn't disclose the exact formula, she provided me with an ingredient list and showed me the results of their experiments. The before and after shots of Irene were just as you described, only I saw them in reverse. She'd gone from looking like a little old lady to looking almost like a young model with one application."

Helen shook her head in disbelief. "You sound like a sales rep."

Sammi grinned. "Probably because I'm convinced. This has got to be the biggest advancement ever in women's cosmetics. I'm actually thinking of volunteering to test it."

"It sounds too good to be true—still, if it made that much difference in Irene, I'm sure it will be a best seller.

"Did you find anything else?" Helen asked, wanting to get back to the autopsy.

"As far as I'm concerned the case is closed. There's no way to determine who or what caused the infection, but there wouldn't have been an infected wound had it not been for the shooting. Paul could file a complaint against the hospital for malpractice, but he's already told me he won't pursue it. The gunman bears the primary responsibility, and he's dead."

"And you're certain he's the one."

"Absolutely. He had a scrape on his arm where he brushed against the concrete wall after he shot at you and Irene. The bloodstains are a match. I can definitely put him at the crime scene. In fact, I had a long talk with Jason, and he agrees with my findings."

Helen remained silent, and Sammi frowned. "I know you think someone at Edgewood may have helped Irene's death along, but the theory doesn't hold up."

"Hmm."

"I know that look. You're still not satisfied."

"No, I'm not." Helen told her about the discussion she'd had with Chris. "There may be nothing going on, but I'd like to make certain. The precipitating events seem too well orchestrated."

"What are you going to do?"

"Check myself in as a patient. From what I understand, Edgewood Manor is one of the best rehab centers around."

"You're not serious." Sammi tossed Helen an incredulous look.

"Oh, but I am. I know you did your best to find out what happened to Irene, but you and I both know there are ways to kill people that can't always be detected in an autopsy. Aside from that, it's entirely possible Irene was targeted because she knew too much. She was about to hand me what she considered proof of her husband's murder, which leads me right back to Edgewood. I won't rest until I've proven to myself that nothing sinister is going on out there."

Sammi sighed and shook her head. "All right, I won't try to

talk you out of it. As I recall, you always were the stubborn one. But keep me posted, okay? I mean, if you do find something, you're going to need backup." She made a left through the gates of Edgewood Estates, pausing at the guardhouse. "And just for the record, I think you're chasing the wind."

Helen noted that she hadn't seen the guard who checked their credentials before. They meandered along the winding road to a large angular building with a bright blue-green tiled roof. The sign in front introduced it as Edgewood Estates Community Center. When they pulled into the circular drive, one of three young men in black-and-white chauffeur uniforms welcomed them and helped the two women out of the car.

Sammi reluctantly handed over the keys and watched until the rear bumper disappeared around the corner. She smiled when she caught Helen's gaze. "New car jitters. You know how it is, the first ding is always the most traumatic."

"I know exactly what you mean. I recently got a new paint job on my '55 Thunderbird, and I almost hate taking it out of the garage."

Chris and Jennie, who'd driven in just ahead of them, were waiting at the door. Even though she'd noticed the large expanse of windows from the outside, she was unprepared for the open garden feel of the interior.

"Chris, this is . . . breathtaking." It looked like the lobby of an opulent hotel, filled with lush tropical plants. To her right a waterfall cascaded into one end of an Olympic-sized pool, surrounded by at least a dozen therapy pools. The bottom of each pool was a work of art in floral mosaics. To the left, a vast stone fireplace covered one wall in front of a large conversation pit carpeted in a creamy beige. Several guests were seated on the forest green leather chairs and sofas.

"I knew you'd like it." Jennie hung an arm around Helen's

neck. "Maybe you and J.B. could buy a condo out here, Gram. Then I could invite my friends."

Helen chuckled. "It's tempting, but I've got a perfectly nice home at the beach, and I intend to stay there." She turned to Chris. "This is magnificent. Has it been here long?"

"Grandfather had it built three years ago when they decided to expand Edgewood to include the condominiums. He believed the last years of a person's life should be the best."

"It's a nice theory." Sammi pursed her lips in a cynical smile. "But most older people don't have the money to live like this."

"Some do." Chris shrugged and placed a hand on Helen's back, steering her toward the far end. "Come on, the reception's outside."

A series of four wide sliding glass doors opened onto an expansive patio and garden area. Two tables stood end to end, covered in white tablecloths and laden with an assortment of food. The catered affair looked more like a wedding feast than a funeral. Some of the guests had already lined up at the buffet.

"My parents are over there." Chris nodded toward a couple standing off to one side, then began walking toward them. David Chang had the look of a middle-aged executive—shorter than Chris, though just as lean. His gaze scanned the crowd and lingered a moment on Helen. He nodded in acknowledgment, then bent his head and said something to his wife. If she looked, Helen couldn't tell. A black veil covered Mai Lin Chang's face.

"You go ahead and meet them, Helen," Sammi said. "I'll catch up with you later." Sammi wandered over to a couple standing at the buffet table. The blond man bore a striking resemblance to Paul Newman. She hadn't seen him before but recognized the woman with him. Stephanie Curtis, the head nurse at Edgewood Manor, looked as though she could have used Mai's veil to cover her blotchy face and puffy eyes.

"Chris, who's the man with Stephanie?"

"Oh, that's Jack Owens. He's on staff at Edgewood Manor."

As if sensing she was being watched, Stephanie looked up and caught Helen's curious gaze. She held eye contact for a moment, giving Helen an almost hostile look, then turned back to Jack and Sammi.

"I wonder what that was about," Helen murmured.

"Did you say something?" Jennie asked.

"Nothing important." Helen turned her attention back to Jennie and Chris and allowed him to escort her across the lawn to where his parents stood.

Fourteen

Mom, Dad, this is Grandma's friend, Helen Bradley," Chris said, making the appropriate introductions, then added, "She's also Jennie's grandmother."

Helen reached forward to grasp David Chang's extended hand, then Mai's. "Thank you for allowing me to come."

"I'm glad you did." David glanced at Helen's arm. "I feel badly that you were injured as a result of my mother-in-law's confused state. How are you feeling?"

"Not bad. I'll need several weeks of rehabilitation. An injury like this takes time. In fact, I've been considering Edgewood Manor's rehab program."

"That would be a good choice, Mrs. Bradley," Mai said. "I think you should come as our guest."

David seemed a bit surprised by his wife's offer but quickly recovered. "I agree."

"That's very kind. I hadn't even considered holding you responsible." Helen hadn't expected to get into the facility so easily—and certainly not with an invitation.

"Please, it is the least we can do after what you've been through. As I said, we feel somewhat responsible for your misfortune. If we had been more diligent in watching Mother, this wouldn't have happened. You see, she'd been doing so well—" Mai paused to reach under her veil and wipe away her tears, giving way to anguished sobs.

"Darling, you mustn't blame yourself." David grasped his wife's shoulders and guided her to a nearby chair.

After a few moments, Mai recovered enough to speak again. "Forgive me." She looked up at her husband. "I think I'd like to lie down awhile."

"I'll have Chris run you up to the house." He turned to his son and spoke in hushed tones. All Helen could make out were the words "bed" and "sedative."

"Sure." Chris glanced at Jennie. "I'll be back in about twenty minutes."

"No problem."

Chris escorted his mother down the concrete path that led along the back of the building to the parking lot.

David watched until they turned the corner, then looked back at Helen. "My wife is taking her mother's death very hard."

"I shouldn't wonder—losing both parents within such a short period of time."

"Yes. Ah . . . about your therapy. Why don't you come around ten tomorrow? We have a room available, so if you'd like to check in . . . "

"That would be fine as long as I can get a ride out."

"I can bring you, Gram," Jennie offered.

"It's all set then." David Chang bowed slightly. "I hope you will excuse me, Mrs. Bradley, but I must see to our other guests."

Helen nodded and turned to Jennie. "You've been awfully quiet since we arrived. Are you feeling okay?"

"Just watching. You know how you've always taught me to observe people's actions."

Helen smiled. "And have you discovered anything?"

"Nothing specific. Just a feeling. This place is so unreal, sometimes it seems I'm watching a movie."

"In what way?" Helen looked behind her and sat down on the chair Mai had just vacated.

Jennie shrugged. "I don't know.... It's all so staged—even the people. Take the Changs, for example. They seem really nice and everything, but I think they're having some problems. The family isn't as together as they want people to believe."

"Life hasn't been exactly normal for the Changs lately. I'm sure they're all under a great deal of stress. Death is not an easy thing to endure."

"Yeah, but we've been through a lot too, with Dad being missing for so long and Nick's kidnapping. I don't know, something isn't right. When Chris talks about his parents, there's this sarcastic tone in his voice."

"I noticed that when he was talking to Sammi."

"Oh, her." Jennie glanced toward the woman in question. "He has good reason not to like your friend, Gram. According to Chris, Dr. Fergeson was trying to break up his grandparents' marriage. Now that his grandfather is dead, she's working on the uncle."

"Paul? Are you certain?" Though Helen had lost contact with her friend, she had a difficult time seeing Sammi as a husband snatcher—particularly when Andrew Kincaid must have been twenty years her senior.

"That's what Chris said. See, Paul is supposed to be engaged to one of the scientists who works here—Adriane Donahue. She's really nice, Gram—and smart. I met her the first day I came out here." Jennie scanned the crowd. "She's over there, near the far end of the pool—the lady sitting by herself. Want to meet her?"

"Absolutely."

They wove their way around the milling guests, across the lawn, the patio, and the tiled pool area. While they walked, Jennie shared the information she'd gleaned from Adriane during her tour. "The work she's doing is super complicated. Adriane has developed this computer chip that can stimulate the brain to make new brain cells. She's been experimenting with animals and says it should be ready to use on humans soon."

"Did she say how it would be used?"

"I probably should let her tell you, but she says it can be programed to identify defective brain cells, destroy them, and create new ones."

"You're right. It does sound complicated and a bit strange."

They stopped talking as they neared the table. Adriane Donahue seemed engrossed in whatever she was reading. The shoulder pads on her beige pinstriped business suit and cream silk blouse made her head seem a couple sizes too small for her body. With her long dark hair slicked back and gathered at the back in a pearl barrette, she looked like an executive who'd paused for a brief lunch.

Adriane glanced up and smiled as they approached. "Jennie, how nice to see you again." She wasn't a classic beauty, Helen noted—not like Sammi.

"Hi." Jennie glanced at the papers on the table. "I hope we're not disturbing you, but I wanted you to meet my grandmother, Helen Bradley."

"I was just reviewing my notes on the project I told you about the other day." Adriane's striking blue gaze studied Helen through glasses that overwhelmed her small nose and heart-shaped face. She stretched out a hand. "Mrs. Bradley, I've heard so much about you."

"I'm afraid I know very little about you, although I did meet Paul the other day. I understand you two are engaged."

Adriane opened her mouth, then closed it as if censoring an unkind remark. "At the moment, yes." She straightened and cleared her throat. "We'd planned to be married next week—even put a down payment on a house, but with both Paul's parents dying, we've had to postpone our plans indefinitely." She glanced down at her clenched hands. "Paul needs time to work things out in his personal life as well as with Edgewood Estates."

Helen let her gaze drift to Sammi, who now seemed to be deep in conversation with Paul Kincaid. Maybe there was some truth in the rumor after all. Helen thought about asking Adriane, then decided against it. She'd check it out with Sammi first.

Adriane looked from Helen to Jennie. "So Jennie is your grand-daughter. Such a small world."

"Yes, it is." Helen eyed one of three chairs. "Do you mind if we sit down?"

"Oh, please." She gave Helen an empathetic look. "Are you in pain? Can I get you anything?"

"Actually, I was about to ask Jennie to bring me some water or punch so I can take some medication." She glanced up, shielding her eyes against the bright noon sun. "Would you mind, dear?"

"I'm on it. Would you like anything, Adriane?"

She handed Jennie her cup. "Thanks, just dump this and get me some fresh coffee."

Adriane's gaze followed Jennie to the buffet tables. "She's a sweet girl. You must be proud."

"Oh, I am." Helen glanced at the papers on the table. "Jennie told me you've developed a computer chip that can destroy dead brain cells and create new ones. It sounds fascinating."

"And a little like science fiction?"

"Well, I have to admit, I am skeptical."

Adriane adjusted her glasses. "Much of what scientists do can sound frightening at first, Mrs. Bradley. Eventually new advances become routine. We're experimenting with several animals right now, but soon we hope to implant the chip in humans." Adriane's tone softened as she warmed to her subject. "If preliminary tests are any indication, we'll soon be able to heal the brain. By destroy-ing damaged cells and creating new ones to take their place, we could conceivably eliminate senile dementia and brain damage caused by strokes. The possibilities are phenomenal, not only for the older population, but for people of all ages who have suffered brain damage of any kind." Adriane's smile doubled in volume.

"I can see why you're excited."

"Sometime, perhaps when your arm is better, you can come out to the lab. I'll give you a tour of the facility and show you the procedures we go through to develop new products."

"I'd like that. As a matter of fact, I'll be coming out tomorrow." Helen told Adriane about Mai and David's offer.

"I hope you will seriously consider staying. You will receive better care here at Edgewood than anywhere else in the country."

"So I've been told." Helen glanced over at Jennie, who was making her way back to the table. "This project of yours—you haven't tested it on humans at all?"

"Not yet. We have a long detailed process to go through first. It can be extremely tedious, but we follow the rules to the letter. If we don't, we could lose our funding from the state and federal government—as well as our reputation."

"Sounds complicated."

"It is, and the paper work is outrageous. But we've made great strides and may get clearance to use the chips in humans as early as next year."

"Are you working with someone else on the project?"

A look of pain crossed her face. "I was. Dr. Kincaid—Andrew. He'd been my mentor since I started working here. I . . . I couldn't have done it without him."

"Wasn't he working on a cure for Alzheimer's as well?"

"Yes, a medication. Unfortunately, we haven't been able to locate the later stages of his work." Adriane shook her head. "He was a wonderful man, Mrs. Bradley."

"Here you go." Jennie set the drinks down. "The food looks great and I'm starved. Want me to get you a plate too, Gram?"

"Sure." When Jennie left, Helen lifted her handbag to her lap and dug around for her pain pills. After taking them and drinking half the fruit-flavored punch, she steered their conversation back to Andrew Kincaid.

"Andrew's death must have been difficult for you."

"Yes. He was like the father I never had." Adriane paused to sip on her fresh coffee. "We were all pretty devastated by his death— maybe because it was so unexpected."

Helen chewed on her lower lip, wondering how far to take the conversation. "Adriane, would you mind if I asked you some questions about Andrew's and Irene's deaths?"

"Of course, although I'm not certain I can answer them."

"As you probably know, Irene called me prior to her death and arranged a meeting. She insisted that Andrew had been murdered. I realize now she had Alzheimer's, but even so, there are a number of things that don't add up."

"Such as?"

"Her death. The gunshot wound isn't what killed her. Infection did. I can't help but wonder why. The break-in at her apartment, the timing of the supposed thief who shot us. The only way I can make sense of it is to assume that Irene was lucid and that she really did have some condemning evidence on the disk she'd planned to give me."

"I can certainly understand why you might be suspicious, Mrs. Bradley, but the one thing you can be sure of is that no one at Edgewood would have killed Andrew. To my knowledge he had no enemies. Dr. Kincaid was a great man. I can also assure you that he died as a result of a heart attack—that was established by our staff as well as by the medical examiner. As for Irene, I have no explanations for what happened to her. I only know that we worked very hard to save her. Unfortunately, we're not miracle workers."

"You're probably right, but humor me for just a moment. Suppose Irene had found some condemning evidence. Can you think of anyone who might have gained from Andrew's death?"

Adriane frowned and shook her head. "No, I can't and I won't. Your questions are very disturbing. I—" Adriane started to stand, then sank back into her chair. "Do you really think Irene had the evidence she claimed? Did you see the disk?"

"I didn't actually see it, but she told me she had it. I think it's too soon to dismiss her allegations."

"That's why you want to come to Edgewood, isn't it? To investigate."

"In part. I feel terrible about Irene's death. She asked for my help, and I owe it to her to look into her side of the story. There may be nothing, then again—"

"Yes, I see your point. Perhaps a more thorough investigation would be in order."

Jennie arrived just then with two plates laden with fruits, vegetables, crackers, and slices of a variety of meats and cheeses.

While they ate, Adriane gathered her papers and excused herself, saying she needed to get back to work. Before leaving she scribbled her home phone on a business card and set it on the table near Helen's plate. "I'm not sure I approve of what you're doing, but if I can help in any way, please call."

Helen thanked her and turned back to an especially delicious serving of mini-meatballs covered with a sweet-and-sour sauce and speared a second one with her decorative blue toothpick.

"What doesn't she approve of?" Jennie asked.

"My investigation."

"You told her?"

"There's been too much publicity about my involvement in the case to try to disguise my interest."

"Are you still planning to stay here?"

"Mmmm. I'll check in tomorrow."

"Great. I start my job then, too. This will be so cool. We haven't worked on a murder case together since you took me to Dolphin Island in Florida—"

"Whoa. Back up a minute." Helen lowered the piece of cheddar she'd been about to eat. "What's this about a job?"

"While I was getting food I talked to the personnel manager. She said she'd checked out my application and I got the job. I'll be working as an aid at the manor. It's perfect."

"Jennie, perfect isn't the word I'd use. I can't let you—"

"Gram, please." Jennie's deep blue gaze bore into hers with stubborn intensity. "It won't be dangerous. I'll only be there during the evening shift—that's all they have open right now. I won't even ask any questions if you don't want. I'll just keep my eyes and ears open, and let you know what I find out. By working at the manor, I'll be able to get into places you can't—like file rooms and stuff. Come on, Gram, please say yes."

"Oh, my darling girl. What am I going to do with you?" Helen stuffed a square of cheddar in her mouth. Jennie made a good argument. Having her there could be invaluable—it could also be risky. Still . . . "I'll tell you what. We'll talk to your mom and dad, and if they agree, you can do it. We'll need to draw up some guidelines, though."

"Thanks." Jennie grinned.

"You seem pretty sure of yourself."

"They'll say yes. I already told them about my filling out the application, and they think the experience would be good for me."

"And did you mention the reason you were doing this?"

"Not all of it. I just said I wanted a chance to work with older people." Jennie must have read the skepticism in Helen's face because she hesitated and added, "I do, you know. That day I came out to Edgewood for a tour, I felt really sad for some of the people in the nursing home. Chris said it was hard to find good help because the wages are low. They pay more than most of the other nursing homes around, but I guess they still end up with aids who really don't care about the residents."

Helen couldn't help but smile. Jennie was going to make a wonderful lawyer.

Jennie looked over Helen's shoulder and cringed. "Uh-oh. Chris's uncle is heading this way, and he looks as if he's been eating lemons. Wonder what he wants."

Helen twisted around in her chair and watched Dr. Kincaid approach. "Mrs. Bradley, my sister told me you were here."

Although his tone was pleasant, anger emanated from him. "How is she?" Helen asked.

"Resting. I understand you'll be coming to Edgewood as a client soon." His comment sounded like a threat.

"Yes." Helen stood. "As a matter of fact, I'll be out tomorrow."

"I'm not the type of person who minces words, so let me set the record straight. I don't want you here. If I had any say on the matter, I would withdraw my sister's guilt-induced invitation. Regardless, I will not allow you to upset my family nor the staff here with your foolish allegations about my parents being murdered."

"Not even if they were?" Helen flinched as Paul clenched his fists and leaned toward her.

"I told you once and I'll tell you again, they were not. As you already know, the medical examiner found no evidence of foul play. The police are satisfied and so am I."

But I'm not. Helen didn't say the words aloud, thinking it might be better not to antagonize him further. "I hope you're right, Doctor. I really do."

Fifteen

Sammi came up behind Helen and Paul. "Right about what?"

"It doesn't matter." Paul ran a hand through his hair. "Look, Mrs. Bradley, there is nothing sinister going on here, and the last thing we need at Edgewood is someone making accusations. We're a high profile organization—with a good reputation. If you plan on doing anything to tarnish that, I'll—"

"Paul, take it easy—you look as if you're about to explode." Sammi set her coffee cup on the table and looped her arm through his. "Helen isn't coming out here to make trouble. She just wants to clear up questions she has about Irene's and your father's deaths. Besides, it will help bring closure to her own trauma. To be honest, I might do the same thing in her shoes. After all, Irene did ask her to investigate."

"The police have done a fine job of that and you did the autopsies yourself."

"And we didn't discover anything to incriminate anyone at Edgewood. I doubt Helen will either, but she does raise some valid points."

"Dr. Kincaid," Helen said, "it's entirely possible that I'm wrong, but what if your stepmother was right? What if someone did murder your father and then, seeing Irene as a threat, came after her? Wouldn't you want to know? Wouldn't you want the murderer brought to justice?" Helen watched his expression change as he considered her question.

"What I want is to get beyond this tragedy as quickly as possible." Paul folded his arms across his chest. "You can check yourself into the manor for therapy as my sister's guest. But leave it at that. My family has been through a lot over the last few weeks. We're all eager to bury our dead and concentrate on the living." He paused. "Now, Mrs. Bradley, I think you've caused enough trouble today, and I'd like you to leave." With that he spun around and walked off.

Jennie bounced to her feet, tipping over her plastic chair in the process. "I can't believe that guy." She bent to pick up the chair.

"Doesn't have much of a bedside manner, does he?" Sammi shook her head. "But don't worry. I hear his bark is a lot worse than his bite."

"He's grieving, I suspect." Helen stared at the big man's retreating figure. "The anger—blaming me for Irene's death. He's been through a lot." Helen massaged her aching arm. "Much as I'd like to stick around, I think I'll take his suggestion and go home— that is if you don't mind, Sammi. I have a lot to do before I check in here tomorrow." She glanced up when a raindrop hit her head. The blue sky was quickly turning gun-metal gray.

"So you've definitely decided to come, despite the good doctor's protests?"

"Oh yes. I'm more convinced now than ever that something's going on here." Helen turned to Jennie. "Would you like to ride back with us?"

"No, that's okay. Chris should be here any minute." Jennie stacked the plates and gathered up the napkins. "Don't worry, Gram," she added. "I'll be fine. I'll see you when I get home."

A few minutes later Helen and Sammi settled into her car and wove their way back through Edgewood Estates and out onto the highway toward Portland. The rain was dripping steadily now, and Sammi switched her wipers from intermittent to low.

Though she would have preferred closing her eyes for a quick nap, Helen thought she'd better pursue the rumors about

Sammi's quest for the Kincaid men and their money.

"I had an interesting talk with Adriane Donahue."

Sammi's lips curled in a churlish smile. "Let me guess, she's accusing me of trying to steal Paul."

"Actually, I heard you were after Andrew first, but when he died, you set your sights on his son."

Sammi sighed. "That woman is so insecure. What I had for Andrew was sheer admiration. I'm interested in their work and their minds, Helen, not their bodies."

"I'm glad to hear it. What do you think gave her the impression you and Paul had something going?"

"The time we've spent together, I imagine. Paul and I met several times to discuss the autopsies and in the process have become good friends. He's been extremely preoccupied lately, what with his work at Edgewood and his parents' dying. He just hasn't had time to deal with her. Adriane tends to be a high maintenance kind of woman. And she's steamed about him postponing their wedding."

"Is he still planning to marry her?"

"He hasn't said anything to make me think otherwise. To be honest, I wish he would break it off. She's not his type."

"Do you think she's marrying him for his money?"

"I did at first, but now I'm not so sure. Paul, as you've seen for yourself, can be pretty intense. I don't know many women who'd put up with that, even for his millions."

When they pulled into Susan's driveway twenty minutes later, Helen thanked Sammi for her help.

"No problem. Did you want me to take you out to Edgewood tomorrow? I have to testify in court in the afternoon, but my morning is free."

"I'd like that. How about picking me up at nine?"

"Sounds good. Wait a sec . . . " Sammi glanced at the water

pouring across the windshield, twisted in her seat, and reached for her umbrella. "I'll walk you to the door. Two seconds in this downpour and you'll be soaked to the skin."

Minutes later Helen waved good-bye, then lingered at the porch railing, enjoying the sound of rain on the roof and the pungent scent of wet dirt and grass as water soaked the thirsty ground.

The front door opened behind her. Susan joined her at the rail and leaned against it. "Want some tea?"

"Sounds lovely." Helen shivered. "It's gotten downright cold out here. If you don't mind, I think I'll change into a sweat suit first."

"Sure. Need any help?"

Helen declined the offer and ducked into her room to exchange her linen suit for her favorite pale pink sweats—a birthday present from J.B. The soft reverse fleece brought back warm memories of a cozy fire and candlelight. She brushed her hand against the material's downy texture and closed her eyes.

"I miss you," she spoke to the man whose picture filled her mind. J.B. had come down to her home at the beach the evening of her birthday last December, bringing instructions for a new assignment and the gift. Her heart constricted as she remembered the tenderness in his eyes, the warmth of his lips brushing against hers for the first time.

Grabbing a tissue from the nightstand, Helen soaked up the moisture on her cheeks. "Please be safe, darling," she whispered to J.B.'s fading image, then hurried into the kitchen.

"It's about time you got here." Nick grabbed her hand and pulled her to the table. "Mommy said I had to wait for you 'fore I could eat."

Helen chuckled and slid onto the chair Nick pulled out for her. "Thank you, sweetheart. It's nice to feel wanted."

"He and his father are two of a kind when it comes to good-ies." Susan set out fresh-baked hazelnut and chocolate chip scones with coddled cream, berry preserves, and lemon curd.

"Yep. Me and my dad like brownies best." Nick stuffed a good-sized chunk of scone in his mouth.

After sampling the delicious scones and sipping the warm fragrant tea, Helen told Susan about Mai Lin Chang's offer to stay at Edgewood and her decision to accept.

"You don't have to do this. We love having you here."

"I know you do. And I love visiting, but not now. You and Jason have enough worries without adding me to the list."

"Does Jason know?"

Helen nodded. "And Jennie. I have an appointment with Dr. Chang at ten."

"Did you need me to take you?"

"I don't believe so. Sammi said she would."

"I don't suppose it will do any good for me to protest."

"No good at all."

Helen finished her tea, then excused herself, saying she needed to pack.

Sometime later she heard the phone ring. Her heart snapped into a faster rhythm at the thought of J.B. Wishful thinking, she told herself, then tucked a pair of tennis shoes into a side pocket of her carry-on.

"Helen." Susan tapped on the door and opened it. "Telephone for you."

"Thank you." Helen closed the door before saying hello.

"Helen?"

"Yes." It wasn't J.B., but Helen recognized the deep baritone voice immediately. "Tom Chambers. How are you?"

"Been better. Knee's acting up on me. Otherwise I'm okay." Helen imagined the mid-sized man with the bay window stomach leaning back in his chair, feet on the desk, and an unlit cigar in his thick fingers. He'd given up smoking six years ago—just hadn't gotten around to giving up the cigars. "Hey, Jason called a few days ago—told me about the shooting. I meant to get by, but things have been kinda crazy around here with J.B. gone. Just wondered how you were doing."

"Fairly well. Have you heard from J.B.?"

"That's part of my reason for calling. See, when you got shot, I thought I'd better get word to him."

"You talked to him?" Helen sank into the cushioned chair.

"No. Apparently he's heading up some big project over in the Middle East—not sure just where—Beirut maybe. Seems some rebel group over there has been holding half a dozen U.S. and British citizens in an underground military facility for years."

"They sent him in to rescue the prisoners?" Helen's heart dropped to her feet.

"Looks that way. They claim it's too risky to try to contact him, so I guess we wait. They'll let him know about you as soon as they can. Wish I could tell you more, but you know how it is."

"Yes, I know how it is." She sighed. "What I don't understand is why they would ask J.B. He's almost ready to retire."

"Wondered that myself. Probably has something to do with his background in British Intelligence. Besides, he's one of the best in the business. Ah, look, Helen, I probably told you more than I should, but I thought you had a right to know. This is top secret stuff. Any kind of leak could jeopardize the mission."

"I understand. I appreciate your calling."

"Sure, no problem."

"Tom," Helen stopped him before he could hang up. "I'll be leaving here tomorrow morning. I plan to spend a couple weeks out at Edgewood Manor to rehabilitate my arm and shoulder. Jason can get messages to me, but let me give you the number out there in case you talk to J.B. or need to get a hold of me quickly." She dug the wallet out of her handbag and read off the phone number.

"Got it. I'll keep in touch."

After their good-byes, Helen stared at the phone for a long time before pressing the button to disconnect. In a way she wished Tom hadn't called. Sometimes it was better not knowing too many details. She breathed a prayer for her husband and the mission that had taken him away. Now more than ever she wished he could have taken her along.

Morning, with its still gray skies, came far too soon. Helen had gone to bed exhausted and awakened the same way. Snatches of violent dreams, reminiscent of war, still lingered. All night she'd hung on the periphery of the ongoing dream—gunfire, screams, blood. In the dreams, she'd lain among the wounded, bleeding, crying for J.B., reaching out to him. He stood only a few feet from her—just across the room talking to three men in uniform, but he didn't seem to hear her.

Then the world exploded. She felt herself floating alone in utter darkness. Even now, knowing it had only been a dream, Helen could still feel the aching isolation.

After a quick breakfast, she showered, dressed, and finished packing. Sammi showed up at nine-fifteen. Having already said her good-byes to Susan and the children, Helen was more than ready to leave.

She opened the door just as Sammi reached for the doorbell.

"Sorry I'm late. Had some paper work to catch up on before I could leave the office. I'm testifying in a murder case this afternoon."

"No problem." Helen set her suitcase on the porch, retrieved her handbag, then closed the door.

"Is this everything?" Sammi picked up the suitcase and looked around.

"That's it. I'll have Jason pick up some clothes from the apartment later. This is all I need for now."

Minutes later they were on their way. Helen gazed out the car window at the bank of purple-gray clouds hovering on the horizon. "Looks like another storm is rolling in."

"Rain. That's the one thing I hate about this area. Makes me want to move back to California." Sammi turned on the wipers and the defogger.

"It's not so bad—except in the winter when we don't see the sun for weeks at a time." Helen frowned at the sky. "According to the weather report last night, we were supposed to have morning clouds, then sunshine. This must be the storm front that was supposed to miss us."

Sammi chuckled. "Don't tell me you believe in weather forecasts."

"Only when they promise good weather."

The winds hit when Sammi turned onto Highway 84 and headed east. Heavy rains and high gusts up to sixty miles per hour—according to the radio broadcast—soon slowed traffic to a crawl. The wind buffeted the car, practically lifting it off the pavement. Sammi clung white-knuckled to the steering wheel for several miles. "I can't do this. I'm getting off at the next exit. I think there's a factory outlet just off the road. Maybe we can get a cup of coffee—providing we don't get blown away trying to make it from the car to the restaurant. I need to relax for a few minutes."

"Good idea. Hopefully the storm will let up while we're waiting."

Sammi parked near a deli and they raced for the covered walk that ran the full length of the stores. The wind and rain rammed them, nearly throwing them against the building. Sammi pulled at the glass door with both hands, holding it open for Helen, then squeezing inside. The door banged shut behind them.

"I am definitely moving south." Sammi brushed at her wind-blown hair with her fingers, then shrugged out of her lightweight green jacket and hung it over a chair by an empty table. "I've been in hurricanes with less force than this."

"At least it isn't cold." Helen unbuttoned her jacket but left it on.

They made their way to the front of the deli to place their orders. About half a dozen customers sat at small round tables, while others were browsing through the attached gift shop. The waitress, who looked to be about eighteen, greeted them with a gum-snapping "I'll be with you in just a sec." She set a breakfast platter of biscuits and gravy on the table in front of a young man with a swatch of wiry orange hair. The striped shirt and tie and absence of a coat suggested he might be a clerk in one of the eclectic assortment of stores nearby.

Wendy, according to her name pin, bopped back behind the counter. "Okay, ladies, what can I get for ya?"

"I'll have a regular coffee." Sammi dug into her handbag and retrieved a wallet.

"I'll get it," Helen insisted. "It's the least I can do for having you drive me around in this weather." Helen glanced at the handwritten menu items behind the counter. "I'll have an almond latté—single, tall."

"Thanks." Sammi dropped her wallet into her bag, turned around, and leaned back against the counter.

"Ooo . . . it looks just awful out there," Wendy exclaimed as she poured Sammi's coffee and set it on the counter, then began preparing Helen's drink on the espresso machine.

"It is," Helen told her. "Which is why we're in—"

An earsplitting explosion cut her off. The windows bowed and shattered, spraying shards of glass into the store. Helen's cry of alarm joined those of Sammi, the waitress, and the other customers.

Sixteen

A deadly calm followed the explosion. Splinters of glass began to drip from the ceiling, making an almost musical sound as they pinged against the glass-littered floor. For several eternal seconds, Helen lay on her stomach, too stunned to think. It was hot. The stench of burning rubber and fuel rolled in with clouds of black smoke and stung her nostrils.

The deli's piercing fire alarm shattered the stillness. Sprinkler heads in the ceiling spurted out cold water, then picked up momentum. Within seconds Helen was drenched and cold. From outside she could hear people shouting. A cacophony of frantic voices competed with the bleating fire alarm.

"My daughter is in there! I need to get her out!"

"Stay back, lady!"

"Someone call 9-1-1!"

"They're on the way."

A whimpering sound from behind the counter brought Helen's attention back inside. From another part of the store someone moaned. A child was crying. Helen got to her knees. Her arm hurt from the fall. Other than a burning pain on the back of her head, she was okay. She touched the throbbing area and winced when she felt shards of glass in her hair. A patch of hair on the back of her head was matted and damp. She glanced down at her blood-streaked palm.

Sammi moaned. "My face—"

Helen whipped around and knelt beside her friend. "It's okay, Sammi, I'm here." Sammi was sitting, back against the counter like a lifeless rag doll. A mixture of blood and water streamed from multiple cuts on her cheeks, nose, and forehead. Helen brushed Sammi's bangs aside to get a better view of the head wound and the chunk of glass still imbedded there.

She searched her scrambled brain for advice. Did she leave it in or pull it out? Removing it might create a bigger problem, as she had no idea how deep the piece was imbedded. She left it in. Reaching for a napkin dispenser that had fallen to the floor, Helen grabbed a handful and began dabbing at the blood on Sammi's face.

"How bad is it?" Sammi raised her hand to her left temple.

Helen stopped her. "Don't touch it. There's a piece of glass still in there. Are you hurt anywhere else?" Helen gently patted her arms and legs and did a quick check for other injuries.

"I . . . I don't think so. What about you?"

"I'm all right. Just lie still. I'll see to the others."

"No, I'm okay. Let me help triage." Glass crunched as Sammi struggled to her feet.

"Wh-what happened?" Wendy crept out from behind the counter, her hair a drenched mess clinging to the sides of her face. Aside from the look of sheer terror, Wendy appeared to have escaped the blast without a scrape. Others were not so lucky.

Helen scanned the room, not knowing who to assist first. One woman lay on her stomach, legs pinned by a toppled shelf. She started toward the woman when she spotted the boy with the orange hair. He had been sitting too close to the window. He now lay in a pool of blood under the table.

Wendy screamed when she saw him. "Tommy! Oh, please, no!"

Helen held the girl back while Sammi knelt beside him.

She came away a moment later, face whiter than it should have been. "He's dead." Sammi closed her eyes and slumped to the floor.

Helen released the frantic waitress and hurried to Sammi's side. Her pulse was thready, weak. She'd probably collapsed from shock or loss of blood—or maybe an injury neither of them had detected. Helen rolled Sammi onto her back and wiped the water from her face. "Come on, stay with me, Sammi." Taking her jacket off, Helen balled it up and placed it under Sammi's feet. "Wendy, can you turn off the sprinklers?"

Wendy didn't move.

Sammi moaned, "Sorry, I—"

"Shh. Don't try to talk. I shouldn't have let you get up."

It had taken the fire department only four minutes to respond to the call, but to Helen it had seemed far longer. Half a dozen EMTs swarmed in carrying medical supplies and boards. Two of them paused to check the dead boy, then moved over to the woman pinned under the shelving.

One of the technicians drew Helen away from Sammi's side and directed her to a chair while two others concentrated on Sammi. "Looks like you did okay." He quickly checked her head wounds. "Bleeding's stopped. Doesn't look like you'll need stitches, but with all that glass, better have a doc look at it." He checked her pupils and pulse. "How are you feeling otherwise?"

"A little shaky, but okay." Helen fought off an onslaught of dizziness. "I think." Reality, along with her cold wet clothing, seeped into her bones and set her limbs to trembling. She took a deep breath of smoke-filled air to dispel her body's reaction to the trauma. Her lungs rebelled in a fit of coughing.

The EMT grabbed her as she went down and settled her on the floor. "We'll be taking you in. Gotta get your friend in the wagon first, though. Got some more rigs on the way." After instructing Helen to lie still and not move, he summoned for help.

She glanced toward Sammi. The EMTs had already hooked up an IV and were placing her on a stretcher. "Could I ride with her?"

He shook his head. "Better if we take you in separately in case there's trouble. You can catch up to her in the hospital."

To her left rescuers had managed to pull the woman from under the shelf. They immobilized her and took her out on a board, the wind and rain hampering their efforts to reach the ambulance.

"What are you doing?" Helen asked when two technicians laid her out on a stretcher and put her in a neck brace.

"Need to make sure you don't have a spinal cord injury," one explained.

Outside the black smoke was clearing, but the rain continued to pour. Sirens howled and lights flashed as more official vehicles arrived. Police and sheriff's deputies were taping off the area to secure the crime scene and keep the gathering onlookers at bay. There would be a full-scale investigation, of course. A forensics team would be streaming into the deli, gathering evidence and taking photographs, trying to gain some understanding.

Helen finally closed her eyes, not to sleep, but to wonder. What had caused the blast? A gas line? An act of terrorism?

An hour later Helen had been treated and released with minor cuts and bruises. Sammi had been taken into surgery. While she waited for an opportunity to see her friend, Helen hunted down a pay phone and called Susan. When no one answered, she left a message on the answering machine outlining what had happened and assuring them she was okay. She then called Jason, but he'd already gotten word and was on his way to the hospital.

When she arrived back in the waiting room, she was accosted by news teams from what must have been every television and radio station in Oregon. Lights flashed and popped, cameras whirred. Melody James, a reporter Helen recognized from a local television station, shoved a microphone in Helen's face. "I understand you were inside the building when the car exploded. Can you tell us what it was like?"

Helen raised her arm to protect her eyes from the bright lights. "Car? I don't—"

A deputy sheriff stepped in front of the mike and camera. "Not right now, folks. You'll have time to ask questions later." He hurriedly escorted Helen through a set of double doors and into an office. "Have a seat in here, ma'am. We'd like to ask you a few questions. Someone will be with you in a minute."

Helen stared at the cold murky brown liquid in the Styrofoam cup. She didn't care much for industrial coffee and had taken it mostly to warm her hands. It hadn't worked. She set the cup aside. The local police had already questioned her. Unfortunately, they hadn't been willing to pass along any of their information to her. She heard the door open but didn't bother turning around.

"Helen?"

"Tom!" Helen turned toward the familiar voice. "What are you doing out here?"

He closed the door. "Are you kidding? We're all out here—state, city, county, federal. Probably every law enforcement agency in the Portland area. Not every day you get a bombing." He shook his head. "Anyway, I should be asking you that. You trying to get yourself killed or something? First the shooting, now your car blows up—what gives?"

"My car?" Helen rubbed her forehead, trying to dispel her confusion.

"You didn't know?"

"A reporter said something about a car exploding. It—it was Sammi's car?"

"Witnesses said it was a black Cadillac—newer model. Described you and another woman getting out of it just a few minutes before it blew."

"Are you sure it was a bomb? I mean—maybe the car was defective or someone rammed the gas tank."

Tom shook his head. "Oh, it was a bomb all right. That much we know. It'll take a while to figure out what kind or who did it and why. None of the witnesses remembers seeing anyone around the car or tampering with it after you went in, which may mean one of two things. Either they aren't very observant or the bomb was already on the car when you pulled in. I'd lay odds on the second."

"But that means Sammi and I were—" Helen paused as the realization hit.

"What?"

"If it hadn't been for that storm, Sammi and I wouldn't have stopped there." Helen took a drink of the bitter brew and grimaced. "We'd have been on the highway when the bomb went off. And . . . we'd have both been killed."

Seventeen

Tom ran a hand through what little hair he had left. "You stepped on anyone's toes lately?"

Stunned, Helen ran back through recent events, trying to come up with a motive for hers and Sammi's murder. "A few." Paul Kincaid came to mind, as did several prison inmates she'd helped put away.

Tom pulled a cigar out of his pocket and fingered it. "Better start making a list of possibles."

Helen glanced at her watch—eleven-thirty a.m. Had it not been for the storm and the explosion, she'd have been at Edgewood at that very moment, speaking with David Chang and getting ready to tour the facilities. Was someone at Edgewood wanting to keep her away permanently?

Tossing Helen a determined look, Tom asked, "So, who wants you dead?"

"Hard to say. Like you, I've managed to accumulate a few enemies over the years."

"Comes with the territory. Start with the most recent."

Helen brought him up to date on Irene's death and Paul Kincaid's reaction to her being at Edgewood.

"So you think this Kincaid guy might have wanted you out of the way?"

"Out of the way, yes, but a bombing? Killing me while I'm on my way to Edgewood would only fuel interest in the case. Kincaid wouldn't want that. If he were going to kill me, he would choose a more subtle method than a car bomb." She shook her head. "It's too high profile."

"No kidding. It's probably already being reported on the national news."

"I doubt Kincaid would want to run the risk of Edgewood getting any more bad press."

"Sounds like we're dead-ending here. Maybe we ought to look back a ways. Who else have you antagonized?"

"Your guess is as good as mine. The last case I worked on in an official capacity was with the DEA. A drug ring was operating as a travel agency up in Canada. Unofficially, I recently tripped up a fellow officer who got greedy. As far as I know he's still in prison."

"Well, make a list for me. I'll check them out. In the meantime, watch your back." He glanced out the office window, then back at Helen. "What about your friend—what is her name?"

"Sammi Fergeson."

"Right. I understand she's a deputy medical examiner."

"Yes." Helen frowned, remembering something Sammi had told her this morning. "She was scheduled to testify in a murder case this afternoon."

"So she could just as easily have been the target."

"It makes more sense. As a forensic pathologist, she's called in as an expert witness in dozens of murder cases a year. She's undoubtedly made a few enemies." Helen frowned. "And there's another consideration. If someone were after me, how would they know I'd be in Sammi's car?"

"If she didn't tell anyone she was picking you up, the bomb may well have been meant for her." Tom pulled a small spiral notebook and pen from his breast pocket and made a notation. "I'll ask her about it. In fact, I think I know which trial she was talking about. Jim Perry—the guy's smoother than satin sheets."

"Hmm. I've been following the case. Perry is in jail, but he could easily have hired a hit."

Tom tucked the notebook away. "Looks like we've got a lot of angles to pursue here. Complications like this I don't need."

Helen smiled. Despite his grumbling, Tom thrived on complex cases. She felt relieved knowing he'd be involved. Before he left, Helen supplied him with a detailed list of possible suspects and in the end decided to include Paul Kincaid.

Jason walked in shortly after Tom left. He stared at her for a moment—his gaze mingled with fear, anger, and relief. "You could have called me," he accused.

"I did. As soon as I was released." Helen wrapped her arms around him and rested a head on his shoulder. "You were already on your way."

Jason held her tight. "Is it always going to be like this for us? Knowing that at any moment one of us might be blown to kingdom come?"

Helen felt his Adam's apple move up and down against her head as he struggled for control. "First Dad and now you. Maybe Susan is right—I am asking too much of her to marry someone like me. They may all be better off if I just left."

Helen stepped back. "Jason McGrady. I can't believe you said that."

He sighed. "I've been giving it some serious thought. But never mind that. I think we'd better talk about what happened here."

"How did you find out about it so quickly?" Helen stepped back.

"Tom radioed me when he found out you were one of the victims."

"If it's any consolation, I don't believe the bomb was meant for me."

"That's what Tom said." Jason nodded toward the door. "We talked before I came in."

"Good, then I won't have to repeat myself." Helen sank into the chair behind the desk. "Jason, I know you're busy, but would you mind driving me out to Edgewood?"

"Now?" He frowned. "You still want to go out there?"

"More than ever."

Jason looked like he wanted to argue but didn't.

They fought their way past reporters and managed to check in on Sammi, who had just come out of surgery. She was still out cold from the anesthesia, but her condition had stabilized.

After stopping at a convenience store for snacks and drinks, Jason and Helen were on their way. The wind had died down to a gentle breeze. Sunlight and patches of blue sky penetrated layers of gray.

For the first few minutes they continued to speculate on the bombing. When they exited the freeway at Corbett, the conversation drifted back to the Kincaids.

"You'll be happy to know I'm not closing the case yet. There are some loose ends—like the break-in prior to the mugging." Jason took a sip of root beer and set the can in a drink holder on the console. "Like you, I feel uncomfortable with the coincidences." He smiled. "Besides, I've been getting a lot of pressure from some VIPs telling me to archive it."

"Really?"

"Apparently Kincaid has some friends in high places. 'Course, that's a red flag for me. The chief isn't too happy with me, but he's willing to give me a few more days to come up with some solid evidence. Fortunately, he doesn't like being pressured either."

"I must say I'm relieved."

"Mother, there's something else we need to discuss."

"I'm not sure I like the sound of that."

"It's got to do with you and Jennie. I honestly don't know what to do with you two . . . ."

"What do you mean?"

"For starters, I find it awkward having my mother and daughter trying to solve my cases for me. Normally I'd order you to stop getting involved. Thing is, you're not normal."

Helen chuckled. "Thanks a lot."

"What I mean is, you were a great homicide detective and you're a terrific agent. And Jennie—what can I say? She's got the makings of a top-notch lawyer or cop or whatever she decides to be."

"But . . . ?"

"You're coming out here to rehabilitate, and Jennie says she's coming here to work. I know perfectly well you're both here to snoop. I could forbid Jennie to take the job, but what good would it do? She'd end up resenting me. And I know better than to try to dissuade you."

"I'm not too crazy about having Jennie out here either, but look at the positive side. With me here, I can look after her, and you'll have an excuse to come out as often as you like in an unofficial capacity. Kincaid apparently wants the case closed. Fine—let him think it is."

"You have a point, but I still feel like I should be warning you off."

"Before your disappearance, you always used to come to me for advice. We'd talk things out and—"

"And I'd go away feeling better. We didn't always come up with the solution, but you helped me see the problems more clearly." He nodded and grinned. "It's good to be home."

———

At Edgewood Estates, Andi greeted Helen like an old friend. "Got you on the list this time, Mrs. Bradley. In fact, Dr. Chang just called to see if you'd showed up. You get slowed down by that explosion in Troutdale?"

"As a matter of fact, we did." Jason signed in on the sheet and handed it to Helen, then told Andi that Helen had been injured in the blast.

"No kidding? You look okay."

"I was lucky, just some minor cuts. How did you hear about it?"

Andi nodded toward the guardhouse. "Police radio scanner. I'm a volunteer deputy for Clackamas County when I'm not working here. Like to keep track of what's going down."

Helen signed in and checked the signatures on the list of check-ins. "Andi, do you have everyone sign in?"

"Sure do. I'm a nut for security—like to know where people are at all times."

"So if Paul Kincaid were here this morning, he'd have signed this?" Helen handed the clipboard back.

"Would have. Dr. Kincaid hasn't come in yet. He called around eight—said he had some business at the medical examiner's office. Did you want to see him? I can call him on his car phone and find out when he'll be back."

Helen's stomach tightened. "No, that's all right. I'll catch him later."

"Okay—you're all set then. I'll call Dr. Chang and let him know you're coming."

When the gate opened, Jason put the car in first gear and drove through. "So Dr. Kincaid was at the ME's office this morning."

"I take it you plan to question him about the bombing."

"You got that right. Looks like your Dr. Kincaid might not be as worried about his reputation as you seem to think."

Eighteen

Mrs. Bradley, I must say I'm surprised you came." Dr. Chang met her at the door to the manor, and after meeting Jason, he escorted them inside. "Andi told me you'd been injured."

Helen nodded. "I was in the deli when the bomb went off."

"Deli?" He offered her a chair in the waiting room and took a seat next to her. "Forgive me if I seem confused, but I understood it was a car."

"It was." She explained what had happened. "My injuries are minor, so I decided to come here straight from the hospital. I hope you don't mind."

"Not at all. I'm pleased you decided to accept our offer." Dr. Chang didn't look especially pleased. He smiled briefly, then turned toward Jason. "You're welcome to stay and tour the facilities as well. We like having the family participate as much as possible."

"Appreciate the invitation, Doc, but I have to get back to work. Don't worry, we'll be visiting Mom a lot while she's here. If there's anything we can do, you let us know."

Jason gave her a one-armed hug and kissed her cheek. "I'll see you tonight."

When he'd gone, Dr. Chang picked up the thread of their conversation about the bombing. "You mentioned that Dr. Fergeson had sustained some injuries. How is she?"

"Still being evaluated, but the doctor assured me she'd be fine."

Dr. Chang nodded, his dark eyes registering concern. "Well, then, I suppose we should get you settled. I'll have one of our other doctors admit you. I'd do it myself, but something's come up in the lab that requires my attention." He left the room and came back in less than two minutes with Stephanie and an empty wheelchair.

The head nurse had apparently purchased a new uniform—one that was better suited to her growing figure. From the fullness of the pastel pink top, Helen suspected that Stephanie's rounded tummy entailed more than overeating.

"I believe you've met Miss Curtis."

"Yes, how are you?"

The nurse ignored the question. "I understand you'll be staying with us for a while." She glanced around. "Did you have a suitcase?"

Helen grimaced. "I did have. It's gone—in the explosion. My laptop and . . . I can't believe I didn't think about it until just now."

"That's understandable." Dr. Chang gave her an empathetic smile. "You've had a major crisis." He turned to Stephanie. "We need to get her admitted. Take her into the exam room. I'll talk to Dr. Lawson. Do we have her room ready?"

"Yes—134."

"Good. That has one of our best views. I'll leave you then—and try not to worry. You're in capable hands."

Stephanie assisted Helen into the wheelchair and rolled her out of the waiting area and down the long hall. One of the residents shuffled toward them, using a carved wooden cane for balance. His snow-white hair and beard and red suspenders reminded Helen of Santa Claus—until he spoke.

"Mornin', Miss Stephanie," he drawled. His sky-blue gaze dropped to Helen. "Now don't tell me y'all are checkin' in here. Young beauty like you?" He chuckled and winked.

Helen liked him immediately.

"Now you quit your flirting, Henry," Stephanie said, sounding almost animated. "Mrs. Bradley is here for our rehab program." To Helen she said, "Don't mind old Henry here. He flirts with every woman in the place. That southern charm of his even makes me feel young and pretty."

"Why, Miss Stephanie, you are young and pretty. Nothin' more beautiful than a pregnant woman, I always say."

"How—" Stephanie glanced down at her rounded abdomen. "Uhh . . . thank you, Henry. Now if you'll excuse us, I need to get our new patient admitted."

"Surely, I will." He dipped his head and winked again. "Reckon I'll be seeing you at dinner, ma'am."

Helen grinned. "Reckon so, Mr.—what was the last name?"

"Butler, ma'am, Rhett Butler." He shuffled down the hall whistling Dixie.

Helen glanced up at Stephanie. "Rhett Butler?"

Stephanie smiled, looking friendly for the first time since they'd met. "He was an actor in his younger days. This morning he's doing *Gone With the Wind*. We never know who he'll be next. Sometimes he's himself, but most of the time he loses himself in characters he's read about or played. They're always southern, though—in that at least, he's consistent."

Being admitted to Edgewood was a matter of filling out a six-page form questioning everything from prescriptions to bowel regularity and listing every disease known to the human race. When Helen had finished the questionnaire, the administrative assistant asked whether or not she had a living will. If not, did she want one.

"I'll think about it," Helen said.

"Okay, I'll put down 'no' for now." The woman opened a file cabinet and pulled out a thick gray folder.

"This is your admitting packet. In it you'll find information on Edgewood and what we do here. There's also a brochure that explains living wills and one on our retirement package. We have a wonderful program for retirees that guarantees life-long care. If you have any questions, our business manager will be happy to answer them for you."

Helen tucked her packet beside her and waited. A few minutes later Stephanie showed up again. About halfway down the corridor a wiry woman in a wheelchair whipped out of her room and nearly collided with them. Her wrinkled face sank inward at the mouth. She pinched her lips together and leaned forward in a mutinous pose.

"Did you lose your dentures again, Iris?"

"Nope—just don't want to wear 'em. They hurt my gums." She clamped her lips together again as if to say you can't make me.

"I know they're uncomfortable, but you'll never get used to them at this rate."

"Don't want to." She bent her elbows and grabbed hold of the wheels, then shoved off and sped down the hallway in the same direction Henry had taken.

"Speed limit's five miles an hour, Iris," Stephanie called after her, the words unheeded.

"She's quite a character." Helen watched her a moment, then turned back around when Stephanie pushed her forward again.

"A terror. She's eighty-five years old and popping wheelies— one of these days she's going to hurt herself or one of the other residents."

"I must say you have some rather colorful patients."

"We get all kinds here. Actually, people like Iris and Henry make our jobs more . . . interesting." Stephanie wheeled her into a room that looked like a beauty shop.

"This is our stying salon." Stephanie locked the wheelchair brakes. "We have licensed beauticians fix our residents' hair twice a week. I thought you might like to have yours washed by one of our staff nurses."

"Washed?" Helen felt the back of her head where the blood was still caked. "Oh, dear, I . . . um . . . forgot. Normally I don't arrive at appointments in such disarray. I guess I should have gone home first."

Stephanie's full lips parted in an empathetic smile while she helped Helen into the salon chair. "Don't give it a second thought." She glanced toward the door and smiled. "Good, here's Thelma now."

A woman the size of a refrigerator filled the doorway. "Got here as quick as I could. Miss Ellsworth's gone and pulled out her IV again. Bled all over creation before I could get to her." Thelma's stark white uniform made her dark skin appear even darker. "I put a dressing on it and cleaned her up."

Stephanie sighed and looked at her watch. "Great. That's all I need. As soon as you finish with Mrs. Bradley, take her into exam room two and call Dr. Lawson."

"Sure will." A grin broke across Thelma's face as she chuckled and shook her head. "This place is feelin' more like a zoo every day." She turned her attention back to Helen, took one look at the matted mess of hair, and frowned. "Okay now, let's get you cleaned up." She released a lever and tilted the chair back. "What's this I hear about an explosion?"

Thelma directed a gentle warm spray of water over Helen's head and in a few moments, her tense body settled into the padded chair. Helen closed her eyes and retold her story.

"If that doesn't beat all," Thelma said as Helen finished. "What's this world comin' to? All this killing." She sighed. "Wouldn't be at all surprised to find out it was a prank pulled by some drug-crazed hoodlums. Nothing surprises me these days."

"Hmm." Helen listened as Thelma expounded on the prevailing violence of children in today's society. In a way she wished Thelma's theory about the explosion were true, but the events leading up to it strongly suggested that either Helen or Sammi—or both—had been deliberate targets.

All too soon, Thelma turned off the water, draped Helen's head in a towel, and raised the chair to an upright position. "All set."

"Have you worked here long?" Helen asked.

"Two years. Worked at a hospital for ten years before that."

"Do you like it here?" Helen transferred back to the wheelchair.

Thelma shrugged. "It's like any other job. Some days good—some not so . . . " Thelma wheeled Helen to a bank of mirrors, picked up a brush, and pulled a dryer from its well. Without asking for preferences, she began blow drying and styling Helen's hair. "It was better before Dr. Kincaid passed away. Dr. Paul isn't at all like his daddy."

"Really?" Helen hoped the nurse would elaborate, but she didn't. Thelma clamped her jaw as though she'd already said too much.

"You do that very well." Helen watched her hair turn from wet and limp to fluffy.

"Used to be a hairdresser. One of the reasons they hired me, I expect. I fill in when the regulars aren't here."

Helen smiled. "A woman of many talents."

Thelma turned off the dryer and set it aside, then whisked the brush through Helen's hair, carefully working around the abrasions. The short blunt cut fell into a natural style. She caught Helen's gaze in the mirror and smiled. "Not bad if I do say so myself."

"It's wonderful." Helen tipped her head from side to side, admiring Thelma's handiwork.

"You have good hair."

Thelma wheeled her into the hall and down an empty corridor. Depositing Helen in room two, then handing her an open-backed gown. "Just put this on, honey, and I'll let Dr. Lawson know you're here." She set the wheelchair near the door and left.

———

Twenty minutes later, Helen scooted off the paper-lined exam table and pulled a current copy of Newsweek out of the oak magazine rack on the wall and thumbed through it while she waited in the uncomfortably cool exam room.

She'd been ruminating over her lost computer the entire time and repeatedly told herself it could be replaced. In part that was true. Insurance would cover a new laptop, and she had most of her work on her desktop at home—her beach home—but the unfinished articles she'd been working on the last few days would have to be rewritten.

The door opened and Helen tossed the magazine onto the chair where she'd set her clothes.

"Mrs. Bradley." A woman wearing a lab coat, blue jeans, and Birkenstocks entered. "I'm Dr. Lawson." She'd pulled her wavy dishwater-blond hair into a leather clasp at the back of her head. "I understand you were involved in some kind of explosion. And let's see, we're admitting you for rehab on your arm?" She set the clipboard down, leaned against the counter, and settled a skeptical gaze on Helen's shoulder. "Which is from a gunshot wound?"

"Yes."

"I know it's probably a really stupid question, but how did all this happen to you?"

"It's a long story." Helen briefly outlined both incidents. "I understand Edgewood has an excellent rehabilitation program."

Dr. Lawson nodded, a smile stretching her already thin lips.

"Which is why I'm here." She moved to Helen's side and began probing her injured arm. "You've been wearing a sling?"

"Faithfully." Helen winced as the doctor raised the arm up and out of Helen's comfort zone.

"Show me what exercises you've been doing."

Helen went through the routine she'd developed. "I've been working with five-pound weights."

"You've got pretty good range of motion. I'm going to recommend pool exercises as well as some work on the weights. We'll combine that with a daily massage and some ultrasound therapy. I'd say three—maybe four—weeks and you'll be good as new."

"Will you be working with me?"

"Occasionally. I run the department, and that keeps me pretty busy. In the meantime, I'm tracking all the clients—trying to see what works and what doesn't."

"Sounds like you enjoy your work."

"Oh, I do. Keeping older people active helps them live longer and more productive lives. Of course we don't only deal with the elderly. We often have younger residents who have physical limitations and disabilities."

"Have you been here long?"

"Five years. I was a trained physical therapist before going to med school. Thanks to Andrew Kincaid, I'm going for a second Ph.D. in geriatric rehab." She frowned. "Unfortunately, now that he's gone I don't know if they'll continue to fund the program."

"Why's that?"

"Money."

Helen wanted to know more, but Dr. Lawson glanced at her watch. "I'd better get over to physical therapy. I have an appointment with one of my greatest successes. You're welcome to come watch. It'll give you an idea of what we do."

"I'd like that."

"Great. I'll tell Stephanie and she can have someone bring you down."

Helen had just finished dressing when Thelma came in with the wheelchair and insisted Helen climb into it.

"I really don't need this thing."

"Maybe not, but Dr. Chang said we should keep you in it today—because of that explosion. No sense taking any chances."

"Are you taking me down to physical therapy?"

"Yes, ma'am. Dr. Lawson is putting Lars through his paces. And that is a sight to behold."

"Why's that?"

"Mr. Olsen is ninety-two years old. A year or so ago he had a stroke and his family gave him up for dead. But Lars and the good Lord had other plans."

Edgewood Manor's physical therapy department looked like a state-of-the-art fitness center. Mirrors lined the walls and treadmills, stair steppers, and stationary bicycles filled the area to her left. Royal blue exercise mats occupied the center of the room, where a large number of residents, mostly seniors, were trying to mimic a bouncy middle-aged aerobic instructor to the tune of "La Bamba." Off to the right a white-haired man with a torso every bit as muscular as an Olympic gymnast's was doing arm curls.

Helen nodded toward him. "Now don't tell me that's Lars Olsen?"

"That's him."

"What do you think of our facility, Mrs. Bradley?" Dr. Lawson came up behind her, making eye contact in the mirror.

"Very impressive." Helen nodded toward the man. "I'm having trouble believing your Mr. Olsen is a day over fifty, though."

The doctor beamed. "Wonderful specimen, isn't he? Lars!" she shouted above the music. "Come here a minute—I'd like you to meet someone."

Lars set the weight in its holder and moved toward them. His left foot dragged slightly as he walked.

"Did Thelma tell you he's had a stroke?" Dr. Lawson asked.

"Yes. He seems to be doing quite well."

"His entire left side was paralyzed when he first came to us."

"I'd say you are a miracle worker."

"Ya—that she is." The big Scandinavian grinned down at her, revealing a beautiful set of what must be false teeth.

Dr. Lawson introduced them.

"Vill you be joining us then?" Lars glanced down at her sling before fixing his bright blue gaze on Helen's.

"Yes, and the sooner the better. I need my arm back."

"Vell, if anyone can fix you up, the Doc here can." After an awkward pause and a few more comments on the attributes of Edgewood, Lars went back to his exercising.

"I don't suppose you'd be willing to share the secret of your success. I'd love to be that fit at ninety."

"Better. We'll be putting you on a similar regimen. We treat the whole body here at Edgewood. The doctors from the various departments work as a team, outlining what's best for each patient. When I have more time I can answer some of your questions. Right now, however, I need to get back to my patient. You're welcome to stay and watch."

"Thanks." Helen waved her on, watched for about ten minutes, then accepted Thelma's offer to take her back to her room.

As promised, Room 134 had a spectacular view of the Columbia River Gorge.

"Can I get you anything before I go? A snack or something to drink?"

"No, thank you. I'm fine."

Glad to be alone again, Helen settled into a blue-gray recliner and fell asleep.

When she awoke the room was in shadows. Someone had lowered the blind.

Helen heard a faint scraping that sounded like a drawer opening and closing. "Who's there?"

No one answered.

Sure someone was in the room, Helen reached for the lamp next to the chair. It clattered to the floor and left her groping at the air.

Nineteen

Helen's heart hammered in her chest. Someone was in the room with her. She pressed herself against the chair, waiting for her attacker to strike—staring into the darkness, wishing the chair were facing the door rather than the window.

Nothing happened.

Seconds later the door swished open. Overhead lights came on, obliterating the shadows. "Mrs. Bradley?" A soprano voice splintered the stillness. "Time for dinner.

"Mrs. Bradley? Are you all right?" A woman in a floral pastel uniform came into Helen's view. She frowned at the lamp. "My goodness, what happened?"

"I'm . . . I'm not sure. I thought I heard someone in my room . . . ." Helen squinted, still trying to adjust to the light.

"You did, honey—me. I came down to see if you'd like to join the residents for dinner."

"I . . . I could have sworn someone was here before you came in. They knocked the lamp out of my hand. Did you see anyone leave?"

"No. But you look like you just woke up. Maybe you were a little disoriented and misjudged the distance. It happens." She pulled the lamp upright and straightened the shade. "No harm done."

"Thank you." Helen frowned. The intrusion had seemed so real. Now she wondered if the incident had been the product of an overactive imagination.

"I'm Lucy Walker. You're assigned to me this shift."

Helen put the incident behind her and focused on the aid. Lucy's smile was nearly as wide as her pixielike face. With her short shaggy haircut and petite figure, she looked a bit like Peter Pan. Helen guessed her to be around thirty, maybe more. Around here it was hard to tell.

"So would you like to eat in the dining room, or do you want me to bring you a tray?"

Helen opted for the dining room, since it would give her a chance to visit with the other residents. When Lucy brought the wheelchair, Helen insisted on walking. "I need the exercise."

"All right, but I'll walk with you—just in case."

By the time Helen arrived, the well-lit dining room had only a few empty seats. Not that it mattered. According to Lucy, residents sat in assigned seats at every meal to cut down on the confusion and provide continuity.

Like everything else at Edgewood, the large room had been simply but elegantly decorated. Dusty rose tablecloths and matching cloth napkins along with floral centerpieces provided cheery colors. The arrangement and layout of the room with its numerous round tables resembled the banquet room of a pricey hotel. The residents varied in age, Helen noticed—a handful appeared younger than herself—however, most looked to be sixty and over.

Lucy escorted Helen to a table near the wall of windows that overlooked a central courtyard and offered an unhindered view of the river. She recognized two of her seatmates—Iris, who was now wearing her teeth, and the therapy protégé, Lars Olsen.

"She can't sit there," a scratchy voice proclaimed when Lucy pulled out a chair next to a woman who had barely enough skin to cover her bones. "That's Ruthie's place."

"Now, Gladys," Lucy patted the woman's shoulder. "You know Ruthie's no longer with us. Everyone, this is our new resident, Helen Bradley."

NOW I LAY ME DOWN TO SLEEP

"Oh yes, I saw you earlier in the exercise room," one of the women said. "I'm Betty Salter."

Helen eased into her chair. "The aerobics instructor."

Betty blushed. "Just one of the many things I do around here to earn my keep."

Helen started to ask what she meant when Lucy intervened. "I'll introduce everyone, then you're on your own. On your right is Gladys Seavolt, then Lars Olsen, Iris Johanson, Betty Salter and her husband, Jim, Daniel Mays, and Lydia James. Now, if you'll excuse me, I'll go get your dinners."

"Welcome to our table." Betty lifted her water glass in a toast.

"She's sitting in Ruthie's place." Gladys glared at Helen, eyes hard as black marbles.

"You'll have to forgive Gladys," Jim said. "Ruthie was her sister, and she's only been gone a few days."

"Was she discharged or—"

"Died," three of them echoed.

"I'm sorry." Helen picked up her fork and pushed around the salad that had been placed there earlier.

"She fell down the basement stairs." Jim, a lean man with parchment white skin, reached for a roll and a pat of butter from the basket in front of him before passing it on.

"She was pushed." Gladys picked up her fork and stabbed a chunk of lettuce.

An anxious look passed between the other residents. Lars leaned toward Gladys and murmured something in her ear. A warning to keep her mouth shut?

Daniel Mays cleared his throat. "Don't believe everything you hear in this group, Helen. Gladys has trouble discerning fact from fiction."

Helen made a mental note to speak with Gladys privately. Fiction and reality had a tendency to become interwoven here at

Edgewood, and Helen wanted an opportunity to judge the woman's mental capacity for herself.

"So tell us what brings you out here." Betty seemed anxious to steer the conversation into safer channels. "Did you come voluntarily or did your family . . . ahh . . . place you?"

Helen bristled at the idea of being placed anywhere. "Strictly voluntary, I can assure you. I came to take advantage of their rehabilitation program."

"You fall too?" Iris asked, her teeth clicking as she spoke.

"In a manner of speaking. Actually, I was shot." Helen went on to explain her encounter with Irene and the gunman.

Lars beamed his recognition. "Ya. I thought your name sounded familiar. I read about you."

"We did too." Betty and Jim joined the conversation, probing for more details. The excited buzz came to a halt when Lucy arrived with a serving cart. She dispensed their meals, then moved to the table beside them. Other staff members—Helen counted seven—were moving about the room serving their charges as well. One of those was Jennie. Her granddaughter seemed more at home here than Helen did as she smiled and chatted with residents at a table across the room. Jennie caught sight of Helen and waved, giving her an I'll-catch-you-later look.

The moment Lucy left the area, Iris took out her teeth and set them beside her plate. "Fool things," she grumbled.

"For heaven's sake, Iris, put your teeth back in." Betty elbowed her. "We have a guest."

"Do you think I care?"

Helen held back a smile and sampled the white mound on her plate. It looked like steamed fish. Though it had been overcooked, the fish tasted remarkably good dipped in the accompanying dill sauce. She also had rice and an assortment of sautéed vegetables.

Iris, Helen noted, had mashed potatoes and puréed vegetables.

After taking a few bites, Helen ventured back to their interrupted conversation. "I understand Irene worked here as a volunteer."

"Oh yes," Lydia, the woman on her left, spoke for the first time since Helen's arrival. "She was such a dear. Used to come in and chat with us. It's hard to believe she's gone."

"Yes, it is." Helen longed to question them about Irene and the goings on at Edgewood, but it was too soon. Or so she thought.

"They killed her." Iris paused to gum a forkful of mashed potatoes. "They'll kill us all eventually."

Helen's head snapped up. "You mean Irene?"

"Ruthie. But now that you mention it, they might've done in Irene, too."

"That's quite an accusation. Do you have proof?"

"Of course she doesn't." Betty rolled her eyes and sighed. "There are certain residents who seem to have forgotten that death is imminent. As the famous George Bernard Shaw once said, 'The statistics on death are quite impressive. One out of one people die.' And this is a nursing home, for heaven's sake."

"Humph . . . " Iris picked up her teeth and stuffed them back into her mouth. "You mark my words, missy. Ruthie wasn't the first to have an 'accident,' and she sure won't be the last."

"We'd best keep our mouths shut, old woman," Gladys muttered, "or we just might end up next on the list."

"Hi, everyone." Lucy arrived with trays of dessert. "Oh, Iris, you still have your teeth in. I am so proud of you. See, it wasn't so bad."

Iris flashed her a wide grin.

"We have strawberry-kiwi tarts tonight, and they are excellent. Non-fat too, of course. All of our desserts are," she added for Helen's benefit. "Who wants coffee or tea?" Lucy took their orders and left again.

"I must say, this is the most stimulating conversation I've had in a while." Helen sliced into her tart.

Daniel chuckled. "It's not always like this. Gladys suffers from a type of paranoia brought on by senile dementia. Unfortunately, she's convinced Iris and some of the others that the nursing staff are a band of thieves and murderers."

Helen raised an eyebrow. "I see."

"You listen to Daniel. He's a doctor, you know." Lars pierced a strawberry. "It's all a bunch of malarkey. If they was killing people for the insurance, like Iris here seems to think, they'd of gotten rid of me a long time ago. I figure I cost them a lot more than they'll be able to collect when I'm gone."

"Insurance?" Helen was wishing she'd brought a note pad. She was getting far more information than she'd expected.

"Many of us name Kincaid Enterprises as beneficiaries on our insurance policies and in our wills," Lydia explained. "It's all very legal and altruistic. I've done it."

"Ya—me too."

"And I." Daniel nodded. "I wish I could do more. It's good to know that when I die, I'll be leaving a portion of my estate to a worthy cause."

"Do you mind my asking how much that amounts to?" Helen asked.

"Four million plus whatever the funds have earned in the last year."

Helen gasped at Daniel's figure. "That's quite a donation. And the rest of you?"

"I've stipulated $500,000," Lydia offered. "But I'm thinking of increasing it."

"That's a little rich for our blood," Jim said. "Betty and I can't afford much. We've already signed over all of our assets, just so I can stay here. We're not charity cases, but they're not making any money off us either."

"Betty, you said earlier you were 'earning your keep.' What did you mean by that?"

"Well, as Jim said, we don't have a lot of money. Most of it went to pay for Jim's hospital bills. You see, he has a rare blood disorder."

"I have AIDS." Jim settled a challenging gaze on his wife, then on Helen. "And no, I'm not a homosexual or a drug user. In fact, I'm a retired pastor and have always been faithful to my wife. I have no idea how I contracted the virus."

Betty placed a hand on her husband's hand, momentarily stilling his Parkinson-like tremor. "Our church didn't believe him and we were encouraged to take an early retirement. At any rate, Jim's condition was steadily worsening until we found out about the research being done by Kincaid Laboratories."

"They're doing research on AIDS? I thought their focus was gerontology."

"It is," Daniel interjected. "But acquired-immune deficiency isn't just a disease for the younger generation. It's affecting more and more middle-aged and older people as well."

"So their research brought you here?" Helen turned back to Jim.

"Yes. We found an ad in the paper for volunteers to test a new drug and applied. I agreed to be a guinea pig for them, and they give me room and board for as long as I need it."

"And I work wherever I'm needed to help pay my expenses so I can stay with Jim."

"And the treatment? Is it working?"

"I'm not cured. But their regimen has improved the quality of my life. I'm starting to gain weight and feel more energetic."

"I keep hearing about these wonderful treatments. Are you getting some kind of wonder drug? What are they giving you?"

"It's different for all of us." Lydia placed her napkin on the table. "We go through a battery of tests to determine what our bodies need. Then they determine what vitamins, minerals, herbs, and so on are required to bring us into a more healthy state. It's a very complicated process."

"Could you give me an example of what you're taking?"

"We're really not allowed to tell anyone what medications we're on."

"That's so the family won't know you're being poisoned," Gladys rasped.

And on they went again. The fight against the rational and the irrational. Gladys and Iris insisting Edgewood was the epitome of evil. Jim, Betty, Lars, Daniel, and Lydia making it sound like heaven on earth. Helen had a hunch the truth lay somewhere in between. Her dinner partners had given her much to dissect, only she didn't get a chance to do much thinking above the clamor of debate.

Jason was waiting in her room when she came back from dinner. He'd stretched out in the recliner and fallen asleep. Watching him tugged at Helen's heart. Sleep erased the worry lines from his face, giving him a boyish look. Where had the time gone? It seemed like only yesterday when she'd held him in her arms and read to him and soothed his fears.

She started to brush back the lock of dark hair that had fallen across his forehead but pulled back her hand. Careful not to wake him, Helen crept to the door and reached for the switch to turn off the overhead lights. That's when she noticed the laptop sitting on the desk—hooked up and ready for use. All the comforts of home—almost.

Helen left word with the receptionist that she'd be in the day room. The large spacious area consisted of several sofas and chairs for entertaining visitors and playing games. She was just passing the front door when Susan and Nick arrived.

After hugs and kisses and reassurances that she hadn't been seriously hurt in the explosion that morning, Helen gave them a tour of the physical therapy department, told them about her exercises, then led them to the gardens outside.

The manicured grounds stretched along the front of the manor, sloping gently downward until they met a low boxwood hedge bordering a steep cliff. An asphalt walk meandered down to a circular garden with a panoramic view of the river.

Nick started romping across the wide expanse of lawn. Helen and Susan found a pair of redwood benches under a giant maple and sat down to enjoy the vista.

"I washed the clothes you left at the house and bought a couple outfits. I can get you more later," Susan said. "Did you want me to bring them to your room?"

"Thanks, but we can do that later. Jason's asleep in there."

"Jason's here?" Susan bit her lower lip. "I hadn't heard from him today."

"I'm not surprised. He must have come straight from work. He brought a replacement for the computer I lost in the explosion."

"That was sweet of him."

"Yes. Yes it was."

"Helen. I . . . I've made a decision and I'd like to tell you before I talk to Jason." Susan's gaze dropped to the ground.

"Oh?" Helen braced herself for the worst.

"I'm almost afraid to say it, but I think I'm ready to take Jason back."

"Susan, that's wonderful."

She smiled. "I suppose it is. I do love him—more than I ever thought possible. These last few weeks I've worked very hard at making some adjustments in my own thinking and my expectations. It's working. Instead of nagging at him to be with us more, I'm trying to just relax and enjoy our time together. We're talking—about everything. We never used to do that."

"You haven't told him yet?"

"No. I want Jennie and Nick to be there when I do."

Helen swallowed back the lump in her throat. "You know I couldn't be happier."

"Happier about what?" Jennie came up behind them and wrapped her slender tan arms around Helen's neck.

"None of your business." Susan playfully swatted her daughter on the bottom. "You're too nosy for your own good."

Jennie giggled and came around beside them. "It's Dad, isn't it? You're getting back together."

"Maybe."

"I knew it. I'm going to tell him."

"Wait a minute. How's the job going?" Susan asked.

"Great. I am learning so much. I think I'm really going to like work—"

A piercing scream interrupted Jennie midsentence. Iris, arms and legs flailing, passed by them in her wheelchair, careening without control at a dangerously fast speed. Jennie tore out after the run-away chair with its terrified passenger.

"Iris!" Lucy shrieked.

The wheelchair came to an abrupt halt at the hedge. Iris didn't. Helen and the others watched, horrified, as Iris flew over the hedge and disappeared from view.

Twenty

Jennie, wait!" Helen scrambled to the precipice where her granddaughter, one leg already over the shrubs, started after the elderly woman.

Iris lay unmoving on a rocky ledge about six feet below. Helen closed her eyes for a moment, holding tight to Jennie's arm and offering up a silent prayer. "Don't try to go down there. Go inside and have someone call a rescue unit."

"Mrs. Bradley's right, Jennie," Lucy gasped. "You go ahead. I'll stay here."

Jennie hesitated a moment, then tore up the walk and into the manor.

"This is all my fault." Lucy wrapped her arms around herself as she stared at the still figure below them. "I should have been watching her more closely. I thought I'd strapped her in, but she's like Houdini. She moves so fast. I was afraid she'd end up doing something like this." The last of her words ended in a whine.

A crew of doctors and nursing staff responded immediately, as did a rescue unit bearing the name Edgewood Community Fire & Rescue. Two retirement-age men identified as voluntary EMTs pulled rock-climbing paraphernalia out of their rig and within minutes were on the ledge beside Iris.

"She's alive." The words drifted up to the onlookers as the two men checked Iris for injuries. Within five minutes, the men had her on a stretcher secured with ropes and hooks and gave the signal to haul her up.

"Take her inside," Adriane Donahue ordered the moment rescue workers hauled Iris up the precipice and onto the lawn. "We'll do what we can here, then send her into Portland if necessary."

Adriane, looking crisp and professional in her lab coat, had been one of the first doctors to arrive on the scene. David Chang and Paul Kincaid came next.

Helen followed the group through the maze of hallways and into the trauma room, which she identified by the block letters on the door. It looked like an emergency unit with two gurneys separated by curtains. Equipment and supplies lined the wall. They transferred Iris to a gurney and went to work. Helen wondered if this was where they'd brought Andrew Kincaid when he'd had his heart attack. If she had any question as to these doctors' competence, it disappeared as she watched them work.

"There's something . . . " Iris's arm came up. She clutched Dr. Chang's coat in a bloody grip. "I gotta tell ya . . . ."

"It's all right, Iris." Dr. Chang gently cradled her hand in his and brushed wispy white bangs from her forehead. "You just rest now. You can tell us all about it later."

"No, now . . . "

Helen didn't hear any more. Lucy noticed she'd been standing there and ushered her outside. "I'm sorry, Mrs. Bradley, but you can't be in here. I know you're worried about her, but rules are rules. I'll keep you posted on her progress."

As Lucy opened the door and slipped back into the trauma room, Helen glanced inside and caught Paul's cool gaze. He abruptly left his patient and joined her in the hallway. "Mrs. Bradley, I see you've decided to come to Edgewood after all."

His expression softened a bit. "I . . . I need to apologize for the way I behaved at the funeral. I've been under a tremendous amount of stress lately. As Adriane and Sammi both pointed out to me, I was out of line."

Helen nodded. "Yes, you were, but I can certainly understand why." She looked past him into the trauma room.

"You saw what happened to Iris?" he asked.

"Not all of it. She apparently had been traveling too fast and lost control."

"So you didn't see anyone push her?"

"No, did she say that?"

He pulled the door closed behind him and led her across the hall to an exam room. Once inside he shut the door and turned to her. "Mrs. Bradley, I didn't want you to come here, primarily because I didn't want to bring any more embarrassment upon my family. My stepmother made accusations that were—well, unfounded. Neither she nor my father was murdered. It's ludicrous to even consider that one of our doctors could have been involved in something so evil."

He leaned against the exam table, crossed his long legs at the ankle, and folded his arms. "But you are right about one thing. There is something odd going on here."

"So I noticed."

"I mean besides Iris."

Helen did too but didn't say so.

"Adriane and I had a long talk after the funeral. We decided that since you were coming anyway, we'd ask you to discreetly look into some of the problems we've been having. A few too many incidents have occurred recently to pass them off as normal."

"Like Ruthie?"

"Yes. Like Ruthie and now—" He sighed. "Iris claims someone pushed her. Fortunately, she is a tough old bird. I think she'll pull through. I'd hate to think of these injuries as resulting from anything other than accidents; still, they are cause for concern. And there have been rumors of theft and abuse."

"What can I do that you can't? Surely you know better than I what's going on."

"You'd think so, but for some reason no one is talking. They are either unaware of a problem or they are frightened—except for Iris and a few other women."

"Gladys?"

Paul nodded.

"But no one believes them."

"The others—those who don't have a history of dementia—insist there is no problem."

"I see. And you think since I'm a resident, they might be more open with me?"

"Precisely." He straightened and reached for the door handle. "I think it would be best if this stayed between the three of us—Adriane, you, and myself. Although I like to think our staff is above reproach, I can't be sure."

"I'll let you know if I see anything. In the meantime, I need to get back to my family." Helen ducked under his arm when he opened the door.

An hour later, Helen waved good-bye to Jason, Susan, and Nick while Jennie headed back inside to finish her shift. The warm feeling of seeing Jason and his family together again dissipated as their cars disappeared around the bend. Helen wrapped the light jacket more tightly around herself and hurried along the path toward the well-lit manor.

Earlier Lucy had come out to assure them that Iris would be okay. The woman had sustained multiple injuries—cuts, bruises, and a concussion. Not enough, apparently, to warrant transport to a more sophisticated trauma center in Portland.

The chilly evening wind whipped around Helen. Try as she might, she couldn't shake the image of Iris careening toward that ledge. The feisty old woman who refused to wear her teeth and popped wheelies as she raced down the hall knew how to handle a wheelchair. It seemed unlikely that she had lost control.

She was pushed. The words Gladys had spoken during dinner and that Paul had repeated tore through Helen's mind in neon colors. She pulled open the door and stepped inside.

"There you are." Lucy came toward her, the bounce in her step greatly diminished. "I was just going to ask if you wanted a snack or anything."

"No, I'm still full from dinner."

"Lydia, Betty, and Jim are in the day room. They were looking for a fourth to play pinochle."

"Thanks, but I think I'll go to my room. I'm rather tired."

"I understand. You've had quite a day."

"That's an understatement. By the way, have you seen Jennie?"

"The new aid? She's your granddaughter, isn't she?"

"Yes."

"Jennie's going to be tied up for a while. She's in an orientation class. I can probably get her if you need to talk to her."

"No, no. Don't bother. I'm sure she'll stop by my room before she goes home."

Once in her room, Helen unpacked the bags Susan had brought. Pulling out the sweats J.B. had given her brought a smile to her lips. Thankfully they'd been in the wash and she hadn't brought them with her this morning. Some things couldn't be replaced.

She set the photos—one of her and J.B. on their honeymoon cruise and a family portrait—on the dresser. Fortunately, the tape of her husband's last phone message to her had been in her handbag and not in the car. Helen dropped it into the tape recorder Jason had brought and pressed play.

J.B.'s warm baritone reached out to caress her. She closed her eyes, imagining him in the room with her, holding her in his powerful arms. She longed to be able to talk to him about Irene and Andrew. His analytical mind could sort through the confusion in short order—maybe.

When the message ended, Helen rewound it and played it again as she unpacked more treasures. Susan had replaced the devotional and Bible that had been lost in the explosion, along with her cosmetics, deodorant, soap, shampoo, and other toiletries.

The ritual of unpacking and turning Room 134 into her temporary home calmed her. Rational thought replaced chaotic images. She wondered if Tom or Jason had come any closer to finding out who had planted a bomb in Sammi's car and why.

Her unpacking chores completed, Helen angled the recliner so she could see the door and the view, then scooped up her laptop and settled into the comfortable chair.

She spent several minutes familiarizing herself with the new computer, glancing through the manual, then she clicked into the word processing program. Rather than begin a new article, Helen opted to journal the week's events, beginning with Irene's phone call.

She was just inputting information about the explosion and wondering about Sammi when the phone rang.

"Helen? It's me, Sammi."

"I was just thinking about you."

"I hope I'm not disturbing you. I meant to call earlier, but I wanted to finish up some reports."

"I'm so glad you did." Helen saved her file, exited the program, and turned off the machine.

"I was hoping to get out there tonight, but I'm too exhausted to move."

"I certainly wasn't expecting you to come out, what with your injury and all. In fact, I'm surprised you're not in the hospital."

"They let me go home after they took out the glass and stitched me up. I'm fine. At least physically. Emotionally I'm not faring quite so well."

"It was rather unsettling, wasn't it?"

Sammi sighed. "I can't stop thinking about it. The explosion—I keep experiencing it over and over. I thought working might help, but . . . "

"I know—the images keep intruding."

"What's worse is knowing one of us was the target." Sammi sighed again. "Most likely me—since no one other than my secretary and Paul knew I was picking you up this morning. That's pretty scary. I talked to Jason today. We were trying to come up with a motive."

"Paul knew . . . ?"

"Yes, but like I told Jason, he has no reason to want either one of us dead."

"What about the murder case you were supposed to testify at today?"

"That's the most logical answer. My testimony has been delayed until tomorrow. And the police have assigned an officer to guard me."

Helen nodded. "I'm glad you're getting some protection."

Sammi yawned audibly and apologized for doing so. "Tell me about your first day at Edgewood. It's so peaceful out there, I almost wish I could check in myself."

"Don't be too quick to do that. All is not as it seems." Helen briefly highlighted her experiences so far. "It's been anything but quiet."

"Nursing home residents can say and do some pretty strange things. Believe me, I know. I spent a lot of time there during the last days of John's illness. If I were you, I wouldn't take Iris's or Gladys's comments too seriously. It sounds as though they are both delusional."

Score another one for the logical side. Helen smiled. "You may be right, but I'd like to find out for myself. Which reminds me. Gladys's sister Ruthie died recently as a result of falling down some stairs. Did you by any chance do the autopsy?"

"Yes. Poor thing. She'd fallen down an entire flight of concrete stairs into the basement. The injuries sustained were consistent with an uncontrolled fall."

"Any explanation as to how that could happen?"

"The nursing staff seems to think she may have been confused and opened the wrong door. It is usually kept locked, but apparently someone had forgotten to check it. There's no way of knowing who, as most of the staff has access to it."

"Just out of curiosity, what's in the basement?" Helen asked.

"A lot, actually. There's a morgue, an autopsy room, a lab, furnace room, archives, sterile supplies—that's about it."

"So it's not a dreary dark cellar."

"Heaven's no." Sammi chuckled.

"Did anyone see Ruthie fall?"

"Apparently not. There isn't much going on down there after hours—especially in the area where Ruthie fell. Those stairs lead directly to the morgue, and unless there's a death . . . "

"How convenient. Gladys seems to think her sister was pushed."

"Yes, I know, but her story didn't pan out. Ruthie was a sweet noncombative eighty-year-old," Sammi went on. "She certainly didn't pose a threat to anyone. I spent a lot of time on the case. When I first saw her body, I thought someone may have beaten her up. Paul wanted a full investigation. We ended up ruling it an accidental death."

"You're certain?"

"Yes. I think if it had been anywhere but Edgewood, I might have been more insistent about the possibility of abuse. But the police and I questioned all the staff members on duty, plus the other patients. At the time, the only accusations came from Gladys. She's not entirely reliable, and Edgewood has never had an abuse-related death before, so we didn't have enough evidence to make a case."

They talked for a few more minutes, then rang off when Sammi's son came home.

Lucy popped in minutes later to make a routine check. "Hi, Mrs. Bradley," she bubbled. "Thought you'd like to know Iris is doing better. I am so-o-o glad. Underneath that crusty shell, Iris is a real sweet lady. At least I know now that it wasn't my fault. One of the aids saw her undo the brakes and take off her seat belt right after I checked her. He fastened her back in, but I guess she got loose again. You know the rest." Lucy lifted her shoulders in a resigned sigh. "I thought you'd like to know. Um . . . you were supposed to have a physical therapy session tonight, but with all that happened, I sort of forgot."

"So did I. Is it too late?"

"It is for the physical therapist, but the facility is open all night. If you'd like to go down, I can take you in about half an hour. I need to finish tucking in my other patients."

"That sounds fine."

Helen went back to her notes, but she felt both stifled and saturated. Too many things to think about—too many avenues to explore. Since Lucy would be arriving any moment to take her to therapy, Helen put her computer away. After changing into an old pair of sweats and tennis shoes, she grabbed her swimsuit, stuffed it into a plastic bag, and sat down to wait. Lucy didn't show. At ten-forty-five Helen scribbled a quick note so Jennie and Lucy would know where to find her and left. She really didn't need help to do her exercises anyway.

Most of the doors on either side of the hallway were closed. The fluorescent ceiling lights had been turned off, leaving a soft glow emanating from the night lights that lined the floor. The nurses and aids seemed to have disappeared. Probably giving reports to the next shift. Helen made her way down the hall and into the wing housing the physical therapy department.

Being familiar with most of the equipment, Helen straddled the treadmill, turned it on, and set the timer for twenty minutes. Then bracing herself, she stepped onto the moving belt and began to walk at a slow steady pace. When she'd gotten used to the machine she increased the speed.

As she walked, Helen sifted through the bits and pieces of information she'd managed to glean so far. She'd learned a lot and needed to determine what steps to take. First on the agenda would be to personally interview Gladys and hopefully Iris to determine just how many of the conflicting messages could be blamed on paranoia and senility. She also wanted to speak with her other table mates privately. Perhaps they'd be more willing to talk in a one-on-one situation.

A movement in the mirror caught her eye.

"Hi, Gram." Jennie plodded into the room and sank onto the floor cross-legged.

"Hi, sweetheart. You look exhausted."

"I am. I can't wait to get home and crawl into bed. Lucy said to tell you she was sorry, but they had a patient die and she couldn't get away."

"Not Iris . . ."

"No. Some woman with cancer. They were expecting it, I

guess. It's still so sad. I'm glad I wasn't taking care of her."

"So am I. Did Lucy tell you a name?"

"Mrs. Philips, I think. Lucy said she'd been wanting to go for a long time and finally got her wish."

"I think a lot of cancer patients feel that way." The possibility of assisted suicide pawed at the periphery of her mind. "Who was her doctor?"

Jennie shrugged. "I have no idea. You're not thinking somebody killed her too, are you?"

Helen turned off the treadmill and joined Jennie on the floor. "To be honest, I'm not sure what to think. This is a nursing home. We certainly can't look at every death as suspiscious."

"That's for sure. On the tour today, we went through the morgue. They average two to three deaths a week—more in the winter. Mrs. Phillips had cancer all through her body—that's what the nurse told me. She'd been sick for a long time."

Wanting to change the subject, Helen asked, "What's the latest on Iris?"

"Still doing okay." Jennie pulled her long dark braid foward and wound it around her finger. "I wish I could have caught her before—before she went over. One of the guys coming on night shift, um—Jack Owens—says she got what she deserved. Maybe she needed to take a header to teach her a lesson. I didn't think that was a very nice thing to say."

"No." Helen frowned, remembering the attractive man she'd seen talking to Sammi and Stephanie at the reception following Irene's funeral. "No it wasn't. He isn't assigned to her, is he?"

"No—they brought in a special trauma nurse to monitor her." Jennie stared into the mirror, her eyes drooping at half mast.

"You'd better get on home before you fall asleep."

"I will. Just wanted to give you a report and leave you with this." She reached into her pocket and dropped a key in her hand.

"What's this for?"

"The basement. I figured you might want to snoop around."

Helen palmed the key, and since she had no pockets, she tucked it into her shoe. "Thank you."

"No problem. When you go down there, you gotta do it at night. That's when the fewest people are working. Lucy says the night crew mostly sits around talking. It should be a piece of cake. I saw it when I went on the tour this afternoon." Jennie hesitated. "We could go now. That way I could be your lookout."

"I don't think so. You need to go home."

Jennie scrambled to her feet. "Okay. Just be careful."

"You too, and drive safely."

"I will." Jennie started to leave, then turned back. "Would you like me to stay with you tonight? It'll make the transition easier for you."

"I'll be fine, Jennie. Stop worrying about me and go home."

Shortly after Jennie left, the night supervisor showed up.

"Mrs. Bradley, isn't it? I'm Amy Kahala. How are those exercises coming?" White teeth glistened against bronzed lips as she smiled. The young woman's skin was a soft nut-brown, and her thick wavy hair had been swept back and secured with a pink bow.

"Almost finished."

"Good. I'm surprised you're still up." Amy picked up the sling Helen had tossed on a bench.

"Too wound up to sleep, I'm afraid."

"I can get you a sleeping pill. You have a standing order if you need one."

"No thanks. I thought I'd sit in the whirlpool for a few minutes. That should relax me."

This time Amy's grin brought dimples. "Wish I could join you." She held up Helen's sling. "Your sling is soiled. I'll get you a new one."

By the time Amy returned with a new sling, Helen had changed into her swimsuit and slipped into the swirling water.

"Sorry to take so long. I wanted to finish making my rounds." Amy set the sling alongside Helen's clothing and hunkered down beside the pool. "I'd love to stay and chat for a while. I like getting to know our new residents. Unfortunately, we're quite busy. If you need anything at all during the night, let us know."

Helen assured her she would, then nestled back against a jet, letting the water beat against her neck and shoulders.

The massaging action of the jets should have relaxed her, but Helen felt a curious unease. Like a police officer on watch, she couldn't let down her guard. Perhaps she too had begun to suffer from paranoia.

After ten minutes Helen gave up, dressed, and headed back to her room. The light was on in Room 128, just down the hall from her—and the door was slightly ajar. She paused for a moment, curious, yet not wanting to intrude.

"No," someone, a man, whimpered. "Please, Jack. Don't hit me again. I'll get more money. Tomorrow. I'll have it then. I promise."

Helen crept closer and pushed at the door, opening it another foot.

A man the size of a linebacker picked Daniel up out of his chair and dropped him onto the bed, pinning his shoulders down. "You'd better have it, or you'll be next. No one crosses me and gets away with it."

Helen bristled. "Don't be too sure."

The big man straightened and turned, his look as menacing as a grizzly. "Who are you?"

Daniel groaned. "Mrs. Bradley, don't . . . "

"Shut up," the man growled at Daniel, then turned back to Helen. In a movement swifter than Helen thought possible for a man his size, Jack Owens stepped between Helen and her only means of escape, yanked her in, and closed the door.

Twenty-one

Jack bared his teeth and raised his fist, still clutching the front
of her sweat shirt.

Helen used the only weapon she had at the moment—direct
confrontation. "I wouldn't do that if I were you, Jack." She caught
his hard brown gaze and held it.

Something flickered in his eyes. Not fear, but perhaps a realization that he'd gone too far.

"Do what, Mrs. Bradley?" He smiled and backed off.

"You were about to hit me."

"Was I?" He shook his head. "Well, well. Looks like we got us
another confused resident. Imagine accusing me of such a thing.
I wouldn't hurt a fly, would I, Danny boy?"

Daniel cowered against the bed. "It . . . it isn't what you think,
Mrs. Bradley. Jack didn't hurt me."

"I know what I saw. And I think I know what's going on.
Sounds like extortion to me. What's the deal, Jack? They pay you
in exchange for not getting beat up?"

"Maybe your eyesight isn't all that good, Mrs. Bradley. You are
going to have a tough time proving those allegations. All the residents here love me, right, Dan?"

"Th-that's right. Jack's the best aid around."

"See, Mrs. Bradley? I have a feeling you'll feel the same way
once you get to know me." He glanced at his watch.

"Don't count on it." Helen reached for the door handle.

Jack's hand closed over hers, pressing her fingers firmly against
the metal. "You'd better run along to bed now." His voice had

became menacingly gentle. "Sometimes, when our residents get confused and we find them wandering around in the halls late at night, we have to use restraints and medications to settle them down. I wouldn't want that to happen to you."

"Neither would I." Helen swallowed to stem the rising fear.

"Good, I'm glad we understand each other." Jack released his hold on her hand and escorted her back to her room. "Sleep tight, Mrs. Bradley, and don't forget to say your prayers." He paused, then went to her dresser and picked up the phone. "Just in case you forgot, we have a strict policy about phone calls here. No calls between ten p.m. and eight a.m. So you won't be tempted, I'll take this." Jack disconnected the wire running from the wall jack to the phone, wrapped it neatly around his hand, and tucked it into his pocket. "Oh, and one more thing. I wouldn't go running to Amy or anyone else around here. It won't do you any good."

Long after he'd gone, Helen could feel his ominous presence. If she'd come face-to-face with the devil himself, she doubted she'd have felt more shaken. Jack Owens was a man without a conscience. How many residents had he been stealing from? How many had he abused? Or murdered. Her thoughts jumped back to Ruthie. No wonder Daniel had been terrified.

But the big question was why hadn't any of the nurses or other aids noticed? Surely Jack didn't have control over the entire staff. According to Sammi, Edgewood had never had a problem with abuse. Had Jack managed to eliminate all of his uncooperative witnesses?

Maybe an even more important question she needed to ask was what could she do about it? Probably nothing tonight—not while Jack was working. She thought about calling Jason at home, but that would mean leaving her room. Not something she relished doing at the moment. Jack might be waiting for her to make just such a move.

Tomorrow she'd call Jason. In the meantime she'd pretend that Jack had succeeded in frightening her into silence. Pretend? He had frightened her. For now she'd sleep—or try to. Though she seldom felt the need for a gun for protection, she wished she'd have thought to have Jason bring her .38. Not that asking would have done any good. It was probably still in the evidence locker. Of course, Helen reminded herself, even if she had it she wouldn't be able to use it for at least another month. The thought did little to cheer her.

Two hours later, the small alarm clock Susan had brought ticked loudly in the blanketing darkness. Its fluorescent green letters announced the time—two a.m., reminding Helen she needed to get some sleep. Not wanting to go to bed in case Jack came back, she'd stretched out in the recliner, tucked a pillow behind her head, and tossed a lap robe over her to keep out the chill. Jack Owens had scared her more than she cared to admit.

"Lord," she whispered. "I can't fight this alone. I don't know what to do."

Pray. The answer—so simple, yet at the same time logical—must have come from God.

The words forming in her mind brought a smile to her lips. How often she'd repeated the simple prayer to her children and grandchildren. Helen pulled the blanket up around her neck, turned onto her side and made her request to the one who could protect her when no one else could.

> *"Now I lay me down to sleep,*
> *I pray the Lord my soul to keep...."*

Sunbeams streamed through the slats of the Venetian blinds, nudging Helen into wakefulness. Events of the night before filtered into her mind. She was still alive. The door to her room opened.

"Land sakes, girl, what'd you do, sleep in that chair all night?"

"Yes, I . . ." Helen stopped. No sense bringing accusations against Thelma's co-worker until she had more facts.

"Well, it's no wonder you had such a rough night. You may want to try your bed next time."

"What makes you think I had a rough night?"

"Now don't you play innocent with me, missy. Jack says you couldn't sleep. Then after he gave you a sleeping pill you got all confused and started hallucinating. You even told him Dr. Kincaid was in Daniel's room beating up on him and trying to steal his money. I'll say this for you—when you hallucinate, you do it in a big way. Jack left a note for the doc to switch you to a different medication."

My, my, Jack must have had a pretty busy night covering his tracks. Helen bit back the urge to defend herself. "I always did have a rather fertile imagination. Must have been a strong pill."

"Oh yes—some of those sleeping pills are wicked if you're not used to them. But don't you worry. You won't be getting that one again." Thelma raised the blinds and opened the window.

Helen lowered the chair's footrest and climbed out. "Any chance of getting a cup of coffee or some tea?"

"Sure—in the dining room. They'll be servin' breakfast at eight—looks like you got about an hour. You need help getting dressed or anything?"

"No, thanks, Thelma. I'll be fine."

When Thelma had gone, Helen dressed in a pair of jeans and a cotton knit T-shirt. First thing she needed to do—even before coffee—was to call Jason. Her gaze darted to the telephone. The cord had been replaced.

Grabbing the receiver, Helen started to dial Jason's number, then hung up. Since all the calls went through a switchboard, it wouldn't surprise her if they were able to monitor phone conversations. She'd better find a pay phone.

The sudden panic she'd felt in the early morning hours slithered away, leaving its poison to seep slowly into her bloodstream. Jack Owens had set into motion a scenario that could easily discredit her. He already had the nursing staff believing she'd been confused. Scenes reminiscent of *One Flew Over the Cuckoo's Nest* scurried through her mind. *Let's hope I don't end up with a lobotomy . . . .*

Helen shook the images away, pulled on a jacket, and dug several quarters out of her handbag. She'd go for a walk. With any luck she'd find a phone somewhere along the way.

A few minutes later she did—just outside the community building where Irene's funeral had been held.

Jason's answering machine clicked on. "Jason, this is your mother. If you're there, please pick up. I need you to check out a guy who works night shift here at Edgewood. The name is Jack Owens." She left word for Tom as well, then called Sammi at home and finally got a real voice.

"Helen, are you all right?"

"For the moment." Helen filled her in on Jack Owens and his attempt to cover his iniquities.

"He was actually abusing a patient?"

"I don't think it's one patient. I have no idea how many, but I intend to find out. And who knows? There may be other staff members involved. I'm not sure it's wise to say anything to anyone out here until I have proof. Somehow I don't think my opinion will be enough."

"I don't know what to say. This is crazy. I had no idea anything like this was going on."

"Was Jack Owens working the night Ruthie died?"

"I don't remember. I'd have to check my files." Sammi paused. "We'd better tell Paul."

"Not yet. I'm having Jason run a check on Jack. And I need to question some of the residents first. Besides, I'm not sure I trust Paul—or anyone else at the moment. I'd appreciate it if you kept our conversation confidential."

"If you say so. Keep me posted on what you find out. And if there's anything I can do . . . "

"I'll let you know."

Helen hung up and began the trek back to the manor. When she reached the main road, a car pulled up beside her.

Rolling down the window, Stephanie asked, "Can I give you a lift?"

Helen started to refuse, then thought better of it. Stephanie might be able to provide some answers.

Once inside the car, Helen thanked the RN, then asked, "How well do you know Jack Owens?"

The question seemed to startle her. She hesitated a moment. "Well enough, I suppose. He . . . he works nights, so I don't see him all that often. Why do you ask?"

"I met him last night." Helen chose her words carefully so as not to reveal her intentions. "And I remember seeing you together after the funeral."

Stephanie gripped the steering wheel a bit harder than necessary to execute a turn. "I talked to a lot of people at the reception, Mrs. Bradley. Is there a problem?"

"Perhaps. I understand he gets a bit rough at times with the residents."

"I see." Stephanie gave her a long hard look. "Who told you this?"

"I'd just as soon keep that confidential for now."

As they pulled into a parking space, Stephanie promised to look into it. Her defensive response left Helen with dozens more questions, and she couldn't help wondering if Jack Owens had some hold over her as well.

Helen thanked her for the ride and hurried inside. After a

quick shower and change, she entered the dining room, where most of the residents were already eating.

"There you are. I was beginning to think I'd have to send out a search party." Thelma set a glass of orange juice, a bran muffin, and a bowl of oatmeal in front of her.

"You needn't have worried. I went for a walk this morning. It's beautiful out there."

"Humph. You might have at least let me know. From now on, when you leave you need to sign out with the receptionist. I know you're only here for rehab, but it's a rule for all our residents."

"I'll do that."

"Good, now would you like anything else to eat?"

Helen glanced at the plates around her and shook her head. "This will be fine. Thanks."

Helen blessed her food and eyed the vacant chair across from her. "Anyone know how Iris is this morning?"

"I stopped by to see her before breakfast." Betty began peeling the wrapper off her muffin. "She's already giving the nurses a bad time, so I expect she'll be okay."

"I'm glad to hear that. Any word yet on how it happened?"

Betty shook her head. The others concentrated a bit more than necessary on their mush. Except for Lars, whose questioning blue gaze shifted around the table coming to rest on Daniel.

"You're all looking rather somber this morning." Helen persisted. "Especially you, Daniel."

No one responded, and Daniel refused to meet her gaze.

"Did Daniel tell you about his encounter with Jack last night?" Still no response. Helen poured milk on her oatmeal and sprinkled on a spoonful of brown sugar. "Judging by your silence, I take it he told you about my interrupting the little chat he and

Jack were having."

"That's all it was, Helen. A chat." Daniel's coffee sloshed over the rim when he returned it to the table. "Jack can seem a bit rough at times, but he's okay."

Lydia threw her napkin on her empty plate. "Give it up, Daniel. We might as well talk to her. At least warn her what'll happen if she tries to blow the whistle."

"Oh, I think I already know. Jack gave me a taste of how miserable he could make things for me. He hasn't asked for money yet, though. I suspect that's coming."

"Not unless you want drugs," Gladys offered.

Helen dropped her spoon. She hadn't expected to find a drug dealer in a nursing home. "What kind of drugs?"

"Don't listen to her. She doesn't know what she's talking about." Jim pushed away from the table. "Come on, Betty. It's time for my treatment."

Betty gave Helen a helpless look and wheeled her husband away.

"I'm not as far gone as folks think I am," Gladys announced. "Ruthie found out what he was doing. That's why he pushed her down the stairs—same goes for Iris."

"That's absurd." Daniel rubbed a shaky hand over his face. "Look, Helen, you're better off not knowing."

"What kind of drugs?" Helen repeated.

Lars gave Daniel an emphathetic look. "Maybe it would be best if you tell her, Daniel. Like I said before—it does no good to keep hiding the truth."

Daniel glanced around, then releasing a heavy sigh, whispered. "Not here. Meet me in the garden at nine-thirty."

Lars nodded in approval, and Helen wondered how he fit into the scheme of things. She made a mental note to ask Daniel later.

Helen spent the next hour in the physical therapy room, going through her exercise routine followed by a massage. At nine-twenty, she tucked the small voice-activated tape recorder into her pocket and headed outdoors. Hopefully she'd be able to get enough concrete evidence to put an end to Jack Owens' reign of terror.

Helen half expected Daniel to dodge their appointment and was surprised when he showed up.

"Let's walk." Without waiting for an answer, he started down the path.

Helen hurried to catch up with him.

They wandered through the garden and ended up on a trail leading into the woods. So far Daniel hadn't talked about anything but the weather. Helen was beginning to wonder if he had something other than confession on his mind. Thinking of him as a victim may have been a mistake.

Twenty-two

They were well away from the buildings before Daniel spoke. "Jack is a supplier. He can get us whatever we want. Pain meds, tranquilizers, alcohol, marijuana, black market stuff. Jim Salter's getting a drug developed by a doctor in Mexico that's supposed to kill the AIDS virus."

"I thought Kincaid Laboratories was treating him."

"They are, but there are limits as to what they can and can't use. The FDA won't allow a drug to go on the market in this country unless it goes through rigorous testing in the United States."

"And for good reason."

"The drug has had good results in Mexico and Jim is a desperate man."

"And Lars?"

Daniel shook his head. "Lars is clean. He'll be moving out of here soon. and Jack wouldn't dare threaten him—he only goes after the weak ones."

"But he knows Jack's been abusing the residents?"

"No. Lars is a friend, Helen. He knows what's going on with me, but that's the extent of it. I asked him to keep his mouth shut and he has."

"What about you?"

"I'm not buying drugs—not entirely. I'm buying a way out."

"Out of here? Why don't you just leave?"

"It's not that simple. I'm dying. They told me three weeks ago. For me it's going to be a long and painful process. I don't want to wait. The night I found out about it, I told Jack. For $10,000 he could get me what I need to end my life in a dignified, pain-free manner."

"Assisted suicide?"

"Yes, but he makes sure it looks like a natural death. It seemed like an answer to prayer. Now I'm not so sure. I didn't know what kind of man he was. He's upped the price to $12,000, and I have a feeling it isn't going to stop there."

"Why don't you turn him in?"

"No! And you mustn't either. I'm only telling you because I want you to know what you're up against. If you try to tell anyone about this conversation, I'll flatly deny it. He . . . he's threatened to kill my wife and daughter if I go to the police. I'm sure he's done the same to others."

"He hit you last night. Why?"

"I pay him in cash installments. Someone stole the $500 I had stashed in my dresser. He didn't believe me. I guess he wanted to teach me a lesson."

"Jack needs to be stopped."

Daniel closed his eyes. "I know this may sound absurd to you, but I don't want him stopped. Neither does Jim—or anyone else who uses his services. He may be heavy handed at times, but desperate times call for desperate measures.

Helen could hardly believe what she was hearing. "What about Ruthie? Did Jack kill her?"

Daniel sighed and looked away. "Most likely. Told me I'd get the same treatment if I didn't cooperate. Gladys says Ruthie overheard him negotiate a deal with another resident and stood up to him. I'm not sure how much of what Gladys says is valid, but she insists he beat Ruthie up and then faked the fall down the stairs to explain the bruises."

Helen felt sick. How could anyone, especially a doctor, know this sort of thing was going on and not put a stop to it? As much as she wanted to bombast the man for his lack of good sense, she pressed on for more answers.

"Do you think he pushed Iris?"

"I don't know. He wasn't on duty, but he did come in to collect his pay—from Edgewood and from me."

"What about Irene and Andrew Kincaid? Did he have a deal with them?"

Daniel shook his head. "Irene maybe, but not Andrew. Andrew was against assisted suicide."

"Does Jack have a partner or is anyone else involved in the same kind of business?"

"Not that I know of." Daniel winced and rubbed his back. "This is about as far as I can go."

"You had the sense to turn around on this trail. Why not turn around on the other one you've taken?"

"It's too late."

"It's never too late." Helen doubted her protests would have an effect, but she had to try. "You mentioned that a person's needs don't stop with age. What about morals? You're a doctor. Surely you . . . "

"Spare the lecture, Helen. I've made my choice, and I'm willing to live with the consequences."

"Ruthie made a choice too—to stand up to a criminal. How can you justify letting her killer go free?"

Daniel didn't answer. They walked in silence until they reached the manicured lawn framing Edgewood Manor.

"Daniel." Helen stopped him. "You may be able to turn the other way. I can't. I won't. My son is with the Portland police. I intend to tell him everything."

"I'll deny it."

"It won't matter. I was hoping you'd help me put an end to

Jack's criminal activity, but as you say, you've made your choice.
I've made mine."

———

Jason was waiting for her when she arrived back in her room.
"Where have you been? Thelma said you were in the garden, but
I couldn't find you anywhere. Wanted to let you know about Jack
Owens—he's an ex-con."

"I'm not surprised." Helen told him about the previous night
and gave him the tape. After listening to it, they went to Dr.
Kincaid. By midafternoon the police had issued a warrant for
Jack's arrest. The tight-lipped network quickly broke down when
residents learned their supplier would no longer be available.

Paul Kincaid paid Helen a visit at four, shortly after she'd completed another physical therapy session. He caught up with her
in the garden, which was fast becoming her favorite place to
receive visitors.

Paul seemed entirely different than when she'd first met him.
Much of the grandeur and stuffiness had gone. His anger had dissipated as well, and he greeted her with a genuine smile. "I wanted to thank you again. It's a relief to have this mess cleared up.
Edgewood has always had a fine reputation, and I'd hate to think
of what might have happened if you hadn't insisted on coming."

"I'm glad I was able to help."

"I must assure you that we don't normally hire people like Jack
Owens. If the personnel office had followed the proper screening
process, Jack never would have slipped through. I'm sure by now
you've heard about his record."

"Jason told me. Do you know if they've made an arrest yet?"

"I don't believe so. But it's imminent. We have police at the gate
in case he comes here. They're watching his home as well."

"Good." Helen watched a jet trail dissipate in the air currents high above them.

"I suppose you'll be going home soon, now that you've brought our criminal to justice."

"Not unless you request it. I rather like the program Dr. Lawson's set up for me. I thought I'd stay for a week or two, then come back as an outpatient."

"I'm delighted. I don't think you'll be disappointed." Paul stood, offering her another smile. "I do have to be going, though. I have some business to take care of before dinner."

Helen watched him until he disappeared inside the manor. A sense of uneasiness stirred within her. Jack would soon be arrested. She'd solved the case. But all was not well at Edgewood. There were still a lot of unanswered questions and loose ends. She wondered for a moment if the business with Jack had been a distraction, something to keep her occupied.

She closed her eyes and let the sun warm her face. A cool breeze ruffled her hair.

"I hope you're using sunscreen."

"Adriane. How nice to see you." Helen ran a hand through her hair. "I've only been out here for a few minutes."

"Ah, but the sun—even in small amounts—can cause age spots and skin cancer."

"So I hear," Helen acquiesced and moved into the shade.

"I understand you are responsible for ridding our fine facility of a criminal."

"One down—who knows how many more to go."

Adriane raised her eyebrows. "You don't think there are more like Mr. Owens?"

Helen shrugged her shoulders. "I hope not." She couldn't help wondering whether she'd only skimmed the slime off the surface of a contaminated pond. Helen leaned forward. "Adriane, the day of the funeral, you offered to show me around Kincaid Laboratories. I would love to see some of the products you and the other doctors have been developing."

Adriane tucked an errant strand of dark hair behind her ear. The wind whipped it back into her face. "I'd love to do that. How about tomorrow—say around ten."

"Perfect."

The rest of the day and evening disappeared in a rush of visitors. Doctors David and Mai Lin Chang dropped by shortly after dinner to offer their thanks and to give her the results of her blood tests. "You are a wonder," David said. "We found nothing wrong."

Mai chuckled. "Which is a rarity for most of our residents. You are not overweight, and you don't have high cholesterol or high blood pressure. All you need to do is continue the therapy for your arm. And perhaps the anti-oxidant packet we've put together. We can tell you more about that when you come to the lab tomorrow."

They'd only been gone a few minutes when her family showed up. "Guess what, Gram?" Nick's eyes held the gleam only having a father could give them. "Dad gets to move back home pretty soon. Momma said."

"That's wonderful." Helen reeled him in for a hug, then looked up at his beaming parents. "Have you two set a date for the wedding?"

"Not yet," Susan said. "We're trying to work it into everyone's schedules."

Jason held his ex-wife and future bride close to his side. "It'll be soon—maybe in a couple of weeks—that is if I don't haul her off to Vegas tonight."

Susan's cheeks turned nearly as red as her hair. "Jason, behave yourself."

Jennie managed a short break and sat with them for a few minutes. The hour passed quickly, and by nine everyone had gone and the residents were beginning to settle in for the night. Though Helen would have preferred crawling into bed, Lucy insisted she do her exercises and stretches, promising to meet her in the physical therapy department in five minutes.

Helen obediently slipped into her sweats, tucked her swimsuit into a towel, and made her way to the exercise room. She paused at Daniel's room, thinking she should see how he was doing, but he wasn't there. Initially he'd been angry with her, but at dinner she did her best to soothe him. According to Jason, he'd been cooperative with the police in supplying information. That was something—especially since he didn't know she'd gotten their conversation on tape. Jason had given her some bad news as well. Jack still hadn't been caught.

Helen hurried into the room, did some stretches, walked for twenty minutes, then began working with the weights. Lucy still hadn't come in, and with her shift nearly over, Helen didn't expect she'd show up at all.

Facing the mirrored wall, Helen watched herself do a series of arm curls—pleased at the degree of strength she'd already regained. Halfway through the second set, Helen stopped. A flash of something had appeared in the mirror. "Jennie?" She turned and smiled, expecting to say good-night to her granddaughter before she headed home.

Instead she caught sight of a gloved hand protruding from the doorway. Unfortunately, the hand was holding a gun.

Twenty-three

Helen dropped to the floor. A section of mirror behind her pinged, splintered. Rolling to the side, she ducked behind the encased wheel on a stationary bicycle. Another bullet rammed the machine beside her.

Helen lay as flat as she could and waited, wishing her arm would stop screaming so she could focus.

Moments later she heard footsteps in the hall. Jennie paused in the doorway, her dark blue gaze darting from the shattered mirror to Helen.

"Gram." Jennie hurried toward her. "Are you all right? I was coming to find you when I heard the noise—it sounded like gun-shots. What happened?"

Helen staggered to her feet and rushed into the hall. "Did you see anyone?"

"No."

To have disappeared that quickly, the assailant must have either ducked into one of the rest rooms or the basement. Since the rest rooms had no outside access, she suspected the latter. "Jennie, call the police and warn the others. Someone just shot at me and may still be in the building."

"I saw a couple of officers out front a while ago. They're still waiting for Jack to show up."

Helen glanced at the shards of glass littering the taupe carpet. "He may already be here." Helen sent Jennie to find the officers with instructions to block all exits. Using her good arm, Helen reached for a five-pound weight to use as a weapon. She quickly checked both bathrooms, then using the key Jennie had given her the night before, she slipped into the enclosed stairwell leading to the basement. She probably should have waited and let the police handle it, but every moment was precious and she didn't want to risk him getting away.

The stairwell lights had been turned off. Helen groped along the wall to find the switch. And did. She sucked in a wild breath and headed down the stairs, through another door, and into a darkened hallway. Grasping the weight in her left hand, she raised her arm in readiness, then moved forward. Filtered light drifted in through the window of a door at the end of the empty hall. The black letters etched into the frosted glass read Medical Records. Helen made her way toward the light. Without warning a double door opened a few feet in front of her. She leaned against the wall, blending into the shadows.

"Here's the death certificate and instructions from the family," a woman said. "Guess she's ready to go."

"You guys have sure had a lot of 'em lately." This came from a man pushing a gurney out of the morgue and into the hall. "Hey. Who turned out the lights?"

Lucy Walker followed him out. "Darned if I know. They were on when I came down. I'd better call maintenance."

"You might want to try the light switch first." Helen stepped out of the shadows toward them, lowering the weight. After giving a brief explanation, she asked, "Did you see anyone?"

"No. This is Bob," Lucy said. "He's from the funeral home—came by to pick up Mrs. Ness."

"Another death?"

"I'm afraid so."

"What did she die from?"

"Old age, I suspect. Poor thing was a hundred and one."

Helen glanced at the black body bag. "I think you'd probably better put her back for the time being—"

The hall lights came on. "Hold it right there!" a police officer shouted. "Hands over your heads."

Helen set the weight on the floor and complied.

Another officer joined the first. The door to the medical records room opened. Dr. David Chang stepped out, then Adriane. A flurry of questions and explanations ensued. Satisfied they hadn't cornered the gunman, the officers began to usher the group upstairs.

Lucy had given a report to the night shift, then came down to sign the body over to Bob. The doctors had been reviewing patient files for research purposes and had been working for the past couple of hours. They hadn't seen or heard anyone. Had it not been for the lateness of the hour and the flush of pink on Adriane's cheeks, Helen might have bought their story. She did believe they hadn't heard anything, she just didn't believe they had been working.

Maybe later she'd question Adriane about her indiscretions, but in the meantime Helen needed to concentrate on tracking down the person—or persons—who wanted her dead.

———

By midnight at least a dozen police officers and sheriff deputies had combed the manor and grounds and turned up nothing. The residents who were awake had been questioned and then banished to their rooms for safekeeping, Helen included. Dr. Kincaid, who'd arrived shortly after being notified by his staff, had called in extra security officers to ensure everyone's safety.

All was quiet now. After much resistance, Jennie had gone home. Helen paced the floor, wondering if she'd ever be able to sleep again. Adrenalin still gnawed at her stomach and defied any effort she made to rest.

The bullets recovered in the physical therapy room had come

from a .25 caliber. At the moment Jack was the primary suspect. Helen wondered again if the explosion in the deli had been meant for her as well as for Sammi. The only connection between the two of them was Edgewood. But to her knowledge Jack hadn't known of her then, so that left a big hole in the puzzle.

So far there'd been three attempts on her life. "Which means," she murmured, "I'd better figure out what's going on before whoever it is succeeds." She just wished she could remember more about the person she'd glimpsed in the mirror.

Easing into the recliner, Helen closed her eyes and tried to recapture the moment. She'd been facing the mirror when she saw something move. The hand. Her mind had been so focused on it and the gun that she'd blocked out everything else. Not that she'd had time to see much. But the gunman had to have taken aim. Why hadn't she seen a face? Somewhere in her gray matter there must be more information. She'd been trained to notice details— even under pressure. So why hadn't she?

Helen leaned back in the chair and willed her mind and body to relax. Concentrating on bringing back the lost images, she took several deep cleansing breaths. Over and over she let the scene replay itself as though it were a video clip. She imagined herself an observer rather than a participant and concentrated.

———

When she awakened hours later, Helen still had no idea who had fired the shots. She was certain, however, that the shooter had been wearing surgical gloves and that it had not been Jack Owens. As she'd done the previous morning, Helen walked to the pay phone and called her son.

Jason agreed with her findings. "Our crime scene analyst says the gun was probably fired by someone shorter—maybe five-five to five-ten."

"A lot of people fit into that category." Helen turned away from the phone and leaned against the glass partition to watch a pair of joggers make their way up the winding hill, then disappear into a grove of trees. "I didn't realize it at first because Jack seemed the logical suspect. Now that I've had a chance to distance myself from it, I've been able to remember some things. The gun was a small semiautomatic and had a short barrel—maybe a Raven—and the shooter was wearing surgical gloves."

"You're sure?"

"Yes, though it may mean nothing. On the other hand, it gives us something to look for. Jack may have had an accomplice working here at the hospital. Or not. I still think the gunman escaped through the basement, ditched the gloves, and came back upstairs via another route."

"I'll get someone out there to look around again. Maybe we'll get lucky."

Jason sounded skeptical and she told him so. "I don't suppose you turned up any leads questioning the staff?"

"Unfortunately, no. Most of them were in the nurses' station for the daily patient report. As you already know, Lucy and the guy from the funeral home were down in the basement when it happened. Jennie was the first to leave the report room."

"So everyone who was in the hospital had an alibi."

"Looks that way." Jason cleared his throat. "I'm thinking if Jack did have an accomplice it was the patient who's a doctor . . . let's see . . ."

"You mean Daniel?"

"Yeah. You'd mentioned that he wasn't in his room when you went past it last night. He's about the right height, and he knew a lot about Jack's activities. I'm heading out there this morning to have another talk with him."

"I suppose that is a possibility." Helen doubted it. "I spoke to Daniel at dinner, and if anything, he'd seemed relieved the ordeal was over."

"Could be, but I can't think of anyone in a better position to let Jack know we were on to him."

After speaking with Jason a few more minutes about family matters, Helen hung up and headed back for the manor. The two joggers she'd seen earlier emerged from a side trail just ahead of her. Adriane Donahue and David Chang—together again.

Adriane slowed and waited for Helen to catch up.

"You're out early this morning," Helen said.

"Best time to run. Clears the head." David sprinted ahead. "You two take your time. I need to get in—early appointment."

Helen studied Adriane, noting the admiration glinting in her eyes as she watched the doctor take off down the trail. "Do you two run together often?"

"Every day. We're old friends. Went to medical school together. David got me a position here shortly after he married Mai. He introduced me to Paul, and you know the rest."

"You've been here a long time, then."

"Sixteen years. They were wonderful years until . . . " She smiled. "Well, let's just say things haven't been the same since Paul's parents died. Now he's so preoccupied with running Edgewood he's—well, that's old news, isn't it? I'm sure things will settle down eventually. In the meantime, I'm keeping pretty busy."

"Adriane, I hope you won't be too upset by my asking, but is there something going on between you and David?"

Her eyes widened. "Oh, you mean last night in the records room? No, not at all—at least not romantically speaking. David and I have been collaborating on an article about reversing senile dementia. Actually, he's writing, and I'm supplying the research."

"Really?"

"You know that micro-computer chip I was telling you about at the funeral?"

Helen nodded.

Excitement glistened in Adriane's eyes as it often did when she spoke of her work. "Well, we're about to go public with it."

"Which means?"

"We begin by submitting the article and calling a press conference. I'm just hoping this business with Jack doesn't interfere. Paul may want to delay the announcement until the abuse business has died down—or at least until the institution is in the clear over it."

They walked for a few yards without speaking. "I noticed you were using the pay phone up at the community center," Adriane said. "Everything all right?"

"Fine. I was just talking to my son."

"The police inspector?"

"Hmm. I realized that the person who shot at me last night wasn't Jack Owens."

"Really? Then who?" Adriane picked up her pace. Helen matched it.

"I don't know. A staff member maybe—though Jason seems to think it could be a patient."

Adriane dropped onto a bench near the path. "I'd hoped all this craziness was over. I've never seen Paul so distraught. It's bad enough that he lost his parents. Now Jack and whoever else may have been working with him are giving Edgewood and Kincaid Laboratories a bad name. It doesn't seem fair."

Helen gazed out over the panoramic vista. "This may not be a good time to ask, but can you still give me a tour of the laboratory facilities today?"

"Of course." Adriane pushed off the bench. "Life does go on, doesn't it? I'll send Chris over for you at ten."

Helen hurried back to the manor and managed a round of exercises before breakfast. Iris joined them at the table, back to her usual outrageous, toothless, talkative self.

"Probably out of the country by now," she said, commenting on the whereabouts of the former aid.

"Wonder who warned him off?" Lydia, like the others who'd been tormented by Jack, had become much more animated and open.

"Well, it wasn't me," Daniel offered. "The police seem to think I tipped him off. Truth is, I'm glad he's gone."

"But what about your plans to—?" Helen asked.

"I've changed my mind. You were right. Suicide isn't the answer. It never was."

"Vel, I'm sure glad to hear that." Lars grinned and shifted his gaze to Helen. "Kept telling him he needed to have faith. You did us a good turn, Helen. I wish now I'd done something myself."

"Perhaps it's better you didn't, Lars," Helen said. "Jack had ways of dealing with people who defied him. Which reminds me. Do you have any idea as to who might have been working with him?" Helen dunked her tea bag, then set it aside.

"I don't think he was working with anybody around here," Daniel said, "leastwise none of the patients. Only aid I ever saw him being cozy with was Lucy. I think they had a thing for each other once when he first came."

"Not just Lucy." Lydia looked up from her cholesterol free scrambled eggs. "That low life was flirting with everything in skirts, including our Stephanie."

Helen slid over Stephanie as a possible accomplice for the moment and hooked up on Lucy. She remembered the incident with the lamp her first day at Edgewood. Could Lucy have been the person in the room? She said she hadn't seen anyone else. Helen replayed the incident. She'd awakened from her nap and heard something. The room was dark, and when she reached for the light it fell to the floor. Suppose Lucy had been snooping in the drawer, then hidden behind the chair. It would have been easy to knock the lamp out of Helen's reach, wait a few moments, then open the door and snap on the light pretending she'd just come in. Lucy hadn't stolen anything at that time—there'd been nothing to steal.

And Lucy had been in the basement. Could she have had time to shoot at Helen, run downstairs, and set up an alibi with Bob? Maybe. She'd have to talk with Jason. The big question was why? Lucy didn't seem to have a mean bone in her body.

"Helen? Helen, dear, are you still with us?" Lydia asked. "You look rather spaced out as my grandson would say."

"I'm fine. Daniel, you may have something. Could Lucy have taken the money you had planned on giving Jack the night I caught him hitting you?"

His brows nearly came together. "I suppose it's possible. I took a shower that evening and was out of the room for several hours playing cards."

"I bet she stole my diamond," Gladys said. "She kept telling me I lost it 'cause it was too big for my finger. I knew that wasn't true."

"Now that you mention it," Betty added, "I've heard several residents complain about thefts recently—money, jewelry.... It's a problem in a lot of nursing homes, so I didn't think much about it. With all the visitors and such, things tend to walk off."

"Hmph." Lars shook his head. "No one ever stole from me."

Danile chuckled. "Lars, there's good reason for that, big guy. If I were a thief, you'd be the last person I'd want to tangle with."

"Why don't you make a list of the missing items, and I'll give it to my son."

After breakfast, Helen made another call to Jason, this time from her room. He'd already left for Edgewood.

When he arrived Helen was waiting in the lobby. "I may have a suspect." She handed him the list of items the residents were missing and began telling him about Lucy. Slipping an arm through his, Helen drew him down to the day room, then outside onto the patio. "With that in mind, is it possible for Lucy to have shot at me, then ducked down to the basement?"

"It's possible. We've got a few minutes discrepancy in her statement, but that could be individual watches. Bob, the fellow from the funeral home, said he'd arrived at eleven and waited ten minutes in the morgue for Lucy. The nursing supervisor said she'd sent Lucy down with the papers at around eleven, but she couldn't give us an exact time. Lucy says she stopped in the bathroom for a couple of minutes before going down."

"Which could have given her time to fire at me, then duck into the basement, turn out the lights, and go into the morgue."

"Okay, she could have done it, but why?"

Helen shrugged. "To get me out of the way, I suspect. Or she may have only wanted to scare me off. I have a hard time seeing her as a murderer. Still, if she's been helping Jack in his drug trade and extortion—not to mention the assisted suicide arrangements—she's capable of anything."

"We'll take her in for questioning. Maybe she'll lead us to Jack." Jason raked a hand through his thick dark hair. "Funny how things tend to come together. We found a .25 caliber Raven registered to Jack Owens and a pair of gloves in a trash bin in the basement rest room, which is, I might add, rather conveniently located one door down from the morgue and close to the exit."

Helen leaned forward to pick a dead blossom from a deep red

geranium. "Speaking of Jack, have you had any leads?"

"Yes, but so far all dead ends."

Jason's cellular phone buzzed. He folded out the mouthpiece. "Yeah, this is McGrady." He glanced at Helen and frowned, then spoke to the caller. "I'll be there in ten minutes."

"What is it?"

After sliding the phone into a holster at his belt, Jason ran a weary hand down his face. "Forget what I said about this thing coming together. Some cyclist just found Jack's body in a ditch off the old scenic highway. Looks like a hit-and-run."

Twenty-four

Mrs. Bradley?" Chris Chang jogged across the lawn toward her. "Adriane sent me over to get you." ⟩

Helen stared at him a moment, still lost in thought over the news of Jack's death.

"Mrs. Bradley? Is everything okay?"

"Just thinking." She took his hand, letting him help her to her feet. She'd been sitting on the bench since Jason had left her, trying to pull together some kind of logical explanation as to why someone had run Jack down. Not that he didn't have enemies.

"About Jack, I'll bet." Chris led her around the front of the building.

"Yes. How did you find out so quickly?"

"Andi told us."

"Did you know him?"

"Not very well. I saw him a few times when he came over to the lab to bring blood work or pick up meds for the patients. Uncle Paul and Dad were talking about him this morning."

"Did Jack come to the lab very often?"

"I don't know. He mostly worked nights, so I wouldn't have seen him. We have a log though, where people have to sign in and out. Kind of like at the gate, except everyone has to write down what they came to get. The police were looking through it this morning."

Once inside the brick building, Helen and Chris were greeted by a security guard stationed in the large marble entry.

"Andi," Helen said. "I didn't expect to see you over here. I thought you worked out at the guardhouse."

"We alternate—makes the job more interesting. How's the arm?"

"Getting better every day."

"Glad to hear that." They spoke a few more minutes, then after signing in, Chris and Helen proceeded down a wide corridor to the left. According to the sign, the research center was to the right. Helen stopped Chris and asked him why they were heading in the opposite direction.

"We'll be going there in a few minutes. Adriane said I should show you the pharmacy first, then bring you over. I guess she wanted to finish up a project before you arrived."

Helen nodded and paused to admire the carved wood staircase. "This is a beautiful building. If I remember right from reading the brochures, this is part of an old college campus."

"Yes. It was built in the 1920s. Grandfather bought the school and the land around it. It was in pretty bad shape, but they restored it."

"Where do these stairs lead? I didn't notice a sign." Helen fingered the blue velvet rope that blocked off access to the stairs. "And why is it roped off?"

"That's our testing facility. Only authorized personnel can go up there. Actually, that's the case with the entire building—except for the pharmacy. It has a separate door on the outside for customers."

Chris moved away from the stairs toward a door at the end of the hall. "Adriane might take you up there, but I wouldn't count on it." He grinned. "Too many trade secrets."

"Anything that might help me find out whether or not your grandparents were murdered?"

"I doubt it. It's mostly a testing facility. The only people allowed in there are the doctors and a few other people with security clearance." He frowned. "Grandpa had his heart attack up there."

"In that case, I'd very much like to see it."

Chris glanced around. "Maybe I could bring you back later—like tonight after dark. I . . . um . . . I'm not supposed to have a key, but I took an extra one that Grandpa had. I like to snoop around sometimes—see what's new."

Helen nodded. "Tonight then."

Chris opened the door, escorted Helen in, and introduced her to a wiry blond woman in her thirties. "I'll let Sheila show you around here, Mrs. Bradley. She can tell you a lot more about it than I can." His gaze shifted to the head pharmacist. "I'll be in the lab. Let me know when you're done."

"Sure," Sheila responded, "but you don't have to come back. I'll deliver her to you."

Sheila dutifully showed Helen around the pharmacy, which, like all pharmacies, stocked hundreds of medications for every ailment imaginable. Some natural remedies—vitamins, minerals, and miscellaneous sundries—were stocked on shelves as over-the-counter items. Prescription medications were kept behind the counter. Sheila introduced her to one other pharmacist and a clerk, both of whom were busy with customers.

"This is quite a facility."

"Yes. We're rather proud of it. Andrew Kincaid developed the pharmacy to service the nursing home as well as the residents in the assisted living and retirement complexes. All Edgewood members receive a discount on their medications and supplies, and most, depending on their health care plan, get the meds free."

"That must be an expensive venture."

"It is. As you can imagine, we dispense a lot of medication here," Sheila explained. "We have around two thousand residents at Edgewood and almost all of them are on meds. Of course, even if they aren't on prescription drugs, they all take our natural therapy packet, which is made up of vitamin and mineral supplements along with various herbs."

"I've heard a great deal about this natural therapy since coming to Edgewood." Helen let her gaze roam over the well-stocked shelves. Most of the products bore the name Kincaid Laboratories.

"Wonderful, isn't it?" Sheila straightened several brown bottles. "Herbs have always been known to have therapeutic effects, but most western doctors tend to stay away from them for the most part. Too illogical, unproven, and unsophisticated."

"Now herbal remedies are all the rage."

"Dr. Chang—Mai—developed our particular packets. She's devoted most of her life to gathering and studying the effects of herbs. We have our own herb garden out back." Sheila chuckled. "Mai is very particular about the herbs being pure—no insecticides. About the only thing we don't grow ourselves is nettles, and around here mother nature provides an abundance."

"Nettles?"

"Right. Who would have thought a plant that triggered such severe reactions on our skin could be so beneficial?"

Helen shuddered, remembering the terrible itchy rash nettles caused when it contacted skin. "I hate to sound skeptical, but what possible use are nettles?"

"They can be dried and put into capsule form or tea to treat hayfever and other allergies. Nettles are also used to treat vaginal infections and are known to lower blood sugar, among other things. The Indians would make a poulstice from the roots to alleviate joint pain. It's even been used on the scalp for treating hair loss."

"This is fascinating. You grow and produce the products here?"

"Sure do. Let me take you out to the processing plant."

Sheila ushered her back into the main hallway. They walked to the end of it and out another door. She stopped just before entering a large warehouse and pointed to her right. "That's Dr. Chang's herb garden over there. We have about fifteen acres planted this year."

Helen's gaze drifted over the rows of various plants and settled on a large patch of foxglove. The hair on the back of her neck snapped to attention. Foxglove was used to make digitalis—a common heart medication and deadly in high doses.

"Sheila, isn't that foxglove?"

"Yes—beautiful, isn't it?"

"You surely don't make your own digitalis preparations."

"Oh no. Ours is strictly for research purposes—and to look at. We get our digitalis from a pharmaceutical company in the Midwest."

"But Dr. Chang—Mai—does use it for research?"

"Yes—I believe so. You'll have to ask her about that. We only get the details once something has been approved by the FDA for sale in the pharmacy."

"I understand Andrew Kincaid had a heart attack. Was he on heart medication?"

Sheila's pleasantry slid into a look of disgust. "Look, Mrs. Bradley, I know what you're getting at. You think Mai killed her father with a lethal dose of digitalis. You can forget that. Yes, he had a heart condition and he was on medication, but Mai would never have killed him—or anyone for that matter. She's totally devoted to saving lives."

"Did you know about Irene's charges that her husband had been murdered?"

"Yes, she'd talked to me about it. Even accused me and my staff at one point."

"So you think she was delusional?"

"Yes, I do. There's no other reasonable answer for her behavior."

Helen wandered through the herb garden for a few minutes with Sheila, learning more about nature's remedies than she particularly wanted to know. It was a complicated area of study. She would never remember all the combinations of herbs and remedies. The one thing she could recall was that "natural" and "safe" were definitely not synonymous. Some of the products had deadly side effects.

As with everything at Edgewood Estates, the production and distribution area was impressive. They produced a wide variety of medicinal herbs and other products including Renovare, Irene's anti-aging face cream. Many of the products were distributed nationwide through a private distribution company and through catalog sales. It was the kind of corporate structure Helen would have expected to see in a big city, not hidden in a sprawling country estate.

"Does the government know about all this?" Helen asked as she and the pharmacist made their way back into the main building.

"Do you mean is all this a legitimate business? Yes. We have inspectors out here on a regular basis. In fact, even more so now that we've applied for a federal grant."

"Oh yes, Adriane mentioned that. Four million, right?"

"Yes, and we have to come up with matching funds. I'm not sure where we are now, but when Andrew died, we were only at two million."

"I take it the grant is rather important?" Helen's voice echoed through the wide marble hallway.

"Vital. If we don't get it, we'll have to close down the research center, which would be like losing a vital organ. We've all had to make major budget cuts. Like the pharmacy, for example—I had to let two people go. It's been tough, but we'll make it. Paul says he'll do whatever it takes to keep us operating." Sheila paused at what looked like an elevator door, only there were no up or down buttons. She pressed a buzzer and announced their presence into a speaker phone mounted on the wall, then inserted a plastic card into the lock mounted in the wall.

The doors swished apart. Chris stood in the opening. Helen turned to thank Sheila for the tour, but the young woman had already gone.

"Come on in, Mrs. Bradley. I'll take you to Adriane's office."

They walked past a bank of computers set on nondescript desks, which took up most of the central part of what resembled a college chemistry lab. A few technicians glanced up from their monitors as they passed. Microscopes, flasks, beakers, and Bunsen burners were the only items Helen could still name. To their left was a door labeled Library. Chris passed that and headed for a door on the opposite side. This opened into a hallway with several offices each marked with the occupant's name. Adriane's was the farthest down, next to the women's rest room, which Helen decided to use before continuing the tour.

"Just knock on her door when you're ready," Chris instructed. "I'll let her know you're here."

When she exited the rest room, Helen noticed another curved staircase similar to the one in the front entry. This one had no rope barring her entry. Curiosity drew her forward, but she stopped at the base of the stairs. Maybe Adriane would take her up during the tour—if not, she'd take Chris up on his offer and come later.

Moments later she sat in Adriane's office.

"I apologize for taking so long." Adriane looked up from the computer screen. "Unfortunately I have a deadline on applying for a new grant, and I need to have it ready for our business manager this morning." She finished typing, engaged the printer, and turned to face her guest.

"No problem. I enjoyed seeing the pharmacy and everything connected with that. Do you apply for many grants?"

"As many as we can. We need them for research on our various projects." Adriane came around to Helen's side of the desk. "Let me show you what we do around here."

For the next thirty minutes Helen met various workers in the lab, toured the massive library, and discovered in part the money and work that went into creating just one new product.

Adriane finished the tour back at her office. Although she'd explained some of the details in testing new products, she'd made no move to take Helen upstairs.

"Oh no, I'm afraid not," Adriane said when Helen asked about it. "You see, we occasionally perform autopsies there and examine cadavers. Not a place to take visitors."

"Sounds rather gruesome."

Adriane sent her a patronizing smile. "It can be unsettling for nonmedical people, but certainly not gruesome—or sinister. We're not developing a Frankenstein out of spare body parts or anything like that."

"I should hope not, but why do you do autopsies here when you have a morgue in the other building?"

"This one is for special cases."

"For example?"

"I can't go into too much detail, but I can assure you that all of our work is above board and entirely legal. For example, we study differences between the brain tissue of persons with Alzheimer's and those whose brains are healthy. We test animals—mostly rats with medications we've developed. Andrew was very close to finding a drug that could significantly slow down the disease process. We're looking into the possibility of transplanting healthy brain tissue in early Alzheimer's patients, while at the same time removing diseased parts of the brain. And of course I've already explained about my own study—using the computer chip."

"Yes." Helen hesitated, trying to decide how to best formulate her question. "I was just wondering if you or any of the other doctors were ever tempted to bypass all the rules and rats and take your experiments directly to people. I would imagine there'd be a number of residents who would eagerly volunteer to be guinea pigs. Like Jim Salter, for example."

Adriane pressed her lips together, looking first at her hands, then letting her gaze drift up to meet Helen's. "As I've said before, Mrs. Bradley, we follow the rules—as difficult as that may be at times. You'd be surprised at the number of people who come to us, begging us to treat them. There are situations where government restrictions are lax. Mai, for instance, can move much more quickly with her herbs and natural products than Paul can with the drug he's developing." Answering the question before Helen could answer it, Adriane added, "Paul's taken over Andrew's project."

It was all legal. She'd heard the claim far too often to find it reassuring.

"Adriane, I assume you've heard about Jack Owens."

"Y-yes." She folded her arms and frowned. "It's frightening, isn't it?"

"Frightening?"

"To think someone so wicked could get a job here and hurt so many people." Adriane shook her head. "I probably shouldn't say this, and I know it may sound cold, but I'm glad he's dead. Whoever hit him did us all a favor."

"Meaning?"

"Well, now there won't be a messy trial. Maybe with Jack dead, we can put this nasty stuff behind us and move on."

"I'm not sure it'll be that easy."

"Oh?" Adriane looked tired and irritated. "Why not?"

"Jack killed Ruthie and abused a number of people. He may even have been involved in Irene's death, but I'm quite certain he didn't kill Andrew. And I know he didn't shoot at me."

"You still believe Andrew and Irene were murdered?"

"Yes, I do." Helen held up her hands. "I know, I know. You're going to remind me that Andrew had a heart attack and Irene succumed to infection."

"Actually, I wasn't going to say that at all. I've been giving their deaths a lot of thought myself, and I think you're right in pursuing the case." She sighed. "I guess I was just hoping Jack did it. I'd hate to think there's another killer at Edgewood."

———

Back in her room, while Helen debated her next move, a knock sounded on her door.

"Hi. I hope I'm not disturbing you. I needed to talk." Sammi wore no makeup. She had on jeans and a baggy shirt that looked like she had slept in it.

Helen backed up to let her in. "You're definitely not disturbing me. What's wrong?"

Sammi clasped her hands and walked to the window, stood there a moment, then spun around. "I just did a preliminary autopsy on Jack Owens."

"And—?"

"Helen, someone deliberately hit him. Officers at the scene found blood on the road at the point of impact, and skid marks indicate acceleration before and after impact. Whoever ran him down stopped the car and dragged him off the road into some bushes."

"When did it happen?"

"Near as I can guess the night before last—probably right after he got off work. Looks like someone was waiting for him."

"No wonder the police couldn't find him. But why kill him? Why not let the police know of his whereabouts?"

"That's what I've been asking myself." Sammi ran a hand through her already mussed hair. "I keep coming up with the same answer. Jack was scum."

Sammi's hazel gaze drifted up to meet Helen's. "Jason told me someone tried to kill you last night."

"Or scare me."

"It's my fault." Sammi bit into her bottom lip and heaved a shuddering sigh.

"Sammi, for goodness sake, what are you saying?"

"I . . . I've resigned my post as medical examiner. When I leave here I'm going to turn myself in."

Twenty-five

Turn yourself in? But why—" Helen stammered. "Sammi, what are you talking about?"

"Don't say anything, please. Just let me finish." Sammi grabbed a tissue from a box on the dresser, blew her nose, and went back to the window.

"I wanted to tell you first—before I talk to the police. I couldn't bear the thought of you finding out from someone else." She took a deep breath before continuing. "Remember I told you that Dr. Kincaid—Andrew—helped me get the position as medical examiner?"

"Yes."

"Well, there was a catch." Sammi paused to dab the moisture from her eyes. "I was to also serve as their pathologist and perform certain autopsies on their residents here at Edgewood with one of their physicians present. Since they are a research facility, they needed to study and report findings on any specialized treatment the residents were undergoing at the time of their deaths. They never asked me to actually falsify reports on the cause of death— I was simply expected to keep certain facts confidential."

"What facts? I'm not sure what you mean. How could you not falsify your reports if you weren't reporting everything you saw?"

Sammi frowned. "I guess I didn't see that as a problem. The main concern they had was keeping their formulas a secret. They didn't want certain ingredients used in their products mentioned in a public report." Sammi turned around and met Helen's questioning gaze. "Yes, they paid me very well, and with college tuition and . . . it was too good an opportunity to pass up. I didn't really think I was doing anything wrong—Andrew had assured me that any experimentation was FDA approved. I never found any indication that what they were doing was dangerous or that it contributed to the cause of death. I trusted Andrew and Paul, but now . . . "

Helen tipped her head to one side. "What made you decide to confess?"

"A guilty conscience. Jack. Knowing there really is a murderer out here besides him. And the explosion. I'm afraid someone here at Edgewood sees me as a threat. You see, there was one experiment I questioned and threatened to make public. I found a tiny device implanted in the base of Irene's skull, just under the skin."

"The computer chip. Adriane told me about it, but she assured me it wasn't being used on humans."

"It shouldn't have been. I confronted Paul. He said Irene had begged Andrew to let Adriane implant one in her. This was before Andrew's death. It had been so successful in laboratory animals, Andrew finally agreed. They all knew about it. Paul offered me a substantial bonus for my silence. He showed me the results of the study. Irene's memory improved dramatically. I could find no link between the implant and her death, so I agreed to keep quiet."

"What about Andrew's death?"

"Like I said before, he died of a heart attack." Sammi seemed calmer now.

"Is it possible he could have been given a lethal dose of digitalis?"

A caustic smile tugged at the side of her mouth. "I take it you've been visiting Mai's herb garden. Since the explosion the thought has gone through my mind a time or two. I don't know. He was taking it for a heart condition. It's possible, but Mai would have had no reason to kill her father."

"Inheritance?"

Sammi shook her head. "Mai has all the money she needs. No. If she killed either parent it would be to keep them from suffering, but I couldn't find any evidence of that."

"What about Mai's husband? What did he have to gain from Andrew's or Irene's deaths?"

"David? I don't know. Look, Helen, I'm really not into playing 'Means, Motive, and Opportunity' right now. I have an appointment with your son in half an hour."

Helen followed her to the door. "I . . . I don't know what to say. Sorry doesn't seem adequate."

"Do me a favor and pray for me, will you? I know I don't deserve your friendship, but—"

"You made a wrong choice, Sammi. That doesn't negate our friendship." Helen held out her arms and Sammi welcomed the embrace. "And I will pray."

"There's one more thing." Sammi stepped back, pausing in the doorway. "Knowing you, I doubt you'll take my advice, but I strongly suggest you get out of here while you still can."

Helen shook her head. "Not just yet. Whoever shot at me yesterday is afraid I'm getting too close."

Sammi nodded. "Like me—and Jack. There's something else I should tell you. Jack found out that I was getting paid on the side and was blackmailing me. To be honest, if I'd seen him on that road at night, I'd have been tempted to run him down myself."

Helen felt sick. "So if he was blackmailing you, he may have been blackmailing others."

"It's entirely possible."

"Looks as though someone is working awfully hard to cover their tracks."

Sammi nodded. "Which means we'd both better watch our backs."

Helen walked with Sammi to her car. She was just going back

inside when Paul rushed out, calling for Sammi to wait. Helen stood in the lobby and watched, releasing a long sigh of relief when he finally moved away from the car and Sammi drove away.

"Mrs. Bradley," Paul said curtly when he came back inside. "I expect Dr. Fergeson told you what she plans to do."

"Yes. I take it you're not too happy about it."

"That's putting it mildly. Let's just say I'm disappointed. Edgewood doesn't need this kind of publicity—"

"Edgewood! Publicity!" Helen sputtered. "Someone is killing people around here, and you're worried about your reputation. Are you really so cold blooded?"

Paul stared at her a moment. A momentary sadness flickered in his blue eyes. "No, Mrs. Bradley. This place is home to a lot of elderly people. We have worked very hard to give them the best care possible in their old age. My father gave his entire life to help these people. I don't want to see it go down the tube. Now, if you don't mind, I have to see what I can do to salvage it."

He turned and walked out the door before Helen could ask him whether he'd commit murder to save his empire.

On the way back to her room, Helen did pray, for Sammi and the other residents at Edgewood. She prayed for herself as well, that she might solve this bizarre puzzle and bring the murderer to justice before he—or she—killed again.

Several minutes later, Helen plugged in her laptop, settled into the recliner, and pulled up the Kincaid file. The notes she'd made earlier had been erased. In their place was written:

> *Because I could not stop for death*
> *He kindly stopped for me.*
> *Emily Dickinson*

Helen closed her eyes, then opened them again, hoping what she'd seen hadn't been real. It was. She turned off the computer, got out of the chair, set the laptop on the dresser, and went to find Thelma. She found her in the day room chatting with Rhett Butler, or whoever the man fancied himself to be at the moment. Helen exchanged greetings with Rhett and several of the other residents before drawing Thelma aside.

"Did you happen to notice anyone going into my room this morning?"

"No, I sure didn't. Why do you ask?"

"Someone used my computer and erased a file." Helen didn't bother to tell her what had been written in its place.

"One of the residents might have wandered in. Who can tell? We've had a terribly busy morning—three new admissions. Doctors coming and going, ordering tests."

"It's all right," Helen said matter-of-factly. "It wasn't anything important." Just a death threat.

Helen went back to her room, determined not to let the note intimidate her. It didn't work. She thought of calling Jason but decided against it. Knowing him, he'd use any means possible to get her out of there—including arrest for obstructing justice. She couldn't let that happen.

Helen paced back and forth in front of the window for several minutes trying to decide what to do next.

The murderer was getting careless. Killing Jack had been a stupid act. Of course not many people realized the capability of a forensics team. They'd very likely track down the car and the killer within a few days—maybe even hours.

"So why not just go home?" Helen asked her reflection in the window.

Because you can't stop thinking about Irene. For some inexplicable reason, she needed to learn the truth. Helen was more convinced than ever that Irene hadn't been delusional when she'd insisted someone was trying to kill her.

At times Helen hated those gut feelings that cropped up during a case and refused to go away, even in the face of reason and evidence suggesting the opposite. But she knew better than to ignore them.

Someone at Edgewood—not the man who'd stolen Irene's purse that night—had made certain Irene took her secret to the grave.

She sighed and turned away from the window. Helen doubted it would help, but she needed to talk to Stephanie again. Irene had died on the head nurse's shift, and Helen felt certain the woman knew more than she was telling.

Unfortunately, Stephanie was out. According to the desk clerk she'd taken a break and would be back soon.

Needing to clear her head, Helen decided to take a walk. After letting Thelma know where she was going and signing out, Helen hurried outside through the neatly manicured gardens to the path she'd taken the day before with Daniel. Had it only been a day? With all that had happened, it seemed more like a week. She hurried to the vista, thinking it would be a wonderful spot to meditate and perhaps give her a new perspective, but the bench was occupied.

"Stephanie?" Helen approached the hunched-over woman in white.

"Oh." She snapped to attention. "I didn't expect . . . I was . . . "

"Crying. I can see that."

Stephanie stuffed a crumpled soggy tissue into her pocket and pulled out a fresh one.

"Do you want to talk about it?"

She shook her head. "What's the use? All the talking in the world isn't going to bring him back or change what's happened.

I wish I'd never met him."

"Him?" Helen lowered herself to the seat.

"Jack." Stephanie paused to blow her nose. "He told me he loved me and we were going to get married. He lost his job as a mechanic and I got pregnant and we needed the money. He asked me to get him a job here. It's my fault he got hired. I . . . I didn't know about his criminal record. He was just such a sweet man." The last sentence ended with fresh tears.

Helen could think of a lot of words to call Jack and none of them was sweet.

Eventually Stephanie's sobs quieted. She lifted her head. "I feel so foolish, Mrs. Bradley. You must think I'm awful, falling in love with a man like him."

"I heard he could be quite nice when he wanted to be."

"That's no excuse. I hate him for what he did to me. I have psychiatric training. I should have seen it. He used me. And to think I wanted a man in my life so much, I—" She buried her face in her hands.

"Did you kill him?"

She raised her head slowly, a blank look in her eyes. "No. But I almost wish I had."

Helen patted her shoulder. "I'm sorry. I had to ask. I want to ask you something else, too. About Irene."

In one deep breath Stephanie seemed to gather herself back together. She adjusted her glasses and except for her red-rimmed eyes and the blotches on her face, one would never have known how distraught she'd been only seconds before. "What about Irene?"

"When we first spoke on the phone, you seemed surprised when I asked if she was confused. You said she hadn't been, then later you changed your mind."

"She was as lucid as you or I when she came in that day. Then later, she changed. It wasn't the fever—at least not then."

"Could it have been a medication?"

"Not to my knowledge. I suppose someone could have given her something, but I don't see wh . . . ."

"When she was lucid, did she tell you anything?"

"I . . . maybe. I remember her grabbing my hand and pulling me close to her. She said she needed to talk to me later—in private."

"So there were others in the room."

"Oh yes. Paul, David, Mai, Adriane, Chris—some staff members, but I don't remember who. Everyone was worried and trying to figure out what to do for her. Irene was so weak and sick."

"Did you ever get to talk to her privately?"

"Yes, but by that time nothing she said made any sense. She seemed afraid of everyone. Wouldn't sleep. She even accused me of poisoning her when I hooked up her antibiotic. We had to keep her sedated or she'd rip out the IVs."

"Did you suspect she might be telling the truth?"

"Not then. I didn't believe for a moment that anyone at Edgewood would harm Irene. Now I'm not so sure. Still, the autopsy would have shown something, wouldn't it?"

"Not necessarily. Let's suppose for a moment someone did poison her. Do you have any idea who?"

Stephanie closed her eyes. "No. I'm sorry Mrs. Bradley, but I need to get back to work. As it is, I'm way over my break time."

"Just one more question. Did Irene say anything to you about a disk?"

She thought for a moment before answering. "I don't remember anything."

Helen stayed on the bench after Stephanie left, wondering just how much of Stephanie's story she could believe. She finally stood, then did some stretching exercises to loosen up her tense shoulders and walked about a mile down the trail before heading back.

When she returned, Jason was waiting for her in the courtyard. He'd stretched out on a lounge chair and didn't bother getting up when she walked toward him. "You're looking rather pleased with yourself," Helen said.

"I am. We just found the car that was used to run down Jack Owens. And we've made an arrest. Looks like my job out here is finished."

Helen folded her arms and raised her eyebrows. "Really? And are you going to tell me who that is?"

"Paul Kincaid."

"What?"

"You heard me." Jason unfolded himself from the chair and stood up. "He's denying it, of course, but we have enough evidence to make an arrest."

Helen frowned. "That may be, but Paul didn't fire those shots at me the other night. In case you hadn't noticed, he's about the same height as Jack."

"True, but he may have hired someone, just like he did to gun down his mother and you. If you'll recall that guy had a record too—and ended up dead before we could apprehend him. I may never be able to make those charges stick, but we've definitely got him on the hit-and-run. His car had bloodstains on the steering wheel—Jack's I'll bet—and he has no alibi. Claims he was home alone. The DA says we have enough evidence to charge him. I'm satisfied."

"Oh, I don't know, Jason. Somehow I can't imagine Paul Kincaid using his own car to kill Jack. Have you talked to Sammi?"

"Sammi?"

Helen's pulse started to race. "She left here over an hour ago. Said she had an appointment with you."

Jason shook his head. "I haven't seen her."

Helen quickly repeated the conversation she'd had with Sammi earlier. "She left here around one. I saw her talking to Paul just before she left. You don't suppose he—" Helen left the sentence unfinished. "When did you arrest him?"

"Just a few minutes ago—down at the gate."

"He was leaving?"

"No. Coming back." Their gazes collided.

"He went after her," Helen gasped.

"Let's not jump to conclusions. Could be she decided to run. It takes a lot of guts for someone in a public position to face the music."

"I don't think so. Sammi wouldn't have confessed everything to me if she intended to skip town. I'm worried."

Jason whipped out his cellular phone and put out an all-points bulletin for Sammi and her car, and he sent an officer to check her residence. After signing off, he told his mother not to worry and gave her a hug. "I'll call as soon as I hear anything," he said, then took off, leaving Helen to grope through a case that seemed to get muddier by the minute.

Twenty-six

Forty-five long minutes after sending Jason to find Sammi, Helen's phone rang. She grabbed it before it could ring again. "Jason?"

"Yeah. Ah . . . listen, Mom. We haven't been able to track Sammi down. No one's seen her since she left Edgewood. We'll keep looking. The guard says Sammi waited for Kincaid just inside the entrance. Then he followed her out. I hate to say this, but I think Dr. Fergeson may have been the one who used you for target practice."

"That doesn't make sense."

"If Kincaid knew about her confession to you, he may have made her an offer she couldn't refuse. Money and a comfortable hacienda in exchange for her silence."

"I doubt that. Why purge her conscience with me if she intended to leave town?"

"Who knows? Anyway, we'll find her—got the state police alerted and we're checking the airlines."

"Keep me posted."

"I will. By the way, you'll be happy to know that Lucy confessed—actually, she didn't have much choice. Our search warrant turned up a bunch of the residents' missing articles. She had enough stuff in her apartment to open a department store."

Helen sighed. "How sad. It's hard to imagine someone would take advantage of older people that way."

"Yeah. I'll say one thing, Mom, when you're right, you're right. I'm glad you decided to investigate. One thing though, she denies having any thing to do with Jack's operation."

Helen felt weary. After saying good-bye to her son, she sank onto the bed, wondering how many more low-life creatures she'd find under the rocks she'd overturned. And now there was Sammi.

She could very well have been the one who shot at her. Helen was beginning to suspect that Chris Chang's assessment of Sammi may have been closer to the truth than her own. Had her old friend been so enamored with the Kincaids and their money that she'd kill to be a part of it?

But the explosion—that didn't make sense. Jason suspected Paul had hired Jack to plant a bomb in Sammi's car, like he'd hired the man to shoot his stepmother. Jack, as it turned out, had worked as a demolition expert with a construction company a few years back.

Helen closed her eyes and massaged her forehead. Paul simply wasn't a logical suspect. She'd thought the same thing before and it still held true. Helen doubted a man so intent on protecting Edgewood would want to call negative attention to himself or his company, yet the explosion and the hit-and-run had done just that. Paul was not a stupid man. He wouldn't have run Jack down with his car and leave a trail of evidence a ten-year-old could follow. It simply did not fit the image of the Paul Kincaid she'd come to know. If her assumptions were true, Paul had been framed.

Helen could almost feel the adrenaline pulse through her body. Paul Kincaid did not kill Jack Owens, and she seriously doubted that he'd killed anyone—he was too busy holding his crumbling corporation together. So who framed Paul and why? Greed? With Paul out of the way, Kincaid Enterprises would fall to Mai and her husband, David Chang.

She wondered how the other doctors were dealing with Paul's arrest. Helen sprang off the bed. No time like the present to find out.

A surprise visit would be best, Helen decided. She signed out of the manor, saying she was going for a walk. And she did. Helen walked out through the day room and into the courtyard, around the building, through the park, and into Kincaid Laboratories. The large marble entry was empty. She could see Andi at the end of the hall talking to the pharmacist—gossiping no doubt about their boss's arrest.

Helen considered creeping around by herself, but without a key she probably wouldn't get very far. Besides, Andi had turned around and was walking toward her.

"Hi, Mrs. Bradley." Andi hitched up the belt weighed down by her gun and holster. "Been meaning to come over to see you, but things have been pretty busy around here."

"They certainly have. I suppose you've heard about Dr. Kincaid's arrest."

Andi nodded. "Sure did—in fact, I'm the one who spotted the dent in his car this morning. Didn't believe my own eyes at first."

"I imagine the other doctors are pretty upset."

"Oh, yeah. They sent all the lab assistants home. They're huddling up at the Changs' house to decide what to do."

"I'd really like to talk with them."

"I don't think they want to be disturbed, but seeing as it's you, I suppose I could call."

Andi did and relayed the message back to Helen that they would be back in around four. A two-hour wait. Helen considered going back to the room but decided her time might be better spent examining the off-limits room upstairs.

"Andi," Helen began, "you mentioned being surprised when you learned Dr. Kincaid owned the vehicle that hit Jack Owens."

"For sure. It still doesn't seem possible."

Helen rested her arms on the counter. "What if I were to tell you I think Dr. Kincaid was framed and the real killer—the one who killed Jack and Irene and maybe even Andrew—is still on the loose."

Andi's eyes widened. "You think that's a possibility?"

"I'm almost certain of it. Which is why I need your help."

"Sure, what can I do?"

"I have been wracking my brain trying to come up with motives. All along I've been thinking money, but that may not be the case at all. I'm thinking someone—maybe one of the doctors or staff members—did something wrong and has been desperately trying to cover their tracks."

"Like killing Irene?"

"Yes, but perhaps even before that. Irene told me she had proof that her husband had been murdered. She claimed she had a disk with evidence that would prove her right. If she was right, and despite the evidence to the contrary, someone did kill Andrew, then—"

"Maybe he caught the person. Like they could have been embezzling money or selling black market drugs like Jack. Old Doc Kincaid would have fired them on the spot and turned them over to the cops. He always told us he ran a clean operation."

"And I think Paul wanted to keep it that way, but things started going wrong. The information got into the wrong hands, and the killer had to keep trying to stop the leak.

"Now it's possible Paul really is responsible," Helen went on, "but what if he isn't? So far four people have been killed—each one because they knew something. I can't help wondering who's going to be next."

"You maybe. You've been asking a lot of questions and someone's already shot at you."

"Yes, and I'm certain that person wasn't Paul." Helen felt certain it wasn't Sammi either. "What I want to do is go back to the beginning. Chris told me his grandfather died up there." Helen pointed toward the ceiling. "He was going to take me up later, but I'm thinking since I have two hours to spare, maybe you could let me go up and look around."

"Oh, I couldn't do that. I mean, I know you're an ex-cop and all, but I have strict orders not to let anyone up there. Besides, the cops checked the place out when Irene started making noises about her husband being killed."

Helen sighed. "I can certainly understand your hesitation. I'd just hoped you'd help me get to the bottom of whatever's going on. I'm sure you want answers as badly as I do."

"You're right about that." Andi reached into a drawer, pulled out a plastic card, and set it on the counter, then turned around to pick up a clipboard.

Helen stuffed the card into her pocket.

Andi turned back around and set the clipboard on the desk. "I don't normally break the rules, Mrs. B., but I got a lot of respect for you. And seeing as you're Lieutenant McGrady's mother, well if I can't trust you, who can I trust?"

Helen promised she'd return the key shortly and hurried up the stairs before Andi could change her mind.

The testing facility looked much like the lab area downstairs. Each of the doctors had separate working areas and desks with equipment, work spaces, and drawers clearly labeled. The windowed wall to the left offered a view of Mt. Hood in the distance. Straight ahead was another stairway—probably leading down to the offices. Next to the stairs was another room. Through the window in the door she could see a number of cages. The laboratory animals.

To her right was a set of double swinging doors and she decided to start there. Helen had no idea what she was looking for and just hoped she'd know if she found it.

The room was set up much like a modern autopsy room. She'd seen only one autopsy during her time on the police force. One had been enough. Helen closed her mind to the image of the medical examiner making the Y cut to expose and remove the internal organs.

The room was frigid and smelled of antiseptic solution. It had recently been cleaned. Purged of any evidence, it offered nothing but a bad memory. Helen backed out of the room and watched the doors swing shut. A few feet down on the same wall were two heavy metal doors that looked like walk-in refrigeration units. The first was a freezer. Helen depressed the handle, holding her breath as she peered inside. She hadn't known what to expect— corpses, maybe, hanging from meat hooks, or body parts. But there was nothing like that. Only shelf after shelf of various tissues from organs, each labeled and placed neatly in cubicles bearing individuals' names and the name of a doctor.

She opened the next door down—a refrigerator set up much the same way. Hundreds of trays of vials and petri dishes sat on shelves, all neatly labeled. Again, nothing unusual for a research lab. She let her gaze drift over the foreign-sounding names. One cabinet was labeled Microbial Causes. Two words jumped out at her staphylococcus and pneumococcus. A staph infection had killed Irene. And she'd had pneumonia.

While it didn't seem unusual for a research lab to be studying microorganisms—in fact, these were probably used to test various antibacterial agents—but suppose someone was using them to kill residents prematurely and Dr. Kincaid found out? Dr. David Chang's name was on the cabinet.

Helen shivered, remembering Irene's insistence that someone was trying to kill her—poison her. Her son-in-law? It was a bone-chilling thought. Still, she had no real proof. These units would be easily accessible by any of the workers who had clearance.

She poked through the cabinets, finding samples of drugs. One cabinet, bearing Mai Chang's name, was filled with bottles. Helen recognized many of them as the herbs Sheila had pointed out—all alphabetized—no foxglove or digitalis, but there was a bottle of hemlock.

Helen shuddered and shut the refrigerator door, then ducked behind a nearby counter when she heard footsteps on the stairs.

An overhead light came on. "Mrs. Bradley?" Mai called. "Are you still here? It's all right. Andi told me she'd given you a key."

Helen straightened and stepped away from the counter. "I hope you won't be upset with her."

"No, not really." Mai rubbed her forehead. "Have you learned anything?"

"Pardon me?"

"Anything that could clear my brother. Andi said you didn't think he was guilty. I know he isn't. She also said you believed my mother may have been right about my father's death."

"I realize it goes against the evidence, but yes, I have reason to believe someone murdered both of your parents."

Mai walked over to the water dispenser near the sink and retrieved two mugs from a nearby rack. She pressed the red button and filled them with hot water, went over to one of the desks, pulled out a chair, and sat down. "Please. Have a seat and tell me more about your theories."

Helen rolled one of the other office chairs closer to Mai's desk. It creaked in protest as she sat down. "You may not like them."

Mai's dark gaze met Helen's. She opened a drawer and lifted out a tin canister, opened it, and drew out two tea bags. "Chamomile. A restful tea. I grow it myself. One of my mother's favorites. I understand you enjoy tea as well."

"Yes, I do. Thank you." Helen accepted one of the tea bags, slid it into the hot water, then dipped it several times.

"She and I usually made a pot in the afternoons." Tears misted her eyes.

"You miss her."

"Very much."

"Did you help her to die?"

Mai's head snapped up. Hot water sloshed out of her cup onto her hand. She grabbed for a tissue and mopped it up.

"I'm sorry. I didn't mean to startle you. Did you burn your hand?"

"I . . . I'm fine." She wasn't fine. Her hand shook when she reached up to tuck strands of straight black hair behind her ear. "I just didn't expect you to ask me something like that...."

"Your brother believes in assisted suicide. I was told Irene did too. I just wondered if you—"

"I do not. I believe it is important to make one's final days as comfortable as possible. But I could never help someone die. I believe that is up to a higher power than myself. My mother did not want to die." Mai glanced down at the red blotchy area on her hand. "I hold myself partially responsible for her death. Perhaps that's why your question upset me so much."

"Responsible? In what way?"

"I wanted her brought out to Edgewood immediately after her injury, but Paul thought it would be best if she stayed at the hospital for a few days. I should have insisted. By the time he brought her here, it was too late. My treatment had no effect."

"Your treatment?"

"Yes. I do a type of herbal cleansing to rid the body of toxins and build antibodies to fight infection. I hoped that along with the antibiotics it would help to heal her."

"Mai, I saw some vials of bacteria in the cooler. Could someone have injected bacteria into her blood stream? I remember Sammi telling me she had an unusual amount of bacteria in her body."

"I find your accusations very upsetting, Mrs. Bradley. We are all dedicated to healing, not destroying life. My husband would never do such a thing."

"I didn't say I thought it was your husband."

"No, but the microbial causes are in his locker."

"Okay, let's leave that for a minute. What about your father?" Helen held her hand up. "I know—heart attack. Could you tell me what happened and where?"

Mai took a sip of tea. "Over there. By the window. I was in my office. My father told me he was going upstairs to look over some files on the progress of the implants on which Adriane and he had been working. He seemed upset about something, but I never learned what it was. Shortly after that, I heard a noise upstairs. I didn't think too much about it at the time." Mai closed her eyes. "I realized later it was my father. If I'd gone to investigate, perhaps . . . " Her voice trailed off.

"Was anyone with him?"

"Adriane was supposed to be, but she didn't arrive until we'd already begun resuscitation."

"Who was the first to reach him?"

"Paul found him and called us." She shook her head. "My brother didn't kill our father, Mrs. Bradley."

"No, but I'm beginning to get a clearer picture of who did. You said Adriane was supposed to be with him."

"Yes, he'd stopped at her office on the way up and told her he wanted to talk to her."

"But she didn't go?"

"No, I don't think so—at least not right away. I heard her tell him she needed to finish some notes while they were fresh in her mind and she'd be up in about fifteen minutes. She felt terrible about that. She kept saying if she'd been there he may have made it through."

"Sammi told me your father and Adriane had implanted the brain rejuvenating device in Irene. How many other residents received one?"

She frowned. "There were no others."

"I think you're wrong about that. My hunch is that your father discovered some disturbing news—that Adriane had used the implant in a number of people. Perhaps that's what he wanted to talk to her about. I think she did come up here and somehow slipped him some digitalis."

"You have quite an imagination, Mrs. Bradley." The voice came from the back stairwell.

"Adriane! I didn't hear you come up." Mai swiveled her chair around, then gasped.

"Obviously." Adriane strolled toward them, the gun in her hand giving proof to Helen's suspicions.

Twenty-seven

Adriane glanced from Mai to Helen. "You're wrong about the digitalis. Andrew did have a heart attack."

"You were with him?" Mai asked.

"It was a difficult decision, really. If I had helped him and he survived, my career would have been ruined. He was going to fire me and turn me over to the authorities—all because I followed his lead. We needed to try the implant on more patients, not just Irene. But he wouldn't allow it. He said letting Irene have the implant had been a mistake and he was going to remove it."

"But why, Adriane?" Mai asked. "Why jeopardize our entire operation? The implant holds a great deal of promise, but until we're certain of how it performs on animals over a long period of time, we can't—"

"You just don't get it, do you, Mai? You have no idea what it's like to wait an eternity for your dream to be realized. You were born wealthy. You married a brilliant man. Your herbal remedies have almost no government restrictions. All I wanted was a chance to prove my implant really worked on humans. And I was getting good results. I pleaded with your father to let me stay, or at least let me transfer to Mexico where I'd have more freedom. He wouldn't listen. So when he collapsed, I had to make a decision—my life or his."

Helen picked up her cup and warmed her hands on it. Maybe if Adriane got close enough she could throw the hot liquid in her face. "Just how far are you willing to go to guard your secret? How many more people will you be forced to kill?"

"I never wanted to kill anyone. I had no choice. When Irene

found that disk—I had to do something. When I couldn't find it in her apartment, I . . . "

"You hired someone to gun her down," Helen finished. "Only he botched the job. Then to make certain he'd never implicate you, you killed him and Irene. Tell me something. How did you know where we'd be?"

"She confided everything to me. I was the one person she trusted. I encouraged her to turn the disk over to a private detective. I even went with her when she called you from the pay phone."

"How could you have betrayed her like that?" Mai gripped the edge of the desk.

Adriane tossed her a disgusted look.

"What about the bombing? Did you hire Jack to plant the bomb in Sammi's car?"

"Jack owed me in exchange for my silence on his little side business with the patients and the unfortunate incidents with Ruthie and Iris. The bomb was his less than brilliant plan. However, no one will ever be able to prove I had any connection to either of those men. I should never have hired them," Adriane sneered.

"Good help is hard to find—especially when you hire known felons."

"So true. But there will be no more botched jobs. I'm taking care of you personally this time. I was hoping it wouldn't come to this. I tried to warn you off, but you didn't seem to get the message. Well, it's too late now, isn't it?"

"Adriane, please—" Mai pleaded.

"You can't possibly get away with this," Helen announced with a great deal more conviction than she felt.

"Oh, but I can. I'm getting quite adept, really. I've already taken care of our little guard downstairs and closed the pharmacy for the day so there'll be no witnesses."

The gun Adriane had trained on them was a standard .38 police issue—the kind Andi had been wearing. "That's Andi's gun, isn't it?"

"How very observant of you. But don't worry. Andi is fine— she'll just have a headache when she wakes up—which is more than I can say for you.

"Now," Adriane continued, "let's get down to business. First you must finish your tea. But before you drink it, we need to add one more ingredient. Mai, will you do the honors, please?" Adriane waved the gun at her, then stepped over to Mai's herb cabinet. She opened it and glanced inside. "Ah yes, there it is. What are you waiting for, Mai? Come get your hemlock."

"Hemlock?" Mai rose and took several unsteady steps toward the cabinet. "But I don't have . . . "

"Of course you do. You've been keeping a bottle just for such an occasion as this. You're terribly distraught. Losing your parents and now having your brother arrested for murder. Your life is crumbling around you. The sad thing is that Mrs. Bradley discovered your little secret and you had to take her with you. It will all be explained in your suicide note. Good girl," Adriane said as Mai grasped the small bottle. "Now take it back to your desk and add a few drops to yours and Mrs. Bradley's tea."

"A murder-suicide." Helen stood and set her cup down on the desk. "There's just one problem. I have no intention of drinking this stuff."

Mai seemed to gain courage from Helen's refusal to comply and set the bottle on the desk unopened. "And I have no intention of pouring it into the tea."

Adriane pulled the lever back on the gun, aiming it at Helen. "Then Mai will have to shoot you, then kill herself."

Helen moved away from the desk. "Put the gun down,

Adriane. Give yourself up."

Adriane waved the gun. "Stay back."

"No. You can kill us, but I guarantee you it won't be the end of it." Helen inched closer. "You're a murderer now—a cold-blooded murderer. You once had a career as a brilliant doctor. Now you have nothing. You'll spend the rest of your life running, knowing somewhere, somehow, someone will discover what you did."

"No. That's not going to happen—" Adriane glanced toward the front stairwell.

Helen had heard it too. Someone was coming up the steps.

"Is everything okay up here?" Jennie called as her head cleared the floor.

Helen seized the moment to deliver an upward kick to Adriane's arm. The gun discharged, sending a bullet through the window. Using her left hand, Helen slammed her fist against Adriane's windpipe. Adriane, arms and legs flailing, fell back, slamming her head against the corner of the cabinet. Her body went limp and the gun dropped to the floor. Helen scooped it up and tucked it in her waistband.

Jennie rushed toward them. "What's going on? I found Andi on the floor behind her desk and—" Her wide-eyed gaze swept over the room and landed on Adriane. "Is she dead?"

"I don't know. Better call for help."

Mai hurried to her colleague's side and checked for a pulse. "She's alive. Bring me the first aid kit—it's in the cabinet beside the sink."

Helen retrieved the kit and knelt on the other side of Adriane.

"I already called 9-1-1 for Andi. They're on the way—so is Dad." Jennie hunkered down next to Helen. A deep pool of blood had formed around Adriane's head. Mai deftly cleaned and bandaged the wound. "Can I do anything to help?"

Helen wrapped her good arm around Jennie's shoulders. "You

already have, darling. You already have."

When they heard the sirens, Helen sent Jennie downstairs to direct them.

Having done all they could for Adriane, Helen focused on the pale drawn face that so closely resembled Irene prior to the shooting. "It isn't over," Helen said.

"I know." Mai hauled in a deep breath. "David is still at the house. Packing, I suppose. He has tickets to Mexico in his brief-case. I overheard them planning to leave separately and meet at the airport. That's when I came down here."

"How long have you known?"

"About the affair? I've suspected it for years. David and Adriane met and dated for a while in med school. With her engagement to Paul I thought her fixation with David was over. Then when Father died and Paul started showing interest in Sammi—I suppose Adriane knew she was losing Paul and made a move for David instead."

"I'm sorry."

Sirens and the clattering of footsteps up the marble stairs oblit-erated Mai's response. Helen hung around long enough to make the necessary explanations, then walked back to Edgewood Manor with Jennie.

"Wow, that was so cool."

"What's that, Jennie?"

"The way you took Adriane down."

"You helped by distracting her." Helen grasped Jennie's hand. "Which reminds me, what were you doing at the lab?"

"Looking for you. I came in early so I could talk to you, but no one knew where you were. One of the residents said they'd seen you coming this way. When I found Andi I knew something was wrong, so—" Jennie shrugged.

Helen thought about lecturing her for walking into a dangerous situation but refrained. Maybe later when she had more energy.

"Well, I guess I'd better get to work." Jennie hesitated. "Are you going to be okay?"

Helen nodded. "I do think I'll lie down for a while, though. I'm suddenly feeling very tired."

Jason showed up an hour later to tell Helen they'd picked up David Chang at the airport and transported Adriane to a hospital in town.

"I imagine David was surprised to see the police instead of Adriane."

"You might say that. He's anxious to save his own skin, that's for sure. Claims he had no clue that Adriane had done anything wrong."

"Hmm. Do you believe him?"

"I don't know at this point. It's going to take a while to figure out who did what. I doubt Adriane was working alone."

"Don't underestimate her, Jason. She's a very resourceful woman."

"So are you, Mom. So are you."

Helen related Adriane's confession. "I'm sure she's the one who fired at me in the physical therapy room."

Jason nodded. "Oh, I meant to tell you—we found Sammi."

"Is she . . . " Helen prepared herself for the worst.

"She's fine. Paul did go after her, but not to pay her off or hurt her. He just advised her to see a lawyer before she turned herself in and offered to help with legal assistance."

A week later, Helen wiggled her toes in the warm sand in Fogarty Creek State Park on the Oregon Coast. The rest of the family would be down in a couple of days. She smiled at the thought of having them all together again.

It had been a grueling week, giving her statements and helping to build a case against Adriane. When David Chang learned what his girlfriend had done, he was quick to cooperate with the police. He admitted to lying the night Adriane had shot at Helen, saying he feared they might both be suspects and that they agreed to provide each other with alibis. Though he denied using the bacteria to kill Irene, he did confess that two of his vials had turned up missing the day after Irene had been shot.

All in all a complicated affair.

Helen's heart still ached when she thought of the Kincaids and all the tragedies they'd been through. Paul had been released and all charges dropped. He, Mai, and Chris were desperately trying to salvage what remained of Kincaid Enterprises. They'd be all right in time—once the publicity died down. Andrew Kincaid had built a solid foundation based on his commitment to help the older generation. Fortunately, the anti-aging products and Mai's herbal remedies were selling better than ever.

Work on the implant had been shelved for now, but Helen had no doubt it would surface again. The implants Adriane had done on five Alzheimer's patients had been removed, which was sad, in a way, as two residents, Gladys and Iris, had shown dramatic improvements—the others had not.

And Sammi. Though her old friend would be facing charges, she was a happy woman. Sammi and Paul were engaged and planned to be married by the end of the year.

The wind tugged at Helen's straw hat, flipped it off, and sent it tumbling over the sand and into the surf. She scrambled out of her lounge chair and ran down the beach to retrieve it. A tall familiar figure with silver hair stooped to pick it up.

Tears pooled in her eyes at the sight of him. "It's about time you got here."

J.B. closed the distance between them and gathered her in his arms. "Helen, luv. Did you miss me?"

"What do you think?" She swatted him on the back with her hat, then kissed him soundly. Helen had a long string of questions for this thrill-seeking husband of hers, and he undoubtedly had some for her as well, but all of that could wait.

The End

PATRICIA RUSHFORD is an award-winning writer, speaker, and teacher who has published numerous articles, and over twenty books, including *What Kids Need Most in a Mom*, *The Humpty Dumpty Syndrome: Putting Yourself Back Together Again*, and her first young adult novel, *Kristen's Choice*. She is a registered nurse and has a master's degree in counseling from Western Evangelical Seminary. She and her husband, Ron, live in Washington State and have two grown children, six grandchildren, and lots of nephews and nieces.

Pat has been reading mysteries for as long as she can remember and is delighted to be writing a series of her own. She is a member of Mystery Writers of America, Sisters in Crime, Society of Children's Book Writers and Illustrators, and several other writing organizations. She is also co-director of Writer's Weekend at the Beach.

Fiction